An Unsuitable Job for a Woman

P. D. James (1920–2014) was born in Oxford and educated at Cambridge High School for Girls. From 1949 to 1968 she worked in the National Health Service and subsequently the Home Office, first in the Police Department and later in the Criminal Policy Department. All that experience was used in her novels. She was a Fellow of the Royal Society of Literature and of the Royal Society of Arts and served as a Governor of the BBC, a member of the Arts Council, where she was Chairman of the Literary Advisory Panel, on the Board of the British Council and as a magistrate in Middlesex and London. She was an Honorary Bencher of the Honourable Society of the Inner Temple. She won awards for crime writing in Britain, America, Italy and Scandinavia, including the Mystery Writers of America Grandmaster Award and the National Arts Club Medal of Honor for Literature (US). She received honorary degrees from seven British universities, was awarded an OBE in 1983 and was created a life peer in 1991. In 1997 she was elected President of the Society of Authors, stepping down from the post in August 2013.

Further praise for *An Unsuitable Job for a Woman*:

'A gripping, classic murder story set against the civilized background of Cambridge.' *Good Housekeeping*

'Solid, well-written, ingenious.' *Guardian*

P. D. JAMES

An Unsuitable Job
for a Woman

FABER & FABER

First published in 1972
by Faber & Faber Limited
Bloomsbury House, 74–77 Great Russell Street
London WC1B 3DA

Published by Sphere Books in 1974
Published by Penguin Books
in association with Faber & Faber in 1990
Published in paperback by Faber & Faber in 2002

This Faber & Faber paperback edition published in 2020

Photoset by RefineCatch Ltd, Bungay, Suffolk
Printed and bound by CPI Group (UK) Ltd, Croydon, CR0 4YY

A CIP record for this book
is available from the British Library

ISBN 978-0-571-35570-9

Author's Note

A crime novelist, by virtue of his unpleasant craft, has the duty to create at least one highly reprehensible character in each book and it is perhaps inevitable that from time to time their sanguinary misdeeds should impinge upon the dwellings of the just. A writer whose characters have chosen to act out their tragicomedy in an ancient university city is in particular difficulty. He can, of course, call it Oxbridge, invent colleges named after improbable saints and send his characters boating on the Camsis, but this timid compromise merely confuses characters, readers and the author alike, with the result that no one knows precisely where he is and two communities are offered opportunities for offence instead of one.

The greater part of this story is unrepentantly set in Cambridge, a city in which, undeniably, there live and work policemen, coroners, doctors, students, college servants, flower sellers, Dons, scientists, and even, no doubt, retired Majors. None of them, to my knowledge, bears the slightest resemblance to his counterpart in this book. All the characters, even the most unpleasant, are imaginary; the city, happily for us all, is not.

P.D.J.

For Jane and Peter
who kindly allowed two of my characters
to live at 57 Norwich Street

Preface to the Modern Classics Edition

Cordelia Gray, young, enthusiastic and intelligent, is partner to an unsuccessful private detective, Bernie Pryde, and when Bernie dies leaving Cordelia nothing but his gun and good wishes, the general feeling is that Cordelia will not be able to carry on alone and that running a detective agency is an unsuitable job for a woman. But Cordelia is anxious to keep faith with Bernie and continue with the agency. Her first job involves her in a particularly difficult case which threatens her very life. It involves her with a group of students at Cambridge University and she comes to feel comradeship and sympathy with the student whose death she is investigating. She is courageous, unsupported and determined to succeed in a job which certainly proves very suitable for a woman.

I wanted to have a young heroine of courage and intelligence who faces the problems of life with a determination to be successful in a job which everybody else thinks she won't be able to do.

P. D. JAMES
Oxford, October 2014

CHAPTER ONE

On the morning of Bernie Pryde's death – or it may have been the morning after, since Bernie died at his own convenience, nor did he think the estimated time of his departure worth recording – Cordelia was caught in a breakdown of the Bakerloo Line outside Lambeth North and was half an hour late at the office. She came up from Oxford Circus underground into the bright June sunshine, sped past the early morning shoppers scanning the windows of Dickins and Jones and plunged into the cacophony of Kingly Street, threading her way between the blocked pavement and the shining mass of cars and vans which packed the narrow street. The hurry she knew was irrational, a symptom of her obsession with order and punctuality. There were no appointments booked; no clients to be interviewed; no case outstanding; not even a final report to be written. She and Miss Sparshott, the temporary typist, at Cordelia's suggestion were circulating information about the Agency to all the London solicitors in the hope of attracting custom; Miss Sparshott would probably be busy with it now, eyes straying to her watch, tapping out her staccato irritation at every minute of Cordelia's lateness. She was an unprepossessing woman with lips permanently taut as if to prevent the protruding teeth from springing from her mouth, a receding chin with one coarse hair which grew as quickly as it was plucked, and fair hair set in stiff corrugated waves. That chin and mouth seemed to Cordelia the living refutation that all men are born equal and she tried from time to time to like and sympathize with Miss Sparshott, with a life lived in bedsitting rooms, measured in the fivepenny pieces fed to the gas stove and circumscribed by fell seams and hand hemming. For Miss Sparshott was a skilled dressmaker, an assiduous attender at the G.L.C. evening classes. Her clothes were beautifully made but so dateless that they were never actually in fashion; straight skirts in grey or black which were exercises in how to sew a pleat or insert a zip fastener; blouses with mannish collars and cuffs in insipid pastel shades on which she distributed without discretion her collection of costume jewellery; intricately cut dresses with hems at the precise length to emphasize her shapeless legs and thick ankles.

Cordelia had no premonition of tragedy as she pushed open the street door which was kept perpetually on the latch for the convenience of the secretive and mysterious tenants and their equally mysterious visitors. The new bronze plaque to the left of the door gleamed brightly in the sun in incongruous contrast to the faded and dirt-encrusted paint. Cordelia gave it a short glance of approval.

Pryde's Detective Agency
(*Props:* Bernard G. Pryde   Cordelia Gray)

It had taken Cordelia some weeks of patient and tactful persuasion to convince Bernie that it would be inappropriate to append the words 'ex-CID Metropolitan

Police' to his name or prefix 'Miss' to hers. There had been no other problem over the plaque since Cordelia had brought no qualifications or relevant past experience to the partnership and indeed no capital, except her slight but tough twenty-two-year-old body, a considerable intelligence which Bernie, she suspected, had occasionally found more disconcerting than admirable, and a half exasperated, half pitying affection for Bernie himself. It was obvious very early to Cordelia that in some undramatic but positive way life had turned against him. She recognized the signs. Bernie never got the enviable front left-hand seat in the bus; he couldn't admire the view from the train window without another train promptly obscuring it; the bread he dropped invariably fell buttered side downwards; the Mini, reliable enough when she drove it, stalled for Bernie at the busiest and most inconvenient intersections. She sometimes wondered whether, in accepting his offer of a partnership in a fit of depression or of perverse masochism, she was voluntarily embracing his ill-luck. She certainly never saw herself as powerful enough to change it.

The staircase smelt as always of stale sweat, furniture polish and disinfectant. The walls were dark green and were invariably damp whatever the season as if they secreted a miasma of desperate respectability and defeat. The stairs, with their ornate wrought-iron balustrade, were covered with split and stained linoleum patched by the landlord in various and contrasting colours only when a tenant complained. The Agency was on the third floor. There was no clatter of typewriter keys as Cordelia entered and she saw that Miss Sparshott was engaged in cleaning her machine, an ancient Imperial which was a constant cause of justified complaint. She looked up, her face blotched with resentment, her back as rigid as the space bar.

'I've been wondering when you would turn up, Miss Gray. I'm concerned about Mr Pryde. I think he must be in the inner office but he's quiet, very quiet, and the door's locked.'

Cordelia, chill at heart, wrenched at the door handle: 'Why didn't you do something?'

'Do what, Miss Gray? I knocked at the door and called out to him. It wasn't my place to do that, I'm only the temporary typist, I've no authority here. I should have been placed in a very embarrassing position if he had answered. After all, he's entitled to use his own office I suppose. Besides, I'm not even sure if he's there.'

'He must be. The door's locked and his hat is here.'

Bernie's trilby, the stained brim turned up all round, a comedian's hat, was hanging on the convoluted hat-stand, a symbol of forlorn decrepitude. Cordelia was fumbling in her shoulder bag for her own key. As usual, the object most required had fallen to the bottom of the bag. Miss Sparshott began to clatter on the keys as if to disassociate herself from impending trauma. Above the noise she said defensively:

'There's a note on your desk.'

Cordelia tore it open. It was short and explicit. Bernie had always been able to express himself succinctly when he had something to say:

'I'm sorry, partner, they've told me it's cancer and I'm taking the easy way out. I've seen what the treatment does to people and I'm not having any. I've made my

will and it's with my solicitor. You'll find his name in the desk. I've left the business to you. Everything, including *all* the equipment. Good luck and thank you.'
Underneath with the inconsiderateness of the doomed he had scribbled a final unfair plea:

'If you find me alive, for God's sake wait before calling help. I rely on you for this, partner. Bernie.'

She unlocked the door of the inner office and went inside, closing the door carefully behind her.

It was a relief to see that there was no need to wait. Bernie was dead. He lay slumped over the desk as if in an extremity of exhaustion. His right hand was half-clenched and an open cut-throat razor had slithered over the desk top leaving a thin trail of blood like a snail's track and had come to rest precariously poised on the extreme edge of the desk. His left wrist, scored with two parallel cuts, lay palm upwards in the enamel bowl which Cordelia used for the washing-up. Bernie had filled it with water but it was now brimful with a pale pinky liquid smelling sickly sweet, through which the fingers, curved as if in supplication and looking as white and delicate as those of a child, gleamed as smooth as wax. The blood and water had overflowed on to the desk and floor soaking the oblong of garish rug which Bernie had recently bought in the hope of impressing visitors with his status but which Cordelia privately thought had only drawn attention to the shabbiness of the rest of the office. One of the cuts was tentative and superficial but the other had gone deep as the bone and the severed edges of the wound, drained of blood, gaped cleanly like an illustration in an anatomy text book. Cordelia remembered how Bernie had once

5

described the finding of a prospective suicide when he was first on the beat as a young constable. It was an old man huddled into a warehouse doorway who had slashed his wrist with a broken bottle – but who had later been dragged back to reluctant half-life because an immense clot of blood had blocked the severed veins. Bernie, remembering, had taken precautions to ensure that his blood would not clot. He had, she noticed, taken another precaution; there was an empty tea cup, the one in which she served his afternoon tea, on the right of the desk with a grain or two of powder, aspirin perhaps or a barbiturate, staining the rim and side. A dried trickle of mucus, similarly stained, hung from the corner of his mouth. His lips were pursed and half open like those of a sleeping child, petulant and vulnerable. She put her head round the office door and said quietly:

'Mr Pryde is dead; don't come in. I'll ring the police from here.'

The telephone message was taken calmly, someone would come round. Sitting beside the body to wait and feeling that she needed to make some gesture of pity and comfort Cordelia laid her hand gently on Bernie's hair. Death had as yet no power to diminish these cold and nerveless cells and the hair felt roughly and unpleasantly alive like that of an animal. Quickly she took her hand away and tentatively touched the side of his forehead. The skin was clammy and very cold. This was death; this was how Daddy had felt. As with him, the gesture of pity was meaningless and irrelevant. There was no more communication in death than there had been in life.

She wondered when exactly Bernie had died. No one now would ever know. Perhaps Bernie himself had not known. There must, she supposed, have been one measurable second in time in which he had ceased to be Bernie and had become this unimportant but embarrassingly unwieldy weight of flesh and bone. How odd that a moment of time so important to him should pass without his knowledge. Her second foster mother, Mrs Wilkes, would have said that Bernie did know, that there was a moment of indescribable glory, shining towers, limitless singing, skies of triumph. Poor Mrs Wilkes! Widowed, her only son dead in the war, her small house perpetually noisy with the foster children who were her livelihood, she had needed her dreams. She had lived her life by comfortable maxims stored like nuggets of coal against the winter. Cordelia thought of her now for the first time in years and heard again the tired, determinedly cheerful voice, 'If the Lord doesn't call on his way out, He'll call on his way back.' Well, going or coming, He hadn't called on Bernie.

It was odd but somehow typical of Bernie that he should have retained a dogged and invincible optimism about the business even when they had nothing in the cash box but a few coins for the gas meter and yet had given up hope of life without even a struggle. Was it perhaps that he had subconsciously recognized that neither he nor the Agency had any real future and had decided that this way he could yield up both life and livelihood with some honour? He had done it effectively but messily, surprisingly so for an ex-policeman versed in the ways of death. And then she realized why he had chosen the razor and the drugs. The gun. He hadn't really taken the easy way out. He could have used the gun, but he had wanted her to have it; he had bequeathed

7

it to her together with the rickety filing cabinets, the antique typewriter, the scene-of-crime kit, the Mini, his shock-proof and waterproof wrist watch, the blood-soaked rug, the embarrassingly large stock of writing paper with the ornate heading *Pryde's Detective Agency – We take Pride in our Work. All* the equipment; he had underlined all. He must have meant to remind her about the gun.

She unlocked the small drawer at the base of Bernie's desk to which only she and he had a key and drew it out. It was still in the suede drawstring bag which she had made for it, with three rounds of ammunition packed separately. It was a pistol, a .38 semi-automatic; she had never known how Bernie had come by it but she was certain that he had no licence. She had never seen it as a lethal weapon, perhaps because Bernie's boyishly naïve obsession with it had reduced it to the impotence of a child's toy. He had taught her to become – at any rate in theory – a creditable shot. They had driven for practice into the depths of Epping Forest and her memories of the gun were linked with dappled shade and the rich smell of decaying leaves. He had fixed a target to a convenient tree; the gun was loaded with blanks. She could still hear the excited staccato orders. 'Bend your knees slightly. Feet apart. Arm full length. Now place the left hand against the barrel, cradling it. Keep your eyes on the target. Arm straight, partner, arm straight! Good! Not bad; not bad; not bad at all.' 'But, Bernie,' she had said, 'we can never fire it! We haven't a licence.' He had smiled, the sly self-satisfied smile of superior knowledge. 'If we ever fire in anger it will be to save our lives. In such an eventuality the question of a licence is irrelevant.' He had been pleased with this rotund sentence and had repeated it, lifting his heavy face to the sun like a dog. What, she wondered, had he seen in imagination? The two of them crouching behind a boulder on some desolate moor, bullets pinging against the granite, the gun passed smoking from hand to hand?

He had said: 'We'll have to go carefully with the ammunition. Not that I can't get it of course . . .' The smile had become grim, as if at the memory of those mysterious contacts, those ubiquitous and obliging acquaintances whom he had only to summon from their shadow world.

So he had left her the gun. It had been his most prized possession. She slipped it, still shrouded, into the depths of her shoulder bag. It was surely unlikely that the police would examine the drawers of the desk in a case of obvious suicide but it was as well to take no risk. Bernie had meant her to have the gun and she wasn't going to give it up easily. With her bag at her feet she sat down again by the body. She said a brief convent-taught prayer to the God she wasn't sure existed for the soul which Bernie had never believed he possessed and waited quietly for the police.

The first policeman to arrive was efficient but young, not yet experienced enough to hide his shock and dis- taste at the sight of violent death nor his disapproval that Cordelia should be so calm. He didn't spend long in the inner office. When he came out he meditated upon Bernie's note as if a careful scrutiny could extract some inner meaning from the bald sentence of death. Then he folded it away.

'I'll have to keep this note for the present, Miss. What did he get up to here?'

'He didn't get up to anything. This was his office. He was a private detective.'

'And you worked for this Mr Pryde? You were his secretary?'

'I was his partner. It says so in the note. I'm twenty-two. Bernie was the senior partner; he started the business. He used to work for the Metropolitan Police in the CID with Superintendent Dalgliesh.'

As soon as the words were spoken, she regretted them. They were too propitiatory, too naïve a defence of poor Bernie. And the name Dalgliesh, she saw, meant nothing to him. Why should it? He was just one of the local uniformed branch. He couldn't be expected to know how often she had listened with politely concealed impatience to Bernie's nostalgic reminiscences of his time in the CID before he was invalided out, or to his eulogies on the virtues and wisdom of Adam Dalgliesh. 'The Super – well, he was just an Inspector then – always taught us . . . The Super once described a case . . . If there was one thing the Super couldn't stand . . .'

Sometimes she had wondered whether this paragon had actually existed or whether he had sprung impeccable and omnipotent from Bernie's brain, a necessary hero and mentor. It was with a shock of surprise that she had later seen a newspaper picture of Chief Superintendent Dalgliesh, a dark, sardonic face which, on her closer scrutiny, disintegrated into an ambiguity of patterned micro dots, giving nothing away. Not all the wisdom Bernie so glibly recalled was the received gospel. Much, she suspected, was his own philosophy. She in turn had devised a private litany of disdain: supercilious, superior, sarcastic Super; what wisdom, she wondered, would he have to comfort Bernie now.

The policeman had made discreet telephone calls. He now prowled around the outer office, hardly bothering to hide his puzzled contempt at the shabby second-hand furniture, the battered filing cabinet with one drawer half-open to reveal teapot and mugs, the worn linoleum. Miss Sparshott, rigid at an ancient typewriter, gazed at him with fascinated distaste. At last he said:

'Well, suppose you make yourselves a nice cup of tea while I wait for the police surgeon. There is somewhere to make tea?'

'There's a small pantry down the corridor which we share with the other tenants on this floor. But surely you don't need a surgeon? Bernie's dead!'

'He's not officially dead until a qualified medical practitioner says so.' He paused: 'It's just a precaution.'

Against what, Cordelia wondered – judgement, damnation, decay? The policeman went back into the inner office. She followed him and asked softly:

'Couldn't you let Miss Sparshott go? She's from a secretarial agency and we have to pay for her by the hour. She hasn't done any work since I arrived and I doubt whether she will now.'

He was, she saw, a little shocked by the apparent callousness of concerning herself with so mercenary a detail while standing within touching distance of Bernie's body, but he said willingly enough:

'I'll just have a word with her, then she can go. It isn't a nice place for a woman.'

His tone implied that it never had been.

Afterwards, waiting in the outer office, Cordelia answered the inevitable questions.

'No, I don't know whether he was married. I've a feeling that he was divorced; he never talked about a wife. He lived at 15, Cremona Road, S.E.1. He let me have a bedsitting room there but we didn't see much of each other.'

'I know Cremona Road; my aunt used to live there when I was a kid – one of those streets near the Imperial War Museum.'

The fact that he knew the road seemed to reassure and humanize him. He ruminated happily for a moment.

'When did you last see Mr Pryde alive?'

'Yesterday at about five o'clock when I left work early to do some shopping.'

'Didn't he come home last night?'

'I heard him moving around but I didn't see him. I have a gas ring in my room and I usually cook there unless I know he's out. I didn't hear him this morning which is unusual, but I thought he might be lying in. He does that occasionally when it's his hospital morning.'

'Was it his hospital morning today?'

'No, he had an appointment last Wednesday but I thought that they might have asked him to come back. He must have left the house very late last night or before I woke early this morning. I didn't hear him.'

It was impossible to describe the almost obsessional delicacy with which they avoided each other, trying not to intrude, preserving the other's privacy, listening for the sound of flushing cisterns, tip-toeing to ascertain whether the kitchen or bathroom was empty. They had taken infinite trouble not to be a nuisance to each other. Living in the same small terraced house they had hardly seen each other outside the office. She wondered whether Bernie had decided to kill himself in his office so that the little house would be uncontaminated and undisturbed.

*

At last the office was empty and she was alone. The police surgeon had closed his bag and departed; Bernie's body had been manoeuvred down the narrow staircase watched by eyes from the half-opened doors of other offices; the last policeman had left. Miss Sparshott had gone for good, violent death being a worse insult than a typewriter which a trained typist ought not to be expected to use or lavatory accommodation which was not at all what she had been accustomed to. Alone in the emptiness and silence Cordelia felt the need of physical action. She began vigorously to clean the inner office, scrubbing the blood stains from desk and chair, mopping the soaked rug.

At one o'clock she walked briskly to their usual pub. It occurred to her that there was no longer any reason to patronize the Golden Pheasant but she walked on unable to bring herself to so early a disloyalty. She had never liked the pub or the landlady and had often wished that Bernie would find a nearer house, preferably one with a large bosomy barmaid with a heart of gold. It was, she suspected, a type commoner in fiction than in real life. The familiar lunch-time crowd was clustered around the bar and, as usual, Mavis presided behind it wearing her slightly minatory smile, her air of extreme respectability. Mavis changed her dress three

13

times a day, her hair style once every year, her smile never. The two women had never liked each other although Bernie had galumphed between them like an affectionate old dog, finding it convenient to believe that they were great mates and unaware of or ignoring the almost physical crackle of antagonism. Mavis reminded Cordelia of a librarian known to her in childhood who had secreted the new books under the counter in case they should be taken out and soiled. Perhaps Mavis's barely suppressed chagrin was because she was forced to display her wares so prominently, compelled to measure out her bounty before watchful eyes. Pushing a half pint of shandy and a Scotch egg across the counter in response to Cordelia's order, she said:

'I hear you've had the police round.'

Watching their avid faces, Cordelia thought, they know about it, of course; they want to hear the details; they may as well hear them. She said:

'Bernie cut his wrist twice. The first time he didn't get to the vein; the second time he did. He put his arm in water to help the bleeding. He had been told that he had cancer and couldn't face the treatment.'

That, she saw, was different. The little group around Mavis glanced at each other, then quickly averted their eyes. Glasses were momentarily checked upon their upward way. Cutting one's wrist was something which other people did but the sinister little crab had his claws of fear into all their minds. Even Mavis looked as if she saw his bright claws lurking among her bottles. She said:

'You'll be looking for a new job, I suppose? After all, you can hardly keep the Agency going on your own. It isn't a suitable job for a woman.'

14

'No different from working behind a bar; you meet all kinds of people.'

The two women looked at each other and a snatch of unspoken dialogue passed between them clearly heard and understood by both.

'And don't think, now he's dead, that people can go on leaving messages for the Agency here.'

'I wasn't going to ask.'

Mavis began vigorously polishing a glass, her eyes still on Cordelia's face.

'I shouldn't think your mother would approve of you staying on alone.'

'I only had a mother for the first hour of my life, so I don't have to worry about that.'

Cordelia saw at once that the remark had deeply shocked them and wondered again at the capacity of older people to be outraged by simple facts when they seemed capable of accepting any amount of perverse or shocking opinion. But their silence, heavy with censure, at least left her in peace. She carried her shandy and Scotch egg to a seat against the wall and thought without sentimentality about her mother. Gradually out of a childhood of deprivation she had evolved a philosophy of compensation. In her imagination she had enjoyed a lifetime of love in one hour with no disappointments and no regrets. Her father had never talked about her mother's death and Cordelia had avoided questioning him, fearful of learning that her mother had never held her in her arms, never regained consciousness, never perhaps even known that she had a daughter. This belief in her mother's love was the one fantasy which she could still not entirely risk losing although its indulgence had become less necessary and less real with each passing year. Now, in imagination, she consulted her mother. It was just as she expected: her mother thought it an entirely suitable job for a woman.

The little group at the bar had turned back to their drinks. Between their shoulders she could see her own reflection in the mirror above the bar. Today's face looked no different from yesterday's face; thick, light brown hair framing features which looked as if a giant had placed a hand on her head and the other under her chin and gently squeezed the face together; large eyes, browny-green under a deep fringe of hair; wide cheek bones; a gentle, childish mouth. A cat's face she thought, but calmly decorative among the reflection of coloured bottles and all the bright glitter of Mavis's bar. Despite its look of deceptive youth it could be a secret, uncommunicative face. Cordelia had early learnt stoicism. All her foster parents, kindly and well-meaning in their different ways, had demanded one thing of her – that she should be happy. She had quickly learned that to show unhappiness was to risk the loss of love. Compared with this early discipline of concealment, all subsequent deceits had been easy.

The Snout was edging his way towards her. He settled himself down on the bench, his thick rump in its appalling tweed pressed close to hers. She disliked the Snout although he had been Bernie's only friend. Bernie had explained that the Snout was a police informer and did rather well. And there were other sources of income. Sometimes his friends stole famous pictures or valuable jewellery. Then the Snout, suitably instructed, would hint to the police where the loot could be found. There was a reward for the Snout to be subsequently shared, of course, among the thieves, and a pay-off, too, for the detective, who after all had done most of the work. As Bernie had pointed out, the insurance company got off lightly, the owners got their property back intact, the thieves were in no danger from the police and the Snout and the detective got their payoff. It was the system. Cordelia, shocked, had not liked to protest too much. She suspected that Bernie too had done some snouting in his time, although never with such expertise or with such lucrative results.

The Snout's eyes were rheumy, his hand around the glass of whisky was shaking.

'Poor old Bernie, I could see he had it coming to him. He'd been losing weight for the last year and he had that grey look to him, the cancer complexion, my dad used to call it.'

At least the Snout had noticed; she hadn't. Bernie had always seemed to her grey and sick-looking. A thick, hot thigh edged closer.

'Never had any luck, poor sod. They chucked him out of the CID. Did he tell you? That was Superintendent Dalgliesh, Inspector at the time. Christ, he could be a proper bastard; no second chance from him, I can tell you.'

'Yes, Bernie told me,' Cordelia lied. She added: 'He didn't seem particularly bitter about it.'

'No use, is there, in being bitter? Take what comes, that's my motto. I suppose you'll be looking for another job?'

He said it wistfully as if her defection would leave the Agency open for his exploitation.

'Not just yet,' said Cordelia. 'I shan't look for a new job just yet.'

She had made two resolutions: she would keep on Bernie's business until there was nothing left with which to pay the rent, and she would never come into the Golden Pheasant again as long as she lived.

*

This resolution to keep the business going survived the next four days – survived discovery of the rent book and agreement which revealed that Bernie hadn't, after all, owned the little house in Cremona Road and that her tenancy of the bedsitting room was illegal and certainly limited; survived learning from the Bank Manager that Bernie's credit balance would barely pay for his funeral and from the garage that the Mini was shortly due for an overhaul; survived the clearing up of the Cremona Road house. Everywhere was the sad detritus of a solitary and mismanaged life.

The tins of Irish stew and baked beans – had he never eaten anything else? – stacked in a carefully arranged pyramid as if in a grocer's window; large tins of metal and floor polish, half-used, with their contents dried or congealed; a drawer of old rags used as dusters but stiff with an amalgam of polish and dirt; a laundry basket unemptied; thick woollen combinations felted with machine washing and stained brown about the crotch – how could he have borne to leave those for discovery?

She went daily to the office, cleaning, tidying, re-arranging the filing. There were no calls and no clients and yet she seemed always busy. There was the inquest to attend, depressing in its detached almost boring formality, in its inevitable verdict. There was a visit to Bernie's solicitor. He was a dispirited, elderly man with an office inconveniently situated near Mile End Station who took the news of his client's death with lugubrious resignation as if it were a personal affront, and after a brief search found Bernie's will and pored over it with puzzled suspicion, as if it were not the document he himself had recently drawn up. He succeeded in giving Cordelia the impression that he realized that she had been Bernie's mistress – why else should he have left her the business? – but that he was a man of the world and didn't hold the knowledge against her. He took no part in arranging the funeral except to supply Cordelia with the name of a firm of undertakers; she suspected that they probably gave him a commission. She was relieved after a week of depressing solemnity to find that the funeral director was both cheerful and competent. Once he discovered that Cordelia wasn't going to break down in tears or indulge in the more histrionic antics of the bereaved, he was happy to discuss the relative price and the merits of burial and cremation with conspiratorial candour.

'Cremation every time. There's no private insurance, you tell me? Then get it all over as quickly, easily and cheaply as possible. Take my word, that's what the deceased would want nine times out of ten. A grave's an expensive luxury these days – no use to him – no use to you. Dust to dust, ashes to ashes; but what about the process in between? Not nice to think about, is it? So why not get it over as quickly as possible by the most reliable modern methods? Mind you, Miss, I'm advising you against my own best interests.'

Cordelia said:

'It's very kind of you. Do you think we ought to have a wreath?'

'Why not, it'll give it a bit of tone. Leave it to me.'

So there had been a cremation and one wreath. The wreath had been a vulgarly inappropriate cushion of lilies and carnations, the flowers already dying and smelling of decay. The cremation service had been spoken by the priest with carefully controlled speed and with a suggestion of apology in his tone as if to assure his hearers that, although he enjoyed a special dispensation, he didn't expect them to believe the unbelievable. Bernie had passed to his burning to the sound of synthetic music and only just on time, to judge by the impatient rustlings of the cortège already waiting to enter the chapel.

Afterwards Cordelia was left standing in the bright sunlight, feeling the heat of the gravel through the soles of her shoes. The air was rich and heavy with the scent of flowers. Swept suddenly with desolation and a defensive anger on Bernie's behalf, she sought a scapegoat and found it in a certain Superintendent of the Yard. He had kicked Bernie out of the only job he had ever wanted to do; hadn't troubled to find out what happened to him later; and, most irrational indictment of all, he hadn't even bothered to come to the funeral. Bernie had needed to be a detective as other men needed to paint, write, drink or fornicate. Surely the CID was large enough to accommodate one man's enthusiasm and inefficiency? For the first time Cordelia wept for Bernie; hot tears blurred and multiplied the long line of waiting hearses with their bright coronets so that they seemed to stretch in an infinity of gleaming chrome and trembling flowers. Untying the black chiffon scarf from her head, her only concession to mourning, Cordelia set off to walk to the tube station.

She was thirsty when she got to Oxford Circus and decided to have tea in the restaurant at Dickins and Jones. This was unusual and an extravagance but it had been an unusual and extravagant day. She lingered long enough to get full value for her bill and it was after a quarter past four when she returned to the office.

She had a visitor. There was a woman waiting, shoulders against the door – a woman who looked cool and incongruous against the dirty paintwork and the greasy walls. Cordelia caught her breath in surprise, her upward rush checked. Her light shoes had made no sound on the stairway and for a few seconds she saw her visitor unobserved. She gained an impression, immediate and vivid, of competence and authority and an intimidating rightness of dress. The woman was wearing a grey suit with a small stand-away collar which showed a narrow band of white cotton at the throat. Her black patent shoes were obviously expensive; a large black bag with patch pockets was slung from her left shoulder. She was tall and her hair, prematurely white, was cut short and moulded to her head like a cap. Her face was pale and long. She was reading *The Times*, the paper folded so that she could hold it in her right hand. After a couple of seconds, she became aware of Cordelia and their eyes met. The woman looked at her wrist watch.

'If you are Cordelia Gray, then you're eighteen minutes late. This notice says that you would return at four o'clock.'

'I know, I'm sorry.' Cordelia hurried up the last few steps and fitted the Yale key into the lock. She opened the door.

'Won't you come in?'

The woman preceded her into the outer office and turned to face her without giving the room even a glance.

'I was hoping to see Mr Pryde. Will he be long?'

'I'm sorry; I've just come back from his cremation. I mean . . . Bernie's dead.'

'Obviously. Our information was that he was alive ten days ago. He must have died with remarkable speed and discretion.'

'Not with discretion. Bernie killed himself.'

'How extraordinary!' The visitor seemed to be struck by its extraordinariness. She pressed her hands together and for a few seconds walked restlessly about the room in a curious pantomime of distress.

'How extraordinary!' she said again. She gave a little snort of laughter. Cordelia didn't speak, but the two women regarded each other gravely. Then the visitor said:

'Well, I seem to have had a wasted journey.'

Cordelia breathed an almost inaudible 'Oh no!' and resisted an absurd impulse to fling her body against the door.

'Please don't go before talking to me. I was Mr Pryde's partner and I own the business now. I'm sure I could help. Won't you please sit down?'

The visitor took no notice of the offered chair.

'No one can help, no one in the world. However that is beside the point. There is something which my employer particularly wants to know – some information he requires – and he had decided that Mr Pryde

22

was the person to get it for him. I don't know if he would consider you an effective substitute. Is there a private telephone here?'

'In here, please.'

The woman walked into the inner office, again with no sign that its shabbiness had made any impression on her. She turned to Cordelia.

'I'm sorry, I should have introduced myself. My name is Elizabeth Leaming and my employer is Sir Ronald Callender.'

'The conservationist?'

'I shouldn't let him hear you call him that. He prefers to be called a microbiologist, which is what he is. Please excuse me.'

She shut the door firmly. Cordelia, feeling suddenly weak, sat down at the typewriter. The keys, oddly familiar symbols encircled in black medallions, shifted their pattern before her tired eyes, then at a blink clicked back to normality. She grasped the sides of the machine, cold and clammy to the touch, and talked herself back to calmness. Her heart was thudding.

'I must be calm, must show her that I am tough. This silliness is only the strain of Bernie's funeral and too much standing in the hot sun.'

But hope was traumatic; she was angry with herself for caring so much.

The telephone call took only a couple of minutes. The door of the inner office opened; Miss Leaming was drawing on her gloves.

'Sir Ronald has asked to see you. Can you come now?'

Come where, thought Cordelia, but she didn't ask.

'Yes, shall I need my gear?'

The gear was Bernie's carefully designed and fitted-out scene-of-crime case with its tweezers, scissors, finger printing equipment, jars to collect specimens; Cordelia had never yet had occasion to use it.

'It depends upon what you mean by your gear, but I shouldn't think so. Sir Ronald wants to see you before deciding whether to offer you the job. It means a train journey to Cambridge but you should get back tonight. Is there anyone you ought to tell?'

'No, there's only me.'

'Perhaps I ought to identify myself.' She opened her handbag. 'Here is an addressed envelope. I'm not a white slaver in case they exist and in case you're frightened.'

'I'm frightened of quite a number of things but not of white slavers and if I were, an addressed envelope would hardly reassure me. I'd insist on telephoning Sir Ronald Callender to check.'

'Perhaps you would like to do so?' suggested Miss Leaming without rancour.

'No.'

'Then shall we go?' Miss Leaming led the way to the door. As they went out to the landing and Cordelia turned to lock the office behind her, her visitor indicated the note-pad and pencil hanging together from a nail on the wall.

'Hadn't you better change the notice?'

Cordelia tore off her previous message and after a moment's thought wrote:

I am called away to an urgent case. Any messages pushed through the door will receive my immediate and personal attention on return.

'That,' pronounced Miss Leaming, 'should reassure your clients.' Cordelia wondered if the remark was sarcastic; it was impossible to tell from the detached tone. But she didn't feel that Miss Leaming was laughing at her and was surprised at her own lack of resentment at the way in which her visitor had taken charge of events. Meekly, she followed Miss Leaming down the stairs and into Kingly Street.

They travelled by the Central Line to Liverpool Street and caught the 17.36 train to Cambridge with plenty of time. Miss Leaming bought Cordelia's ticket, collected a portable typewriter and a briefcase of papers from the left luggage department and led the way to a first-class carriage. She said:

'I shall have to work in the train; have you anything to read?'

'That's all right. I don't like talking when I'm travelling either. I've got Hardy's *Trumpet Major* – I always have a paperback in my bag.'

After Bishops Stortford they had the compartment to themselves but only once did Miss Leaming look up from her work to question Cordelia.

'How did you come to be working for Mr Pryde?'

'After I left school I went to live with my father on the continent. We travelled around a good deal. He died in Rome last May after a heart attack and I came home. I had taught myself some shorthand and typing so I took a job with a secretarial agency. They sent me to Bernie and after a few weeks he let me help him with one or two of the cases. He decided to train me and I agreed to stay on permanently. Two months ago he made me his partner.'

All that had meant was that Cordelia gave up a regular wage in return for the uncertain rewards of success in the form of an equal share of the profits together with a rent-free bedsitting room in Bernie's house. He hadn't meant to cheat. The offer of the partnership had been made in the genuine belief that she would recognize it for what it was; not a good conduct prize but an accolade of trust.

'What was your father?'

'He was an itinerant Marxist poet and an amateur revolutionary.'

'You must have had an interesting childhood.'

Remembering the succession of foster mothers, the unexplained incomprehensible moves from house to house, the changes of schools, the concerned faces of Local Authority Welfare Officers and school teachers desperately wondering what to do with her in the holidays, Cordelia replied as she always did to this assertion, gravely and without irony.

'Yes, it was very interesting.'

'And what was this training you received from Mr Pryde?'

'Bernie taught me some of the things he learnt in the CID: how to search the scene of a crime properly, how to collect exhibits, some elementary self-defence, how to detect and lift finger prints – that kind of thing.'

'Those are skills which I hardly feel you will find appropriate to this case.'

Miss Leaming bent her head over her papers and did not speak again until the train reached Cambridge.

Outside the station Miss Leaming briefly surveyed the car park and led the way towards a small black van.

Standing beside it rigidly as a uniformed chauffeur, was a stockily built young man dressed in an open-necked white shirt, dark breeches and tall boots who Miss Leaming introduced casually and without explanation as 'Lunn'. He nodded briefly in acknowledgement of the introduction but did not smile. Cordelia held out her hand. His grip was momentary but remarkably strong, crushing her fingers; suppressing a grimace of pain she saw a flicker in the large mud-brown eyes and wondered if he had hurt her deliberately. The eyes were certainly memorable and beautiful, moist calves' eyes heavily lashed and with the same look of troubled pain at the unpredictability of the world's terrors. But their beauty emphasized rather than redeemed the unattractiveness of the rest of him. He was, she thought, a sinister study in black and white with his thick, short neck and powerful shoulders straining the seams of his shirt. He had a helmet of strong black hair, a pudgy slightly pock-marked face and a moist petulant mouth; the face of a ribald cherub. He was a man who sweated profusely; the underarms of his shirt were stained and the cotton stuck to the flesh emphasizing the strong curve of the back and the obtrusive biceps.

Cordelia saw that the three of them were to sit squashed together in the front of the van. Lunn held open the door without apology except to state:

'The Rover's still in dock.'

Miss Leaming hung back so that Cordelia was compelled to get in first and sit beside him. She thought: 'They don't like each other and he resents me.'

She wondered about his position in Sir Ronald Callender's household. Miss Leaming's place she had already guessed; no ordinary secretary however long in service, however indispensable, had quite that air of authority or talked of 'my employer' in that tone of possessive irony. But she wondered about Lunn. He didn't behave like a subordinate but nor did he strike her as a scientist. True, scientists were alien creatures to her. Sister Mary Magdalen was the only one she had known. Sister had taught what the syllabus dignified as general science, a hotch-potch of elementary physics, chemistry and biology unceremoniously lumped together. Science subjects were in general little regarded at the Convent of the Immaculate Conception, although the arts were well taught. Sister Mary Magdalen had been an elderly and timid nun, eyes puzzled behind steel-rimmed spectacles, her clumsy fingers permanently stained with chemicals, who had apparently been as surprised as her pupils at the extraordinary explosions and fumes which her activities with test tube and flask had occasionally produced. She had been more concerned to demonstrate the incomprehensibility of the universe and the inscrutability of God's laws than to reveal scientific principles and in this she had certainly succeeded. Cordelia felt that Sister Mary Magdalen would be no help to her in dealing with Sir Ronald Callender; Sir Ronald who had campaigned in the cause of conservation long before his interest became a popular obsession, who had represented his country at International Conferences on Ecology and been knighted for his services to conservation. All this Cordelia, like the rest of the country, knew from his television appearances and the Sunday Colour Supplements. He was the establishment scientist, carefully uncommitted politically, who personified to everyone's reassurance the poor boy who had made good and stayed good. How, Cordelia wondered, had he come to think of employing Bernie Pryde?

Uncertain how far Lunn was in his employer's or Miss Leaming's confidence, she asked carefully:

'How did Sir Ronald hear about Bernie?'

'John Bellinger told him.'

So the Bellinger bonus had arrived at last! Bernie had always expected it. The Bellinger case had been his most lucrative, perhaps his only, success. John Bellinger was the director of a small family firm which manufactured specialized scientific instruments. The previous year his office had been plagued by an outbreak of obscene letters and, unwilling to call in the police, he had telephoned Bernie. Bernie, taken on the staff at his own suggestion as a messenger, had quickly solved a not very difficult problem. The writer had been Bellinger's middle-aged and highly regarded personal secretary. Bellinger had been grateful. Bernie, after anxious thought and consultation with Cordelia, had sent in a bill the size of which had astounded them both and the bill had been promptly paid. It had kept the Agency going for a month. Bernie had said: 'We'll get a bonus from the Bellinger case, see if we don't. Anything can happen in this job. He only chose us by picking our name from the telephone directory but now he'll recommend us to his friends. This case could be the beginning of something big.'

And now, thought Cordelia, on the day of Bernie's funeral, the Bellinger bonus had arrived.

She asked no more questions and the drive, which took less than thirty minutes, passed in silence. The three of them sat thigh to thigh, but distanced. She saw nothing of the city. At the end of Station Road by the War Memorial the car turned to the left and soon they were in the country. There were wide fields of young corn, the occasional stretch of tree-lined dappled shade, straggling villages of thatched cottages and squat red villas strung along the road, low uplands from which Cordelia could see the towers and spires of the city, shining with deceptive nearness in the evening sun. Finally, there was another village, a thin belt of elms fringing the road, a long curving wall of red brick and the van turned in through open wrought-iron gates. They had arrived.

*

The house was obviously Georgian, not perhaps the best Georgian, but solidly built, agreeably proportioned and with the look of all good domestic architecture of having grown naturally out of its site. The mellow brick, festooned with wisteria, gleamed richly in the evening sun so that the green of the creeper glowed and the whole house looked suddenly as artificial and unsubstantial as a film set. It was essentially a family house, a welcoming house. But now a heavy silence lay over it and the rows of elegantly proportioned windows were empty eyes.

Lunn, who had driven fast but skilfully, braked in front of the porch. He stayed in his seat while the two women got out then drove the van round the side of the house. As she slid down from the high seat Cordelia could glimpse a range of low buildings, topped with small ornamental turrets, which she took to be stables or garages. Through the wide-arched gateway she could see that the grounds dropped slowly away to give a far vista of the flat Cambridgeshire countryside, patterned with the gentle greens and fawns of early summer. Miss Leaming said:

'The stable block has been converted into laboratories. Most of the east side is now glass. It was a skilful job by a Swedish architect, functional but attractive.'

For the first time since they had met her voice sounded interested, almost enthusiastic.

The front door was open. Cordelia came into a wide, panelled hall with a staircase curving to the left, a carved stone fireplace to the right. She was aware of a smell of roses and lavender, of carpets gleaming richly against polished wood, of the subdued ticking of a clock.

Miss Leaming led the way to a door immediately across the hall. It led to a study, a room book-lined and elegant; one with a view of wide lawns and a shield of trees. In front of the french windows was a Georgian desk and behind the desk sat a man.

Cordelia had seen his photographs in the press and knew what to expect. But he was at once smaller and more impressive than she had imagined. She knew that she was facing a man of authority and high intelligence; his strength came over like a physical force. But as he rose from his seat and waved her to a chair, she saw that he was slighter than his photographs suggested, the heavy shoulders and impressive head making the body look top-heavy. He had a lined, sensitive face with a high-bridged nose, deep-set eyes on which the lids weighed heavily and a mobile, sculptured mouth. His black hair, as yet unflecked with grey, lay heavily across his brow. His face was shadowed with weariness and, as Cordelia came closer, she could detect the twitch of a nerve in his left temple and the almost imperceptible staining of the veins in the irises of the deep-set eyes. But his compact body, taut with energy and latent vigour, made no concession to tiredness. The arrogant head was held high, the eyes were keen and wary under the heavy lids. Above all he looked successful. Cordelia had seen that look before, had recognized it from the back of crowds as, inscrutable, they had watched the famous and notorious pass on their way – that almost physical glow, akin to sexuality and undimmed by weariness or ill-health, of men who knew and enjoyed the realities of power.

Miss Leaming said:

'This is all that remains of Pryde's Detective Agency – Miss Cordelia Gray.'

The keen eyes looked into Cordelia's.

'We take a Pride in our Work. Do you?'

Cordelia, tired after her journey at the end of a momentous day, was in no mood for jokes about poor Bernie's pathetic pun. She said:

'Sir Ronald, I have come here because your secretary said that you might want to employ me. If she's wrong, I would be glad to know so that I can get back to London.'

'She isn't my secretary and she isn't wrong. You must forgive my discourtesy; it's a little disconcerting to expect a burly ex-policeman and to get you. I'm not complaining, Miss Gray; you might do very well. What are your fees?'

The question might have sounded offensive but it wasn't; he was completely matter-of-fact. Cordelia told him, a little too quickly, a little too eagerly.

'Five pounds a day and expenses, but we try to keep those as low as possible. For that, of course, you get my sole services. I mean I don't work for any other client until your case is finished.'

'And is there another client?'

'Well, not just at present but there very well could be.' She went on quickly:

'We have a fair-play clause. If I decide at any stage of the investigation that I'd rather not go on with it, you are entitled to any information I have gained up to that point. If I decide to withhold it from you, then I make no charge for the work already done.'

That had been one of Bernie's principles. He had been a great man for principles. Even when there hadn't been a case for a week, he could happily discuss the extent to which they would be justified in telling a client less than the full truth, the point at which the police ought to be brought into an inquiry, the ethics of deception or lying in the service of truth. 'But no bugging,' Bernie would say, 'I set my face firmly against bugging. And we don't touch industrial sabotage.'

The temptation to either wasn't great. They had no bugging equipment and wouldn't have known how to use it if they had, and at no time had Bernie been invited to touch industrial sabotage.

Sir Ronald said:

'That sounds reasonable but I don't think this case will present you with any crisis of conscience. It is comparatively simple. Eighteen days ago my son hanged himself. I want you to find out why. Can you do that?'

'I should like to try, Sir Ronald.'

'I realize that you need certain basic information about Mark. Miss Leaming will type it out for you, then you can read it through and let us know what else you require.'

Cordelia said:

'I should like you to tell me yourself, please.'

'Is that necessary?'

'It would be helpful to me.'

He settled again into his chair and picked up a stub of pencil, twisting it in his hands. After a minute he slipped it absentmindedly into his pocket. Without looking at her, he began to speak.

'My son Mark was twenty-one on the 25th April this year. He was at Cambridge reading history at my old college and was in his final year. Five weeks ago and without warning, he left the university and took a job as gardener with a Major Markland, who lives in a house called Summertrees outside Duxford. Mark gave me no explanation of this action either then or later. He lived alone in a cottage in Major Markland's grounds. Eighteen days later he was found by his employer's sister hanging by the neck from a strap knotted to a hook in the sitting-room ceiling. The verdict at the inquest was that he took his life while the balance of his mind was disturbed. I know little of my son's mind but I reject that comfortable euphemism. He was a rational person. He had a reason for his action. I want to know what it was.'

Miss Leaming, who had been looking out of the french windows to the garden, turned and said with sudden vehemence:

'This lust always to know! It's only prying. If he'd wanted us to know, he'd have told us.'

Sir Ronald said:

'I'm not prepared to go on in this uncertainty. My son is dead. *My* son. If I am in some way responsible, I prefer to know. If anyone else is responsible I want to know that too.'

Cordelia looked from one to the other. She asked:

'Did he leave a note?'

'He left a note but not an explanation. It was found in his typewriter.'

Quietly Miss Leaming began to speak:

'Down the winding cavern we groped our tedious way, till a void boundless as the nether sky appeared beneath us, and we held by the roots of trees and hung over this immensity; but I said: if you please we will commit ourselves to this void and see whether providence is here also.'

The husky, curiously deep voice came to an end. They were silent. Then Sir Ronald said:

'You claim to be a detective, Miss Gray. What do you deduce from that?'

'That your son read William Blake. Isn't it a passage from *The Marriage of Heaven and Hell*?'

Sir Ronald and Miss Leaming glanced at each other. Sir Ronald said:

'So I am told.'

Cordelia thought that Blake's gently unemphatic exhortation, devoid of violence or despair, was more appropriate to suicide by drowning or by poison – a ceremonious floating or sinking into oblivion – than to the trauma of hanging. And yet there was the analogy of falling, of launching oneself into the void. But this speculation was indulgent fantasy. He had chosen

35

Blake: he had chosen hanging. Perhaps other and more gentle means were not to hand; perhaps he had acted upon impulse. What was it that the Super always said? 'Never theorize in advance of your facts.' She would have to look at the cottage.

Sir Ronald said, with a touch of impatience.

'Well, don't you want the job?'

Cordelia looked at Miss Leaming but the woman did not meet her eyes.

'I want it very much. I was wondering whether you really wanted me to take it.'

'I'm offering it to you. Worry about your own responsibilities, Miss Gray, and I'll look after mine.'

Cordelia said:

'Is there anything else that you can tell me? The ordinary things. Was your son in good health? Did he seem worried about his work or his love affairs? About money?'

'Mark would have inherited a considerable fortune from his maternal grandfather had he reached the age of twenty-five. In the meantime, he received an adequate allowance from me, but from the date of leaving college he transferred the balance back to my own account and instructed his Bank Manager to deal similarly with any future payments. Presumably he lived on his earnings for the last two weeks of his life. The postmortem revealed no illnesses and his tutor testified that his academic work was satisfactory. I, of course, know nothing of his subject. He didn't confide in me about his love affairs – what young man does to his father? If he had any, I would expect them to be heterosexual.'

36

Miss Leaming turned from her contemplation of the garden. She held out her hands in a gesture which could have been resignation or despair:

'We knew nothing about him, nothing! So why wait until he's dead and then start finding out?'

'And his friends?' asked Cordelia quietly.

'They rarely visited here but there were two I recognized at the inquest and the funeral: Hugo Tilling from his own college and his sister who is a postgraduate student at New Hall, studying philology. Do you remember her name, Eliza?'

'Sophie. Sophia Tilling. Mark brought her here to dinner once or twice.'

'Could you tell me something about your son's early life? Where was he educated?'

'He went to a pre-prep school when he was five and to a prep school subsequently. I couldn't have a child here running unsupervised in and out of the laboratory. Later, at his mother's wish – she died when Mark was nine months old – he went to a Woodard Foundation. My wife was what I believe is called a High Anglican and wanted the boy educated in that tradition. As far as I know, it had no deleterious effect on him.'

'Was he happy at prep school?'

'I expect he was as happy as most eight-year-olds are, which means that he was miserable most of the time, interposed with periods of animal spirits. Is all this relevant?'

'Anything could be. I have to try to get to know him, you see.'

What was it that the supercilious, sapient, superhuman Super had taught? 'Get to know the dead person. Nothing

37

about him is too trivial, too unimportant. Dead men can talk. They can lead directly to their murderer.' Only this time, of course, there wasn't a murderer. She said:

'It would be helpful if Miss Leaming could type out the information you have given to me and add the name of his college and his tutor. And please may I have a note signed by you to authorize me to make enquiries.'

He reached down to a left-hand drawer in the desk, took out a sheet of writing paper and wrote on it; then he passed it to Cordelia. The printed heading read: From Sir Ronald Callender, F.R.C., Garforth House, Cambridgeshire. Underneath he had written:

The bearer, Miss Cordelia Gray, is authorized to make inquiries on my behalf into the death on 26th May of my son Mark Callender. He had signed and dated it. He asked:

'Is there anything else?'

Cordelia said:

'You talked about the possibility of someone else being responsible for your son's death. Do you quarrel with the verdict?'

'The verdict was in accordance with the evidence which is all one can expect of a verdict. A court of law is not constituted to establish the truth. I'm employing you to make an attempt at that. Have you everything you need? I don't think we can help you with any more information.'

'I should like a photograph.' They looked at each other nonplussed. He said to Miss Leaming:

'A photograph. Have we a photograph, Eliza?'

'There is his passport somewhere but I'm not sure where. I have that photograph I took of him in the garden last summer. It shows him fairly clearly, I think. I'll get it.' She went out of the room. Cordelia said:

'And I should like to see his room, if I may. I assume that he stayed here during his vacations?'

'Only occasionally, but of course he had a room here. I'll show it to you.'

The room was on the second floor and at the back. Once inside, Sir Ronald ignored Cordelia. He walked over to the window and gazed out over the lawns as if neither she nor the room held any interest for him. It told Cordelia nothing about the adult Mark. It was simply furnished, a schoolboy's sanctum, and looked as if little had been changed in the last ten years. There was a low white cupboard against one wall with the usual row of discarded childhood toys; a teddy bear, his fur scuffed with much cuddling and one beady eye hanging loose; painted wooden trains and trucks; a Noah's Ark, its deck a-tumble with stiff-legged animals topped by a round-faced Noah and his wife; a boat with limp dejected sail; a miniature darts board. Above the toys were two rows of books. Cordelia went over to examine them. Here was the orthodox library of the middle-class child, the approved classics handed down from generation to generation, the traditional lore of Nanny and mother. Cordelia had come to them late as an adult; they had found no place in her Saturday comic and television-dominated childhood. She said:

'What about his present books?'

'They're in boxes in the cellar. He sent them here for storage when he left college and we haven't had time to unpack them yet. There hardly seems any point in it.'

There was a small round table beside the bed and on it a lamp and a bright round stone intricately holed by the sea, a treasure picked up, perhaps, from some holiday beach. Sir Ronald touched it gently with long tentative fingers then began rolling it under his palm over the surface of the table. Then, apparently without thinking, he dropped it into his pocket. 'Well,' he said. 'Shall we go down now?'

They were met at the foot of the stairs by Miss Leaming. She looked up at them as slowly they came down side by side. There was such controlled intensity in her regard that Cordelia waited almost with apprehension for her to speak. But she turned away, her shoulders drooping as if with sudden fatigue, and all she said was:

'I've found the photograph. I should like it back when you've finished with it please. I've put it in the envelope with the note. There isn't a fast train back to London until nine thirty-seven, so perhaps you would care to stay for dinner?'

*

The dinner party which followed was an interesting but rather odd experience, the meal itself a blend of the formal and casual which Cordelia felt was the result of conscious effort rather than chance. Some effect, she felt, had been aimed at but whether of a dedicated band of co-workers meeting together at the end of a day for a corporate meal, or the ritual imposition of order and ceremony on a diverse company, she wasn't sure. The party numbered ten: Sir Ronald Callender, Miss Leaming, Chris Lunn, a visiting American Professor, whose unpronounceable name she forgot as soon as Sir Ronald introduced her, and five of the young scientists. All the men, including Lunn, were in dinner jackets, and Miss Leaming wore a long skirt of patch-work satin below a plain sleeveless top. The rich blues, greens and reds gleamed and changed in the candlelight as she moved, and emphasized the pale silver of her hair and the almost colourless skin. Cordelia had been rather non-plussed when her hostess left her in the drawing room and went upstairs to change. She wished that she had something more competitive than the fawn skirt and green top, being at an age to value elegance more highly than youth.

She had been shown to Miss Leaming's bedroom to wash and had been intrigued by the elegance and simplicity of the furniture and the contrasting opulence of the adjacent bathroom. Studying her tired face in the mirror and wielding her lipstick, she had wished she had some eye shadow with her. On impulse, and with a sense of guilt, she had pulled open a dressing-table drawer. It was filled with a variety of make-up; old lipsticks in colours long out-of-date; half-used bottles of foundation cream; eye pencils; moisturizing creams; half-used bottles of scent. She had rummaged, and eventually found a stick of eye shadow which, in view of the wasteful muddle of discarded items in the drawer, she had had little compunction in using. The effect had been bizarre but striking. She could not compete with Miss Leaming but at least she looked five years older. The disorder in the drawer had surprised her and she had had to resist the temptation to see if the wardrobe and the other drawers were in a similar state of disarray. How inconsistent and how interesting human beings were! She thought it astonishing that such a fastidious and competent woman should be content to live with such a mess.

The dining room was at the front of the house. Miss Leaming placed Cordelia between herself and Lunn, a seating which held little prospect of pleasurable conversation. The rest of the party sat where they wished. The contrast between simplicity and elegance showed in the table arrangements. There was no artificial light and three silver branched candlesticks were placed at regular intervals down the table. Between them were set four wine carafes made of thick green glass with curved lips, such as Cordelia had often seen in cheap Italian restaurants. The place mats were of plain cork, but the forks and spoons were antique silver. The flowers were set in low bowls, not skilfully arranged but looking as if they were casualties of a garden storm, blooms which had snapped off in the wind and which someone had thought it kind to place in water.

The young men looked incongruous in their dinner jackets, not ill at ease since they enjoyed the essential self-esteem of the clever and successful, but as if they had picked up the suits second-hand or at a fancy dress costumier and were participating in a charade. Cordelia was surprised at their youth; she guessed that only one was over thirty. Three were untidy, fast talking, restless young men with loud emphatic voices who took no notice of Cordelia after the first introduction. The other two were quieter and one, a tall black-haired boy with strong irregular features, smiled at her across the table and looked as if he would like to have sat within speaking distance.

The meal was brought in by an Italian manservant and his wife who left the cooked dishes on hot plates on a side table. The food was plentiful and the smell almost intolerably appetizing to Cordelia, who hadn't realized until then just how hungry she was. There was a dish heaped high with glistening rice, a large casserole of veal in a rich mushroom sauce, a bowl of spinach. Beside it on the cold table was a large ham, a sirloin of beef and an interesting assortment of salads and fruit. The company served themselves, carrying their plates back to the table with whatever combination of food, hot or cold, they fancied. The young scientists piled their plates high and Cordelia followed their example.

She took little interest in the conversation except to notice that it was predominantly about science and that Lunn, although he spoke less than the others, spoke as their equal. He should, she thought, have looked ridiculous in his rather tight dinner jacket but, surprisingly, he looked the most at ease, the second most powerful personality in the room. Cordelia tried to analyse why this was so, but was defeated. He ate slowly, with finicky attention to the arrangement of the food on his plate, and from time to time, smiled secretly into his wine.

At the other end of the table Sir Ronald was peeling an apple and talking to his guest, his head inclined. The green rind slid thinly over his long fingers and curved down towards his plate. Cordelia glanced at Miss Leaming. She was staring at Sir Ronald with such unwavering and speculative concern, that Cordelia uncomfortably felt that every eye present must be irresistibly drawn to that pale disdainful mask. Then, Miss

Leaming seemed to become aware of her glance. She relaxed and turned to Cordelia:

'When we were travelling here together you were reading Hardy. Do you enjoy him?'

'Very much. But I enjoy Jane Austen more.'

'Then you must try to find an opportunity of visiting the Fitzwilliam Museum in Cambridge. They have a letter written by Jane Austen. I think you'll find it interesting.'

She spoke with the controlled artificial brightness of a hostess trying to find a subject to interest a difficult guest. Cordelia, her mouth full of veal and mushrooms, wondered how she would manage to get through the rest of the meal. Luckily, however, the American professor had caught the word 'Fitzwilliam' and now called down the table to enquire about the Museum's collection of majolica in which, apparently, he was interested. The conversation became general.

It was Miss Leaming who drove Cordelia to the station, Audley End this time instead of Cambridge; a change for which no reason was given. They didn't speak about the case during the drive. Cordelia was exhausted with tiredness, food and wine and allowed herself to be firmly taken in hand and placed in the train without attempting to gain any further information. She didn't really think she would have got it. As the train drew out, her tired fingers fumbled with the flap of the strong white envelope which Miss Leaming had handed to her and she drew out and read the enclosed note. It was expertly typed and set out, but told her little more than she had already learnt. With it was the photograph. She saw the picture of a laughing boy, his head half-turned towards the camera, one hand shielding his eyes from the sun. He was wearing jeans and a vest and was half lying on the lawn, a pile of books on the grass beside him. Perhaps he had been working there under the trees when she had come out of the french windows with her camera and called imperiously to him to smile. The photograph told Cordelia nothing except that for one recorded second at least, he had known how to be happy. She placed it back in the envelope; her hands closed protectively over it. Cordelia slept.

CHAPTER TWO

Next morning Cordelia left Cremona Road before seven o'clock. Despite her tiredness the night before, she had made her major preparations before she went to bed. They hadn't taken long. As Bernie had taught her, she checked systematically the scene-of-crime kit, an unnecessary routine since nothing had been touched since, in celebration of their partnership, he had first set it up for her. She put ready the polaroid camera; sorted into order the road maps from the jumble pushed into the back of his desk; shook out the sleeping bag and rolled it ready; filled a carrier bag with iron rations from Bernie's store of tinned soup and baked beans; considered, and finally decided to take, their copy of Professor Simpson's book on forensic medicine and her own Hacker portable radio; checked the first-aid kit. Finally, she found herself a fresh notebook, headed it *Case of Mark Callender* and ruled up the last few pages

45

ready for her expense account. These preliminaries had always been the most satisfying part of a case, before boredom or distaste set in, before anticipation crumbled into disenchantment and failure. Bernie's planning had always been meticulous and successful; it was reality which had let him down.

Finally, she considered her clothes. If this hot weather continued her Jaeger suit, bought from her savings after much careful thought to see her through almost any interview, would be uncomfortably hot, but she might have to interview the head of a college and the dignified professionalism best exemplified by a suit would be the effect to aim at. She decided to travel in her fawn suede skirt with a short-sleeved jumper and pack jeans and warmer jumpers for any field work. Cordelia enjoyed clothes, enjoyed planning and buying them, a pleasure circumscribed less by poverty than by her obsessive need to be able to pack the whole of her wardrobe into one medium sized suitcase like a refugee perpetually ready for flight.

Once she had shaken free from the tentacles of north London, Cordelia enjoyed the drive. The Mini purred along and Cordelia thought that it had never run so sweetly. She liked the flat East Anglian countryside, the broad streets of the market towns, the way in which the fields grew unhedged to the edge of the road, the openness and freedom of the far horizons and wide skies. The country matched her mood. She had grieved for Bernie and would grieve for him again, missing his comradeship and his undemanding affection, but this, in a sense, was her first case and she was glad to be tackling it alone. It was one that she thought she could solve. It neither appalled nor disgusted her. Driving in happy anticipation through the sunbathed countryside, the boot of the car carefully packed with her gear, she was filled with the euphoria of hope.

When she finally reached Duxford village she had difficulty at first in finding Summertrees. Major Markland was apparently a man who thought that his importance warranted omitting the name of the road from his address. But the second person she stopped to ask was a villager who was able to point the way, taking infinite trouble over the simple directions as if fearing that a perfunctory answer would have seemed discourteous. Cordelia had to find a suitable place to turn and then drive back a couple of miles, for she had already passed Summertrees.

And this, at last, must be the house. It was a large Victorian edifice of red brick, set well back, with a wide turfed verge between the open wooden gate leading to the drive and the road. Cordelia wondered why anyone should have wanted to build such an intimidatingly ugly house or, having decided to do so, should have set down a suburban monstrosity in the middle of the countryside. Perhaps it had replaced an earlier, more agreeable house. She drove the Mini onto the grass but at some distance from the gate and made her way up the drive. The garden suited the house; it was formal to the point of artificiality and too well kept. Even the rock plants burgeoned like morbid excrescences at carefully planned intervals between the terrace paving stones. There were two rectangular beds in the lawn, each planted with red rose trees and edged with alternate bands of lobelia and alyssum. They looked like a patriotic display in a public park. Cordelia felt the lack of a flag pole.

The front door was open, giving a view of a dark, brown-painted hall. Before Cordelia could ring, an elderly woman came round the corner of the house trundling a wheelbarrow full of plants. Despite the heat, she was wearing Wellington boots, a jumper and long tweed skirt and had a scarf tied round her head. When she saw Cordelia she dropped the handle of the wheelbarrow and said:

'Oh, good morning. You've come from the church about the jumble, I expect?'

Cordelia said:

'No, not the jumble. I'm from Sir Ronald Callender. It's about his son.'

'Then I expect you've called for his things? We wondered when Sir Ronald was going to send for them. They're all still at the cottage. We haven't been down there since Mark died. We called him Mark, you know. Well, he never told us who he was which was rather naughty of him.'

'It isn't about Mark's things. I want to talk about Mark himself. Sir Ronald has engaged me to try to find out why his son killed himself. My name is Cordelia Gray.'

This news seemed to puzzle rather than disconcert Mrs Markland. She blinked at Cordelia rapidly through troubled, rather stupid, eyes and clutched at the wheelbarrow handle as if for support.

'Cordelia Gray? Then we haven't met before, have we? I don't think I know a Cordelia Gray. Perhaps it would be better if you came into the drawing room and talked to my husband and sister-in-law.'

She abandoned the barrow where it stood in the middle of the path and led the way into the house, pulling off her head scarf and making ineffective pats at her hair. Cordelia followed her through the sparsely furnished hall, smelling of floor polish, with its clutter of walking sticks, umbrellas and mackintoshes draping the heavy oak hatstand, and into a room at the back of the house.

It was a horrible room, ill-proportioned, bookless, furnished not in poor taste but in no taste at all. A huge sofa of repellent design and two armchairs surrounded the fireplace and a heavy mahogany table, ornately carved and lurching on its pedestal, occupied the centre of the room. There was little other furniture. The only pictures were framed groups, pale oblong faces too small to identify posed in straight innominate lines in front of the camera. One was a regimental photograph; the other had a pair of crossed oars above two rows of burly adolescents, all of whom were wearing low peaked caps and striped blazers. Cordelia supposed it to be a school boating club.

Despite the warmth of the day, the room was sunless and cold. The doors of the french windows were open. On the lawn outside were grouped a large swinging sofa with a fringed canopy, three cane chairs sumptuously cushioned in a garish blue cretonne, each with its footrest, and a wooden slatted table. They looked part of a setting for a play in which the designer had somehow failed to catch the mood. All the garden furniture looked new and unused. Cordelia wondered why the family should bother to sit indoors on a summer morning while the lawn was so much more comfortably furnished.

Mrs Markland introduced Cordelia by sweeping her arm in a wide gesture of abandonment and saying feebly to the company in general:

'Miss Cordelia Gray. It isn't about the church jumble.'

Cordelia was struck by the resemblance that husband and wife and Miss Markland bore to each other. All three reminded her of horses. They had long, bony faces, narrow mouths above strong, square chins, eyes set unattractively close, and grey, coarse-looking hair which the two women wore in thick fringes almost to their eyes. Major Markland was drinking coffee from an immense white cup, much stained about the rim and sides, which had been set on a round tin tray. He held *The Times* in his hands. Miss Markland was knitting, an occupation which Cordelia vaguely felt was inappropriate to a hot summer morning.

The two faces, unwelcoming, only partly curious, regarded her with faint distaste. Miss Markland could knit without looking at the needles, an accomplishment which enabled her to fix Cordelia with sharp, inquisitive eyes. Invited by Major Markland to sit, Cordelia perched on the edge of the sofa, half expecting the smooth cushion to let out a rude noise as it subsided beneath her. She found it, however, unexpectedly hard. She composed her face into the appropriate expression – seriousness combined with efficiency and a touch of propitiatory humility seemed about right, but she wasn't sure that she managed to bring it off. As she sat there, knees demurely together, her shoulder bag at her feet, she was unhappily aware that she probably looked more like an eager seventeen-year-old facing her first

interview than a mature business woman, sole proprie-
tor of Pryde's Detective Agency.

She handed over Sir Ronald's note of authority and
said:

'Sir Ronald was very distressed on your account, I
mean it was awful for you that it should happen on
your property when you'd been so kind in finding Mark
a job he liked. His father hopes you won't mind talking
about it; it's just that he wants to know what made his
son kill himself.'

'And he sent you?' Miss Markland's voice was a com-
pound of disbelief, amusement and contempt. Cordelia
didn't resent the rudeness. She felt Miss Markland had
a point. She gave what she hoped was a credible explanation. It was probably true.

'Sir Ronald thinks that it must have been something
to do with Mark's life at university. He left college suddenly, as you may know, and his father was never told
why. Sir Ronald thought that I might be more successful
in talking to Mark's friends than the more usual type of
private detective. He didn't feel that he could trouble
the police; after all, this sort of enquiry isn't really their
kind of job.'

Miss Markland said grimly:

'I should have thought it was precisely their job; that
is, if Sir Ronald thinks there's something odd about his
son's death . . .'

Cordelia broke in:

'Oh no, I don't think there's any suggestion of that!
He's quite satisfied with the verdict. It's just that he
badly wants to know what made him do it.'

Miss Markland said with sudden fierceness:

'He was a drop-out. He dropped out of university, apparently he dropped out of his family obligations, finally he dropped out of life. Literally.'

Her sister-in-law gave a little bleat of protest.

'Oh, Eleanor, is that quite fair? He worked really well here. I liked the boy. I don't think—'

'I don't deny that he earned his money. That doesn't alter the fact that he was neither bred nor educated to be a jobbing gardener. He was, therefore, a drop-out. I don't know the reason and I have no interest in discovering it.'

'How did you come to employ him?' asked Cordelia.

It was Major Markland who answered.

'He saw my advertisement in the *Cambridge Evening News* for a gardener and turned up here one evening on his bicycle. I suppose he cycled all the way from Cambridge. It must have been about five weeks ago, a Tuesday I think.'

Again Miss Markland broke in:

'It was Tuesday, May 9th.'

The Major frowned at her as if irritated that he couldn't fault the information.

'Yes, well, Tuesday the 9th. He said that he had decided to leave university and take a job and that he'd seen my advertisement. He admitted that he didn't know much about gardening but said that he was strong and was willing to learn. His inexperience didn't worry me; we wanted him mostly for the lawns and for the vegetables. He never touched the flower garden; my wife and I see to that ourselves. Anyway, I quite liked the look of the boy and I thought I'd give him a chance.'

Miss Markland said:

'You took him because he was the only applicant who was prepared to work for the miserable pittance you were offering.' The Major, so far from showing offence at this frankness, smiled complacently.

'I paid him what he was worth. If more employers were prepared to do that, the country wouldn't be plagued with this inflation.' He spoke as one to whom economics were an open book.

'Didn't you think it was odd, his turning up like that?' asked Cordelia.

'Of course I did, damned odd! I thought he had probably been sent down; drink, drugs, revolution, you know the sort of thing they get up to at Cambridge now. But I asked him for the name of his tutor as a referee and rang him, a fellow called Horsfall. He wasn't particularly forthcoming but he did assure me that the boy had left voluntarily and to use his own words, his conduct while in college had been almost boringly irreproachable. I need not fear that the shades of Summertrees would be polluted.'

Miss Markland turned her knitting and broke into her sister-in-law's little cry of 'What can he have meant by that?' with the dry comment:

'A little more boredom of that kind would be welcome from the city of the plains.'

'Did Mr Horsfall tell you why Mark had left college?' asked Cordelia.

'I didn't enquire. That wasn't my business. I asked a plain question and I got a more or less plain answer, as plain as you can expect from those academic types. We certainly had no complaint about the lad while he was here. I speak as I find.'

'When did he move into the cottage?' asked Cordelia.

'Immediately. That wasn't our idea, of course. We never advertised the job as residential. However, he'd obviously seen the cottage and taken a fancy to the place and he asked if we'd mind if he camped out there. It wasn't practicable for him to cycle in from Cambridge each day, we could quite see that, and as far as we knew there was no one in the village who could put him up. I can't say I was keen on the idea; the cottage needs a lot doing to it. Actually we have it in mind to apply for a conversion grant and then get rid of the place. It wouldn't do for a family in its present state but the lad seemed keen on roughing it there, so we agreed.'

Cordelia said:

'So he must have inspected the cottage before he came for the job?'

'Inspected? Oh, I don't know. He probably snooped around to see what the property was like before he actually came to the door. I don't know that I blame him, I'd have done the same myself.'

Mrs Markland broke in:

'He was very keen on the cottage, very keen. I pointed out that there was no gas or electricity but he said that that wouldn't worry him; he'd buy a Primus stove and manage with lamps. There's water laid on, of course, and the main part of the roof is really quite sound. At least I think it is. We don't go there, you know. He seemed to settle in very happily. We never actually visited him, there was no need, but as far as I could see he was looking after himself perfectly well. Of course as my husband said, he was very inexperienced; there were one or two things we had to teach him, like coming up to the kitchen early every morning for the orders. But I liked the boy; he was always working hard when I was in the garden.'

Cordelia said:

'I wonder if I might have a look at the cottage?'

The request disconcerted them. Major Markland looked at his wife. There was an embarrassed silence and for a moment Cordelia feared that the answer would be no. Then Miss Markland stabbed her needles into the ball of wool and got to her feet:

'I'll come with you now,' she said.

The grounds of Summertrees were spacious. First there was the formal rose garden, the bushes closely planted and grouped according to variety and colour like a market garden, the name tags fixed at precisely the same height from the earth. Next was the kitchen garden cut in two by a gravel path with evidence of Mark Callender's work in the weeded rows of lettuce and cabbages, the patches of dug earth. Finally they passed through a gate into a small orchard of old and unpruned apple trees. The scythed grass, smelling richly of hay, lay in thick swathes round the gnarled trunks.

At the furthest end of the orchard was a thick hedge, so overgrown that the wicket gate into the rear garden of the cottage was at first difficult to see. But the grass around it had been trimmed and the gate opened easily to Miss Markland's hand. On the other side was a thick bramble hedge, dark and impenetrable and obviously allowed to grow wild for a generation. Someone had hacked a way through, but Miss Markland and Cordelia had to bend low to avoid catching their hair on its tangled tentacles of thorn.

55

Once free of this barrier, Cordelia lifted her head and blinked in the bright sunshine. She gave a little exclamation of pleasure. In the short time in which he had lived here Mark Callender had created a little oasis of order and beauty out of chaos and neglect. Old flower beds had been discovered and the surviving plants tended; the stone path had been scraped free of grass and moss; a minute square of lawn to the right of the cottage door had been cut and weeded. On the other side of the path a patch about two feet square had been partly dug. The fork was still in the earth, driven deep about two feet from the end of the row.

The cottage was a low, brick building under a slate roof. Bathed in the afternoon sunshine, and despite its bare, rain-scoured door, its rotted window frames and the glimpse of exposed beams in the roof, it had the gentle melancholy charm of age which hadn't yet degenerated into decay. Just outside the cottage door, dropped casually side by side, was a pair of heavy gardening shoes encrusted with earth.

'His?' asked Cordelia.

'Who else's?'

They stood together for a moment contemplating the dug earth. Neither spoke. Then they moved to the back door. Miss Markland fitted the key into the lock. It turned easily as if the lock had been recently oiled. Cordelia followed her into the sitting-room of the cottage.

The air was cool after the heat of the garden but unfresh, with a taint of contagion. Cordelia saw that the plan of the cottage was simple. There were three doors, one straight ahead obviously led to the front garden but was locked and barred, the joints hung with cobwebs as if it hadn't been opened for generations. One to the right led, as Cordelia guessed, to the kitchen. The third door was ajar and she could glimpse through it an uncarpeted wooden stairway leading to the first floor. In the middle of the room was a wooden-topped table, the surface scarred with much scrubbing, and with two kitchen chairs, one at each end. In the middle of the table a blue ribbed mug held a posy of dead flowers, black brittle stems bearing sad tatters of unidentifiable plants, their pollen staining the surface of the table like golden dust. Shafts of sunlight cut across the still air; in their beams a myriad of motes, specks of dust and infinitesimal life danced grotesquely.

To the right was a fireplace, an old-fashioned iron range with ovens each side of the open fire. Mark had been burning wood and papers; there was a mound of white ash in the grate and a pile of kindling wood and small logs placed ready for the next evening. On one side of the fire was a low wooden slatted chair with a faded cushion and on the other a wheel-backed chair with the legs sawn off, perhaps to make it low enough for nursing a child. Cordelia thought that it must have been a beautiful chair before its mutilation.

Two immense beams, blackened with age, ran across the ceiling. In the middle of one was fixed a steel hook, probably once used for hanging bacon. Cordelia and Miss Markland looked at it without speaking; there was no need for question and answer. After a moment they moved, as if by common consent, to the two fireside chairs and sat down. Miss Markland said:

'I was the one who found him. He didn't come up to the kitchen for the day's orders so after breakfast I walked down here to see if he had overslept. It was nine twenty-three exactly. The door was unlocked. I knocked, but there was no reply so I pushed it open. He was hanging from that hook with a leather belt round his neck. He was wearing his blue cotton trousers, the ones he usually worked in, and his feet were bare. That chair was lying on its side on the floor. I touched his chest. He was quite cold.'

'Did you cut him down?'

'No. He was obviously dead and I thought it better to leave the body until the police arrived. But I did pick up the chair and place it so that it supported his feet. That was an irrational action, I know, but I couldn't bear to see him hanging there without releasing the pressure on his throat. It was, as I've said, irrational.'

'I think it was very natural. Did you notice anything else about him, about the room?'

'There was a half-empty mug of what looked like coffee on the table and a great deal of ash in the grate. It looked as if he had been burning papers. His portable typewriter was where you see it now, on that side table; the suicide note was still in the machine. I read it, then I went back to the house, told my brother and sister-in-law what had happened and rang the police. After the police arrived I brought them to this cottage, and confirmed what I had seen. I never came in here again until this moment.'

'Did you, or Major and Mrs Markland, see Mark on the night he died?'

'None of us saw him after he stopped work at about six-thirty. He was a little later that evening because he wanted to finish mowing the front lawn. We all saw him putting the mower away, then walking across the garden towards the orchard. We never saw him alive again. No one was at home at Summertrees that night. We had a dinner party at Trumpington – an old army colleague of my brother. We didn't get home until after midnight. By then, according to the medical evidence, Mark must have been dead about four hours.'

Cordelia said:

'Please tell me about him.'

'What is there to tell? His official hours were eight-thirty to six o'clock, with an hour for lunch and half an hour for tea. In the evenings he would work in the garden here or round the cottage. Sometimes in his lunch hour he would cycle to the village store. I used to meet him there from time to time. He didn't buy much – a loaf of wholemeal bread, butter, the cheapest cut of bacon, tea, coffee – the usual things. I heard him ask about free-range eggs and Mrs Morgan told him that Wilcox at Grange Farm would always sell him half a dozen. We didn't speak when we met, but he would smile. In the evenings once the light had faded, he used to read or type at that table. I could see his head against the lamplight.'

'I thought Major Markland said that you didn't visit the cottage?'

'They don't; it holds certain embarrassing memories for them. I do.' She paused and looked into the dead fire.

'My fiancé and I used to spend a great deal of time here before the war when he was at Cambridge. He was killed in 1937, fighting in Spain for the Republican cause.'

'I'm sorry,' said Cordelia. She felt the inadequacy, the insincerity of her response and yet, what else was there to say? It had all happened nearly forty years ago. She hadn't heard of him before. The spasm of grief, so brief that it was hardly felt, was no more than a transitory inconvenience, a sentimental regret for all lovers who died young, for the inevitability of human loss.

Miss Markland spoke with sudden passion as if the words were being forced out of her:

'I don't like your generation, Miss Gray. I don't like your arrogance, your selfishness, your violence, the curious selectivity of your compassion. You pay for nothing with your own coin, not even for your ideals. You denigrate and destroy and never build. You invite punishment like rebellious children, then scream when you are punished. The men I knew, the men I was brought up with, were not like that.'

Cordelia said gently:

'I don't think Mark Callender was like that either.'

'Perhaps not. At least the violence he practised was on himself.' She looked up at Cordelia searchingly.

'No doubt you'll say I'm jealous of youth. It's a common enough syndrome of my generation.'

'It ought not to be. I can never see why people should be jealous. After all, youth isn't a matter of privilege, we all get the same share of it. Some people may be born at an easier time or be richer or more privileged than others, but that hasn't anything to do with being young. And being young is terrible sometimes. Don't you remember how terrible it could be?'

'Yes, I remember. But I remember other things, too.'

Cordelia sat in silence, thinking that the conversation was strange but somehow inevitable and that, for some reason, she didn't resent it. Miss Markland looked up.

'His girl friend visited him once. At least, I suppose she was his girl friend or why should she have come? It was about three days after he started work.'

'What was she like?'

'Beautiful. Very fair, with a face like a Botticelli angel – smooth, oval, unintelligent. She was foreign, French, I think. She was also rich.'

'How could you tell that, Miss Markland?' Cordelia was intrigued.

'Because she spoke with a foreign accent; because she arrived driving a white Renault which I took to be her own car; because her clothes, although odd and unsuitable for the country, weren't cheap; because she walked up to the front door and announced that she wanted to see him with the confident arrogance that one associates with the rich.'

'And did he see her?'

'He was working in the orchard at the time, scything the grass; I took her down to him. He greeted her calmly and without embarrassment and took her to sit in the cottage until it was time for him to stop work. He seemed pleased enough to see her but not, I thought, either delighted or surprised. He didn't introduce her. I left them together and returned to the house before he had the chance to. I didn't see her again.'

Before Cordelia could speak she said suddenly:

'You're thinking of living here for a time, aren't you?'

'Will they mind? I didn't like to ask in case they said no.'

'They won't know, and if they did, they wouldn't care.'

'But do you mind?'

'No. I shan't worry you and I don't mind.' They were talking in whispers as if in church. Then Miss Markland got up and moved to the door. She turned.

'You've taken on this job for the money, of course. Why not? But if I were you I'd keep it that way. It's unwise to become too personally involved with another human being. When that human being is dead, it can be dangerous as well as unwise.'

*

Miss Markland stumped off down the garden path and disappeared through the wicker gate. Cordelia was glad to see her go. She was fidgeting with impatience to examine the cottage. This was where it had happened; this was where her job really began.

What was it that the Super had said? 'When you're examining a building look at it as you would a country church. Walk round it first. Look at the whole scene inside and out; then make your deductions. Ask yourself what you saw, not what you expected to see or what you hoped to see, but what you saw.'

He must be a man then who liked country churches and that at least was a point in his favour; for this, surely, was genuine Dalgliesh dogma. Bernie's reaction to churches, whether country or town, had been one of half-superstitious wariness. Cordelia decided to follow the advice.

She made her way first to the east side of the cottage. Here, discreetly set back and almost smothered by the hedge, was a wooden privy with its latched stable-like door. Cordelia peeped inside. The privy was very clean and looked as if it had been recently repainted. When she pulled the chain, to her relief, the bowl flushed. There was a roll of lavatory paper hanging by a string from the door and nailed beside it a small plastic bag contained a crumpled collection of orange papers and other soft wrappings. He had been an economical young man. Next to the privy was a large dilapidated shed containing a man's bicycle, old but well cared for, a large tin of white emulsion paint with the lid rammed down hard and a clean brush up-ended in a jam-jar beside it, a tin bath, a few clean sacks, and a collection of gardening tools. All were shining clean and were neatly disposed against the wall or supported on nails.

She moved to the front of the cottage. This was in marked contrast to the southern aspect. Here Mark Callender had made no attempt to tackle the waist-high wilderness of nettles and grass which stifled the small front garden and almost obliterated the path. A thick climbing shrub sprinkled with small white flowers had thrust its black and thorned boughs to bar the two ground floor windows. The gate leading to the lane had stuck and would open only wide enough for a visitor to squeeze through. On each side a holly tree stood sentinel, its leaves grey with dust. The front hedge of privet was head-high. Cordelia could see that on either side of the path there had once been twin flower beds edged with large round stones which had been painted white. Now most of the stones had sunk out of sight among the encroaching weeds and nothing remained of the beds but a tangle of wild and straggling roses.

As she took a last look at the front garden, her eye caught a flash of colour half-trodden among the weeds at the side of the path. It was a crumpled page of an illustrated magazine. She smoothed it open and saw that it was a colour photograph of a female nude. The woman had her back to the camera and was bending forward, gross buttocks splayed above booted thighs. She was smiling saucily over her shoulder in a blatant invitation made more grotesque by the long androgynous face which even tactful lighting couldn't make other than repellent. Cordelia noted the date at the top of the page; it was the May edition. So the magazine, or at least the picture, could have been brought to the cottage while he was there.

She stood with it in her hand trying to analyse the nature of her disgust which seemed to her excessive. The picture was vulgar and salacious but no more offensive or indecent than dozens on view in the side streets of London. But as she folded it away in her bag – for it was evidence of a kind – she felt contaminated and depressed. Had Miss Markland been more percipient than she knew? Was she, Cordelia, in danger of becoming sentimentally obsessed with the dead boy? The picture probably had nothing to do with Mark, it could easily have been dropped by some visitor to the cottage. But she wished that she hadn't seen it.

She passed round to the west of the cottage and made one more discovery. Hidden behind a clump of elder bushes was a small well about four feet in diameter. It had no superstructure but was closely fitted with a domed lid made of strong slatted wood and fitted at the top with an iron hoop. Cordelia saw that the cover was padlocked to the wooden rim of the well and the lock, although rusty with age, held firm at her tug. Someone had taken the trouble to see that there was no danger here to exploring children or visiting tramps.

And now it was time to explore the interior of the cottage. First the kitchen. It was a small room with a window over the sink looking east. It had obviously been recently painted and the large table which took up most of the room had been covered with a red plastic cloth. There was a poky larder containing half a dozen tins of beer, a jar of marmalade, a crock of butter and the mouldy heel of a loaf. It was here in the kitchen that Cordelia found the explanation to the disagreeable smell which had struck her on entering the cottage. On the table was an open bottle of milk about half full, the silver top crumpled beside it. The milk was solid and furred with putrefaction; a bloated fly was sucking at the rim of the bottle and still stuck to its feast as, instinctively, she tried to flick it away. On the other side of the table was a twin-burner paraffin stove with a heavy pot on one burner. Cordelia tugged at the close-fitting lid and it came off suddenly, letting out a rich repulsive smell. She opened the table drawer and stirred the mess with a spoon. It looked like beef stew. Chunks of greenish meat, soapy looking potatoes and unidentifiable vegetables floated up through the scum like drowned and putrefying flesh. Beside the sink was an orange box placed on one side and used as a vegetable store. The potatoes were green, the onions had shrunk and sprouted, the carrots were wrinkled and limp. So nothing had been cleaned up, nothing had been removed. The police had taken away the body and any evidence they required but no one, neither the Marklands nor the boy's family or friends, had bothered to come back to clean up the pathetic leavings of his young life.

Cordelia went upstairs. A cramped landing led to two bedrooms, one obviously unused for years. Here the window frame had rotted, the ceiling plaster had crumbled and a faded paper patterned with roses was peeling away with the damp. The second and larger room was the one in which he had slept. There was a single iron bed with a hair mattress and on it a sleeping bag and a bolster folded in two to make a high pillow. Beside the bed was an old table with two candles, stuck with their own wax to a cracked plate, and a box of matches. His clothes were hung in the single cupboard, a pair of bright green corduroy trousers, one or two shirts, pullovers and one formal suit. A few under-clothes, clean but not ironed, were folded on the ledge above. Cordelia fingered the pullovers. They were hand knitted in thick wool and intricate patterns and there were four of them. Someone, then, had cared enough about him to take some trouble on his behalf. She wondered who.

She ran her hands over his meagre wardrobe, feeling for pockets. She found nothing except a slim, brown leather wallet in the bottom left hand pocket of his suit. Excitedly she carried it over to the window hoping that it might contain a clue – a letter, perhaps, a list of names and addresses, a personal note. But the wallet was empty except for a couple of pound notes, his driving licence and a blood donor's card issued by the Cambridge blood transfusion service, which showed his group to be B rhesus negative.

The uncurtained window gave a view of the garden. His books were arranged on the window shelf. There were only a few of them: several volumes of the *Cambridge Modern History*; some Trollope and Hardy; a complete William Blake; school text book volumes of Wordsworth, Browning and Donne; two paperbacks on gardening. At the end of the row was a white leather-bound book which Cordelia saw was the Book of Common Prayer. It was fitted with a finely wrought brass clasp and looked much used. She was disappointed in the books; they told her little beyond his superficial tastes. If he had come to this solitary life to study, to write or to philosophize he had come singularly ill-equipped.

The most interesting thing in the room was above the bed. It was a small oil painting about nine inches square. Cordelia studied it. It was certainly Italian and probably, she thought, late fifteenth century. It showed a very young tonsured monk reading at a table, his sensitive fingers enleafed between the pages of his book. The long, controlled face was taut with concentration, the heavy lidded eyes were fixed on the page. Behind him, a view from the open window was a miniature of delight. Cordelia thought that one would never tire of looking at it. It was a Tuscan scene showing a walled city with towers enclosed by cypresses, a river winding like a silver stream, a gaudily clad procession preceded by banners, yoked oxen working in the fields. She saw the picture as a contrast between the worlds of intellect and action and tried to remember where she had seen similar paintings. The comrades – as Cordelia always thought of that ubiquitous band of fellow-revolutionaries who

67

attached themselves to her father – had been very fond of exchanging messages in art galleries and Cordelia had spent hours walking slowly from picture to picture, waiting for the casual visitor to pause beside her and whisper his few words of warning or information. The device had always struck her as a childish and unnecessarily histrionic way of communicating, but at least the galleries were warm and she had enjoyed looking at the pictures. She enjoyed this picture; he had obviously liked it too. Had he also liked that vulgar illustration which she had found in the front garden? Were they both an essential part of his nature?

The tour of inspection over, she made herself coffee using a packet from his store cupboard and boiling the water on the stove. She took a chair from the sitting-room and sat outside the back door with the mug of coffee in her lap, her head stretched back to feel the sun. She was filled with a gentle happiness as she sat there, contented and relaxed, listening to the silence, her half-closed lids impressed with the visage of the sun. But now it was time to think. She had examined the cottage in accordance with the Super's instructions. What did she now know about the dead boy? What had she seen? What could she deduce?

He had been almost obsessively neat and tidy. His garden tools were wiped after use and carefully put away, his kitchen had been painted and was clean and ordered. Yet he had abandoned his digging less than two feet from the end of a row; had left the uncleaned fork in the earth; had dropped his gardening shoes casually at the back door. He had apparently burnt all his papers before killing himself, yet had left his coffee mug unwashed. He had made himself a stew for his supper which he hadn't touched. The preparation of the vegetables must have been done earlier in the same day, or perhaps the day before, but the stew was clearly intended for supper that night. The pot was still on the stove and was full to the brim. This wasn't a heated-up meal, one left from the evening before. This surely meant that he had only made the decision to kill himself after the stew had been prepared and had been put on the stove to cook. Why should he trouble to prepare a meal that he knew he wouldn't be alive to eat?

But was it likely, she wondered, that a healthy young man coming in from an hour or two of hard digging and with a hot meal waiting should be in that mood of boredom, *accidie*, anguish or despair which could lead to suicide? Cordelia could remember times of intense unhappiness, but she couldn't recall that they had followed purposeful outdoor exercise in the sun with a meal in prospect. And why the mug of coffee, the one which the police had taken away to analyse? There were tins of beer in the larder; if he had come in thirsty from his digging, why not open one of those? Beer would have been the quickest, the obvious way of quenching thirst. Surely no one, however thirsty, would brew and drink coffee just before a meal. Coffee came after food.

But suppose someone had visited him that evening. It wasn't likely to have been someone calling with a casual message as he passed by; it was important enough for Mark to break off his digging even within two feet of the end of a row and invite the visitor into the cottage. It was probably a visitor who didn't like or drink beer

– could that mean a woman? It was a visitor who wasn't expected to stay for supper but yet was at the cottage long enough to be offered some refreshment. Perhaps it was someone on his way to his own evening meal. Obviously, the visitor hadn't been invited to supper earlier or why would the two of them have begun the meal by drinking coffee and why would Mark have worked so late in the garden instead of coming in to change? So it was an unexpected visitor. But why was there only one mug of coffee? Surely Mark would have shared it with his guest or, if he preferred not to drink coffee, would have opened a tin of beer for himself. But there was no empty beer can in the kitchen and no second mug. Had it perhaps been washed and put away? But why should Mark wash one mug and not the other? Was it to conceal the fact that he'd had a visitor that evening?

The jug of coffee on the kitchen table was almost empty and the bottle of milk only half full. Surely more than one person had taken milk and coffee. But perhaps that was a dangerous and unwarranted deduction; the visitor might well have had his mug refilled.

But suppose it wasn't Mark who had wished to conceal the fact that a visitor had called that night; suppose it wasn't Mark who had washed and put away the second mug; suppose it was the visitor who had wished to conceal the fact of his presence. But why should he bother to do that since he couldn't know that Mark was going to kill himself? Cordelia shook herself impatiently. This, of course, was nonsense. Obviously the visitor wouldn't have washed up the mug if Mark were still there and alive. He would only have obliterated the evidence of his visit if Mark were already dead. And if Mark had been dead, had been strung up on that hook before his visitor had left the cottage, then could this really be suicide? A word dancing at the back of Cordelia's mind, an amorphous half-formed jangle of letters, came suddenly into focus and, for the first time, spelt out clearly the blood-stained word. Murder.

*

Cordelia sat on in the sun for another five minutes finishing her coffee, then she washed up the mug and hung it back on a hook in the larder. She walked down the lane to the road where the Mini was still parked on the grass verge outside Summertrees, glad of the instinct that had led her to leave it out of sight of the house. Letting in the clutch gently, she drove it slowly down the lane looking carefully from side to side for a possible parking place; to leave it outside the cottage would only advertise her presence. It was a pity that Cambridge wasn't closer; she could then have used Mark's bicycle. The Mini wasn't necessary to her task but would be inconveniently conspicuous wherever she left it.

But she was lucky. About fifty yards down the lane was the entrance to a field, a wide grass verge with a small copse at one side. The copse looked damp and sinister. It was impossible to believe that flowers could spring from this tainted earth or bloom among these scarred and misshapen trees. The ground was scattered with old pots and pans, the up-ended skeleton of a pram, a battered and rusty gas stove. Beside a stunted oak a matted heap of blankets was disintegrating into the earth. But there was space for her to drive the Mini off the road and under cover of a kind. If she locked it carefully it would be better here than outside the cottage and at night, she thought, it would be unobserved.

But now, she drove it back to the cottage and began to unpack. She moved Mark's few underclothes to one side of the shelf and set her own beside them. She laid her sleeping bag on the bed over his, thinking that she would be glad of the extra comfort. There was a red toothbrush and half-used tube of toothpaste in a jam-jar on the kitchen window ledge; she placed her yellow brush and her own tube beside them. She hung her towel next to his across the cord which he had fixed between two nails under the kitchen sink. Then she made an inventory of the contents of the larder and a list of the things she would need. It would be better to buy them in Cambridge; she would only draw attention to her presence if she shopped locally. The saucepan of stew and the half bottle of milk were a worry. She couldn't leave them in the kitchen to sour the cottage with the stench of decay but she was reluctant to throw the contents away. She considered whether to photograph them but decided against it, tangible objects were better evidence. In the end she carried them out to the shed and shrouded them thickly with a piece of old sacking.

Last of all, she thought about the gun. It was a heavy object to carry with her all the time but she felt unhappy about parting with it, even temporarily. Although the back door of the cottage could be locked and Miss Markland had left her the key, an intruder would have no difficulty in breaking in through a window. She decided that the best plan would be to secrete the ammunition among her underclothes in the bedroom cupboard but to hide the pistol separately in or near the cottage. The exact place cost her a little thought, but then she remembered the thick and twisting limbs of the elder bush by the well; by reaching high, she was able to feel for a convenient hollow near the fork of a branch and could slip the gun, still shrouded in its drawstring bag, among the concealing leaves.

At last she was ready to leave for Cambridge. She looked at her watch; it was half-past ten; she could be in Cambridge by eleven and there would still be two hours of the morning to go. She decided that her best plan would be to visit the newspaper office first and read the account of the inquest, then to see the police; after that she would go in search of Hugo and Sophia Tilling.

She drove away from the cottage with a feeling very like regret, as if she were leaving home. It was, she thought, a curious place, heavy with atmosphere and showing two distinct faces to the world like facets of a human personality; the north, with its dead thorn-barred windows, its encroaching weeds, and its forbidding hedge of privet, was a numinous stage for horror and tragedy. Yet the rear, where he had lived and worked, had cleared and dug the garden and tied up the few flowers, had weeded the path, and opened the windows to the sun, was as peaceful as a sanctuary. Sitting there at the door she had felt that nothing horrible could ever touch her; she was able to contemplate the night alone there without fear. Was it this atmosphere of healing tranquillity, she wondered, that had attracted Mark Callender? Had he sensed it before he took the job, or was it in some mysterious way the result of his transitory and doomed sojourn there? Major Markland had been right; obviously Mark had looked at the cottage before he went up to the house. Had it been the cottage he wanted or the job? Why were the Marklands so reluctant to come to the place, so reluctant that they obviously hadn't visited it even to clean up after his death? And why had Miss Markland spied on him, for surely such close observation was very close to spying? Had she only confided that story about her dead lover to justify her interest in the cottage, her obsessional preoccupation with what the new gardener was doing? And was the story even true? That ageing body heavy with latent strength, that equine expression of perpetual discontent, could she really once have been young, have lain perhaps with her lover on Mark's bed through the long, warm evenings of long-dead summers? How remote, how impossible and grotesque it all seemed.

Cordelia drove down Hills Road, past the vigorous memorial statue of a young 1914 soldier striding to death, past the Roman Catholic church and into the centre of the city. Again she wished that she could have abandoned the car in favour of Mark's bicycle. Everyone else seemed to be riding and the air tinkled with bells like a festival. In these narrow and crowded streets even the compact Mini was a liability. She decided to park it as soon as she could find a place and set out on foot in search of a telephone. She had decided to vary her programme and see the police first.

But it didn't surprise her when at last she rang the police station to hear that Sergeant Maskell, who had dealt with the Callender case, was tied up all the morning. It was only in fiction that the people one wanted to

74

interview were sitting ready at home or in their office, with time, energy and interest to spare. In real life, they were about their own business and one waited on their convenience, even if, untypically, they welcomed the attention of Pryde's Detective Agency. Usually they didn't. She mentioned Sir Ronald's note of authority to impress her hearer with the authenticity of her business. The name was not without influence. He went away to enquire. After less than a minute he came back to say that Sergeant Maskell could see Miss Gray at two-thirty that afternoon.

So the newspaper office came first after all. Old files were at least accessible and could not object to being consulted. She quickly found what she wanted. The account of the inquest was brief, couched in the usual formal language of a court report. It told her little that was new, but she made a careful note of the main evidence. Sir Ronald Callender testified that he hadn't spoken to his son for over a fortnight before his death, when Mark had telephoned to tell his father of his decision to leave college and to take a job at Summertrees. He hadn't consulted Sir Ronald before making the decision nor had he explained his reasons. Sir Ronald had subsequently spoken to the Master, and the College authorities were prepared to take his son back for the next academic year if he changed his mind. His son had never spoken to him of suicide and had no health or money worries as far as he was aware. Sir Ronald's testimony was followed by a brief reference to other evidence. Miss Markland described how she had found the body; a forensic pathologist testified that the cause of death was asphyxia due to strangulation; Sergeant

Maskell recounted the measures he had thought it proper to take and a report from the forensic science laboratory was submitted which stated that a mug of coffee found on the table had been analysed and found harmless. The verdict was that the deceased died by his own hand while the balance of his mind was disturbed. Closing the heavy file, Cordelia felt depressed. It looked as if the police work had been thorough. Was it really possible that these experienced professionals had overlooked the significance of the unfinished digging, the gardening shoes dropped casually at the back door, the untouched supper?

And now, at midday, she was free until half-past two. She could explore Cambridge. She bought the cheapest guide book she could find from Bowes and Bowes, resisting the temptation to browse among the books, since time was short and pleasure must be rationed. She stuffed her shoulder bag with a pork pie and fruit bought from a market stall and entered St. Mary's church to sit quietly and work out her itinerary. Then for an hour and a half she walked about the city and its colleges in a trance of happiness.

She was seeing Cambridge at its loveliest. The sky was an infinity of blue from whose pellucid depths the sun shone in unclouded but gentle radiance. The trees in the college gardens and the avenues leading to the Backs, as yet untouched by the heaviness of high summer, lifted their green tracery against stone and river and sky. Punts shot and curtsied under the bridges, scattering the gaudy water fowl, and by the rise of the new Garret Hostel bridge the willows trailed their pale, laden boughs in the darker green of the Cam.

She included all the special sights in her itinerary. She walked gravely down the length of Trinity Library, visited the Old Schools, sat quietly at the back of King's College Chapel marvelling at the upward surge of John Wastell's great vault spreading into curved fans of delicate white stone. The sunlight pouring through the great windows staining the still air, blue, crimson and green. The finely carved Tudor roses, the heraldic beasts supporting the crown, stood out in arrogant pride from the panels. Despite what Milton and Wordsworth had written, surely this chapel had been built to the glory of an earthly sovereign, not to the service of God? But that didn't invalidate its purpose nor blemish its beauty. It was still a supremely religious building. Could a non-believer have planned and executed this superb interior? Was there an essential unity between motive and creation? This was the question which Carl alone among the comrades would have been interested to explore and she thought of him in his Greek prison, trying to shut her mind to what they might be doing to him and wishing his stocky figure at her side.

During her tour she indulged in small particular pleasures. She bought a linen tea cloth printed with a picture of the chapel from the stall near the west door; she lay on her face on the shorn grass above the river by King's Bridge and let the cold green water eddy round her arms; she wandered among the book stalls in the market place and after careful reckoning bought a small edition of Keats printed on India paper and a cotton kaftan patterned in greens, blues and browns. If this hot weather continued it would be cooler than a shirt or jeans for wearing in the evenings.

Finally, she returned to King's College. There was a seat set against the great stone wall which ran from the chapel down to the river bank and she sat there in the sun to eat her lunch. A privileged sparrow hopped across the immaculate lawn and cocked a bright insouciant eye. She threw him scraps from the crust of her pork pie and smiled at his agitated peckings. From the river floated the sound of voices calling across the water, the occasional scrunch of wood on wood, the harsh call of a duckling. Everything about her – the pebbles bright as jewels in the gravel path, the little shafts of grass at the verge of the lawn, the sparrow's brittle legs – was seen with an extraordinary intensity as if happiness had cleared her eyes.

Then memory recalled the voices. First her father's:

'Our little fascist was educated by the papists. It accounts for a lot. How on earth did it happen, Delia?'

'You remember, Daddy. They muddled me up with another C. Gray who was a Roman Catholic. We both passed the eleven plus exam the same year. When they discovered the mistake they wrote to you to ask if you minded my staying on at the Convent because I'd settled there.'

He hadn't in fact replied. Reverend Mother had tried tactfully to conceal that he hadn't bothered to answer and Cordelia had stayed on at the Convent for the six most settled and happy years of her life, insulated by order and ceremony from the mess and muddle of life outside, incorrigibly Protestant, uncoerced, gently pitied as one in invincible ignorance. For the first time she learned that she needn't conceal her intelligence, that cleverness which a succession of foster mothers had somehow seen as a threat. Sister Perpetua had said:

'There shouldn't be any difficulty over your A Levels if you can go on as you are at present. That means that we plan for university entrance in two years' time from this October. Cambridge, I think. We might as well try for Cambridge, and I really don't see why you shouldn't stand a chance of a scholarship.'

Sister Perpetua had herself been at Cambridge before she entered the Convent and she still spoke of the academic life, not with longing or regret, but as if it had been a sacrifice worthy of her vocation. Even the fifteen-year-old Cordelia had recognized that Sister Perpetua was a real scholar and had thought it rather unfair of God to bestow a vocation on one who was so happy and useful as she was. But for Cordelia herself, the future had, for the first time, seemed settled and full of promise. She would go to Cambridge and Sister would visit her there. She had a romantic vision of wide lawns under the sun and the two of them walking in Donne's paradise. 'Rivers of knowledge are there, arts and sciences flow from thence; gardens that are walled in; bottomless depths of unsearchable councils are there.' By the aid of her own brain and Sister's prayers she would win her scholarship. The prayers occasionally worried her. She had absolutely no doubt of their efficacy since God must necessarily listen to one who at such personal cost had listened to Him. And if Sister's influence gave her an unfair advantage over the other candidates – well, that couldn't be helped. In a matter of such importance neither Cordelia nor Sister Perpetua had been disposed to fret over theological niceties.

But this time Daddy had replied to the letter. He had discovered a need for his daughter. There were no A

Levels and no scholarship and at sixteen Cordelia finished her formal education and began her wandering life as cook, nurse, messenger and general camp follower to Daddy and the comrades.

But now by what devious routes and for what a strange purpose she had come at last to Cambridge. The city didn't disappoint her. In her wanderings she had seen lovelier places, but none in which she had been happier or more at peace. How indeed, she thought, could the heart be indifferent to such a city where stone and stained glass, water and green lawns, trees and flowers were arranged in such ordered beauty for the service of learning. But as regretfully she rose at last to go, brushing the few crumbs from her skirt, a quotation, untraced and unsought, came into her mind. She heard it with such clarity that the words might have been spoken by a human voice, a young masculine voice, unrecognized and yet mysteriously familiar: 'Then saw I that there was a way to hell even from the gates of heaven.'

*

The police headquarters building was modern and functional. It represented authority tempered with discretion; the public were to be impressed but not intimidated. Sergeant Maskell's office and the Sergeant himself conformed to this philosophy. He was surprisingly young and elegantly dressed, with a square, tough face wary with experience and a long but skilfully cut hair style which, Cordelia thought, could only just have satisfied the Force requirements, even for a plain clothes detective. He was punctiliously polite without being gallant and this reassured her. It wasn't going to be an easy interview, but she had no wish to be treated with the indulgence shown to a pretty but importunate child. Sometimes it helped to play the part of a vulnerable and naïve young girl eager for information – this was a role in which Bernie had frequently sought to cast her – but she sensed that Sergeant Maskell would respond better to an unflirtatious competence. She wanted to appear efficient, but not too efficient. And her secrets must remain her own; she was here to get information, not to give it.

She stated her business concisely and showed him her note of authority from Sir Ronald. He handed it back to her, remarking without rancour:

'Sir Ronald said nothing to me to suggest that he was not satisfied with the verdict.'

'I don't think that's in question. He doesn't suspect foul play. If he did, he would have come to you. I think he has a scientist's curiosity to know what made his son kill himself and he couldn't very well indulge that at public expense. I mean, Mark's private miseries aren't really your problem, are they?'

'They could be if the reasons for his death disclosed a criminal offence – blackmail, intimidation – but there was never any suggestion of that.'

'Are you personally satisfied that he killed himself?'

The Sergeant looked at her with the sudden keen intelligence of a hunting dog on the scent.

'Why should you ask that, Miss Gray?'

'I suppose because of the trouble you took. I've interviewed Miss Markland and read the newspaper report of the inquest. You called in a forensic pathologist; you had the body photographed before it was cut down; you analysed the coffee left in his drinking mug.'

'I treated the case as a suspicious death. That's my usual practice. This time the precautions proved unnecessary, but they might not have been.'

Cordelia said:

'But something worried you, something didn't seem right?'

He said, as if reminiscing:

'Oh, it was straightforward enough to all appearances. Almost the usual story. We get more than our share of suicides. Here is a young man who gave up his university course for no apparent reason and went to live on his own in some discomfort. You get the picture of an introspective, rather solitary student, one who doesn't confide in his family or friends. Within three weeks after leaving college he's found dead. There's no sign of a struggle; no disturbance in the cottage: he leaves a suicide note conveniently in the typewriter, much the kind of suicide note you would expect. Admittedly, he took the trouble to destroy all the papers in the cottage and yet left the garden fork uncleaned and his work half-completed, and bothered to cook himself a supper which he didn't eat. But all that proves nothing. People do behave irrationally, particularly suicides. No, it wasn't any of those things which gave me a bit of worry; it was the knot.'

Suddenly he bent down and rummaged in the left-hand drawer of his desk.

'Here,' he said. 'How would you use this to hang yourself, Miss Gray?'

The strap was about five feet long. It was a little over an inch wide and was made of strong but supple brown leather, darkened in places with age. An end was tapered and pierced with a row of metal-bound eye holes, the other was fitted with a strong brass buckle. Cordelia took it in her hands; Sergeant Maskell said:

'That was what he used. Obviously it's meant as a strap, but Miss Leaming testified that he used to wear it wound two or three times round his waist as a belt. Well, Miss Gray, how would you hang yourself?'

Cordelia ran the strap through her hands.

'First of all, of course, I'd slip the tapered end through the buckle to make a noose. Then, with the noose round my neck, I'd stand on a chair underneath the hook in the ceiling and draw the other end of the strap over the hook. I'd pull it up fairly tight and then make two half-hitches to hold it firm. I'd pull hard on the strap to make sure that the knot didn't slip and that the hook would hold. Then I'd kick away the chair.'

The Sergeant opened the file in front of him and pushed it across the desk.

'Look at that,' he said. 'That's a picture of the knot.'

The police photograph, stark in black and white, showed the knot with admirable clarity. It was a bow-line on the end of a low loop and it hung about a foot from the hook.

Sergeant Maskell said:

'I doubt whether he would be able to tie that knot with his hands above his head, no one could. So he must have made the noose first just as you did and then tied the bowline. But that can't be right either. There were only a few inches of strap between the buckle and the knot. If he'd done it that way, he wouldn't have had sufficient play on the strap to get his neck through the

83

noose. There's only one way he could have done it. He made the noose first, pulled it until the strap fitted his neck like a collar and then tied the bowline. Then he got on the chair, placed the loop over the nail and kicked the chair away. Look, this will show you what I mean.'

He turned over a new page of the file and suddenly thrust it towards her.

The photograph, uncompromising, unambiguous, a brutal surrealism in black and white, would have looked as artificial as a sick joke if the body were not so obviously dead. Cordelia felt her heart hammering against her chest. Beside this horror Bernie's death had been gentle. She bent her head low over the file so that her hair swung forward to shield her face and made herself study the pitiable thing in front of her.

The neck was elongated so that the bare feet, their toes pointed like a dancer's, hung less than a foot from the floor. The stomach muscles were taut. Above them the high rib cage looked as brittle as a bird's. The head lolled grotesquely on the right shoulder like a horrible caricature of a disjointed puppet. The eyes had rolled upwards under half-open lids. The swollen tongue had forced itself between the lips.

Cordelia said calmly:

'I see what you mean. There are barely four inches of strap between the neck and the knot. Where is the buckle?'

'At the back of the neck under the left ear. There's a photograph of the indentation it made in the flesh later in the file.'

Cordelia did not look. Why, she wondered, had he shown her this photograph? It wasn't necessary to prove his argument. Had he hoped to shock her into a realization of what she was meddling in; to punish her for trespassing on his patch; to contrast the brutal reality of his professionalism with her amateurish meddling; to warn her perhaps? But against what? The police had no real suspicion of foul play; the case was closed. Had it, perhaps, been the casual malice, the incipient sadism of a man who couldn't resist the impulse to hurt or shock? Was he even aware of his own motives?

She said:

'I agree he could only have done it in the way you described, if he did it. But suppose someone else pulled the noose more tight about his neck, then strung him up. He'd be heavy, a dead weight. Wouldn't it have been easier to make the knot first and then hoist him on to the chair?'

'Having first asked him to hand over his belt?'

'Why use a belt? The murderer could have strangled him with a cord or a tie. Or would that have left a deeper and identifiable mark under the impression of the strap?'

'The pathologist looked for just such a mark. It wasn't there.'

'There are other ways, though; a plastic bag, the thin kind they pack clothes in, dropped over his head and held tight against his face; a thin scarf; a woman's stocking.'

'I can see you would be a resourceful murderess, Miss Gray. It's possible, but it would need a strong man and there would have to be an element of surprise. We found no sign of a struggle.'

'But it could have been done that way?'

'Of course, but there was absolutely no evidence that it was.'

'But if he were first drugged?'

'That possibility did occur to me; that's why I had the coffee analysed. But he wasn't drugged, the P.M. confirmed it.'

'How much coffee had he drunk?'

'Only about half a mug, according to the P.M. report, and he died immediately afterwards. Sometime between seven and nine p.m. was as close as the pathologist could estimate.'

'Wasn't it odd that he drank coffee before his meal?'

'There's no law against it. We don't know when he intended to eat his supper. Anyway, you can't build a murder case on the order in which a man chooses to take his food and drink.'

'What about the note he left? I suppose it isn't possible to raise prints from typewriter keys?'

'Not easily on that type of key. We tried but there was nothing identifiable.'

'So in the end you accepted that it was suicide?'

'In the end I accepted that there was no possibility of proving otherwise.'

'But you had a hunch? My partner's old colleague – he's a Superintendent of the CID – always backed his hunches.'

'Ah, well, that's the Met, they can afford to indulge themselves. If I backed all my hunches I'd get no work done; it isn't what you suspect, it's what you can prove that counts.'

'May I take the suicide note and the strap?'

'Why not, if you sign for them? No one else seems to want them.'

'Could I see the note now, please?'

He extracted it from the file and handed it to her. Cordelia began to read to herself the first half-remembered words:

> *A void, boundless as the nether sky*
> *appeared beneath us . . .*

She was struck, not for the first time, by the importance of the written word, the magic of ordered symbols. Would poetry hold its theurgy if the lines were printed as prose, or prose be so compelling without the pattern and stress of punctuation? Miss Leaming had spoken Blake's passage as if she recognized its beauty yet here, spaced on the page, it exerted an even stronger power.

It was then that two things about the quotation caught at her breath. The first was not something which she intended to share with Sergeant Maskell but there was no reason why she should not comment on the second. She said:

'Mark Callender must have been an experienced typist. This was done by an expert.'

'I didn't think so. If you look carefully you'll see that one or two of the letters are fainter than the rest. That's always the sign of an amateur.'

'But the faint letters aren't always the same ones. It's usually the keys on the edges of the keyboard which the inexperienced typist hits more lightly. And the spacing here is good until nearly the end of the passage. It looks as if the typist suddenly realized that he ought to disguise his competence but hadn't time to retype the whole passage. And it's strange that the punctuation is so accurate.'

'It was probably copied direct from the printed page. There was a copy of Blake in the boy's bedroom. The quotation is from Blake, you know, the Tyger tyger burning bright poet.'

'I know. But if he typed it from the book, why bother to return the Blake to his bedroom?'

'He was a tidy lad.'

'But not tidy enough to wash up his coffee mug or clean his garden fork.'

'That proves nothing. As I said, people do behave oddly when they're planning to kill themselves. We know that the typewriter was his and that he'd had it for a year. But we couldn't compare the typing with his work. All his papers had been burnt.'

He glanced at his watch and got to his feet. Cordelia saw that the interview was over. She signed a chit for the suicide note and the leather belt, then shook hands and thanked him formally for his help. As he opened the door for her he said, as if on impulse:

'There's one intriguing detail you may care to know. It looks as if he was with a woman some time during the day on which he died. The pathologist found the merest trace – a thin line only – of purple-red lipstick on his upper lip.'

CHAPTER THREE

New Hall, with its Byzantine air, its sunken court and its shining domed hall like a peeled orange, reminded

Cordelia of a harem; admittedly one owned by a sultan with liberal views and an odd predilection for clever girls, but a harem nonetheless. The college was surely too distractingly pretty to be conducive to serious study. She wasn't sure, either, whether she approved of the obtrusive femininity of its white brick, the mannered prettiness of the shallow pools where the goldfish slipped like blood-red shadows between the water lilies, its artfully planted saplings. She concentrated on her criticism of the building; it helped to prevent her being intimidated.

She hadn't called at the Lodge to ask for Miss Tilling, afraid that she might be asked her business or refused admission; it seemed prudent just to walk in and chance to luck. Luck was with her. After two fruitless enquiries for Sophia Tilling's room, a hurrying student called back at her:

'She doesn't live in college but she's sitting on the grass over there with her brother.'

Cordelia walked out of the shadow of the court into bright sunlight and over turf as soft as moss towards the little group. There were four of them, stretched out on the warm-smelling grass. The two Tillings were unmistakably brother and sister. Cordelia's first thought was that they reminded her of a couple of pre-Raphaelite portraits with their strong dark heads held high on unusually short necks, and their straight noses above curved, foreshortened upper lips. Beside their bony distinction, the second girl was all softness. If this were the girl who had visited Mark at the cottage, Miss Markland was right to call her beautiful. She had an oval face with a neat slender nose, a small but beautifully formed mouth, and slanted eyes of a strikingly deep blue which gave her whole face an oriental appearance at variance with the fairness of her skin and her long blonde hair. She was wearing an ankle-length dress of fine mauve patterned cotton, buttoned high at the waist but with no other fastening. The gathered bodice cupped her full breasts and the skirt fell open to reveal a pair of tight fitting shorts in the same material. As far as Cordelia could see, she wore nothing else. Her feet were bare and her long, shapely legs were untanned by the sun. Cordelia reflected that those white voluptuous thighs must be more erotic than a whole city of sunburnt limbs and that the girl knew it. Sophia Tilling's dark good looks were only a foil to this gentler, more entrancing beauty.

At first sight the fourth member of the party was more ordinary. He was a stocky, bearded young man with russet curly hair and a spade-shaped face, and was lying on the grass by the side of Sophie Tilling.

All of them, except the blonde girl, were wearing old jeans and open-necked cotton shirts.

Cordelia had come up to the group and had stood over them for a few seconds before they took any notice of her. She said:

'I'm looking for Hugo and Sophia Tilling. My name is Cordelia Gray.' Hugo Tilling looked up:

'What shall Cordelia do, love and be silent.'

Cordelia said:

'People who feel the need to joke about my name usually enquire after my sisters. It gets very boring.'

'It must do. I'm sorry. I'm Hugo Tilling, this is my sister, this is Isabelle de Lasterie and this is Davie Stevens.'

Davie Stevens sat up like a jack-in-the-box and said an amiable 'Hi.'

He looked at Cordelia with a quizzical intentness. She wondered about Davie. Her first impression of the little group, influenced perhaps by the college architecture, had been of a young sultan taking his ease with two of his favourites and attended by the captain of the guard. But, meeting Davie Stevens's steady intelligent gaze, that impression faded. She suspected that, in this seraglio, it was the captain of the guard who was the dominant personality.

Sophia Tilling nodded and said 'Hullo.'

Isabelle did not speak but a smile beautiful and meaningless spread over her face. Hugo said:

'Won't you sit down, Cordelia Gray, and explain the nature of your necessities?'

Cordelia knelt gingerly, wary of grass stains on the soft suede of her skirt. It was an odd way to interview suspects – only, of course, these people weren't suspects – kneeling like a suppliant in front of them. She said:

'I'm a private detective. Sir Ronald Callender has employed me to find out why his son died.'

The effect of her words was astonishing. The little group, which had been lolling at ease like exhausted warriors, stiffened with instantaneous shock into a rigid tableau as if struck to marble. Then, almost imperceptibly, they relaxed. Cordelia could hear the slow release of held breath. She watched their faces. Davie Stevens was the least concerned. He wore a half-rueful smile, interested but unworried, and gave a quick look at Sophie as if in complicity. The look was not returned; she and Hugo were staring rigidly ahead. Cordelia felt that the two Tillings were carefully avoiding each other's eyes. But it was Isabelle who was the most shaken. She gave a gasp and her hand flew to her face like a second-rate actress simulating shock. Her eyes widened into fathomless depths of violet blue and she turned them on Hugo in desperate appeal. She looked so pale that Cordelia half expected her to faint. She thought:

'If I'm in the middle of a conspiracy, then I know who is its weakest member.'

Hugo Tilling said:

'You're telling us that Ronald Callender has employed you to find out why Mark died?'

'Is that so extraordinary?'

'I find it incredible. He took no particular interest in his son when he was alive, why begin now he's dead?'

'How do you know he took no particular interest?'

'It's just an idea I had.'

Cordelia said:

'Well, he's interested now even if it's only the scientist's urge to discover truth.'

'Then he'd better stick to his microbiology, discovering how to make plastic soluble in salt water, or whatever. Human beings aren't susceptible to his kind of treatment.'

Davie Stevens said with casual unconcern:

'I wonder that you can stomach that arrogant fascist.'

The gibe plucked at too many chords of memory. Wilfully obtuse, Cordelia said:

'I didn't enquire what political party Sir Ronald favours.'

Hugo laughed.

'Davie doesn't mean that. By fascist Davie means that Ronald Callender holds certain untenable opinions. For example, that all men may not be created equal, that universal suffrage may not necessarily add to the general happiness of mankind, that the tyrannies of the left aren't noticeably more liberal or supportable than the tyrannies of the right, that black men killing black men is small improvement on white men killing black men in so far as the victims are concerned and that capitalism may not be responsible for all the ills that flesh is heir to from drug addiction to poor syntax. I don't suggest that Ronald Callender holds all or indeed any of these reprehensible opinions. But Davie thinks that he does.'

Davie threw a book at Hugo and said without rancour:

'Shut up! You talk like the *Daily Telegraph*. And you're boring our visitor.'

Sophie Tilling asked suddenly:

'Was it Sir Ronald who suggested that you should question us?'

'He said that you were Mark's friends; he saw you at the inquest and funeral.'

Hugo laughed:

'For God's sake, is that his idea of friendship?'

Cordelia said:

'But you were there?'

'We went to the inquest – all of us except Isabelle, who, we thought, would have been decorative but unreliable. It was rather dull. There was a great deal of irrelevant medical evidence about the excellent state of Mark's heart, lungs and digestive system. As far as I can see, he would have gone on living for ever if he hadn't put a belt round his neck.'

'And the funeral – were you there too?'

'We were, at the Cambridge Crematorium. A very subdued affair. There were only six of us present in addition to the undertaker's men; we three, Ronald Callender, that secretary/housekeeper of his and an old nanny type dressed in black. She cast rather a gloom over the proceedings, I thought. Actually she looked so exactly like an old family retainer that I suspect she was a policewoman in disguise.'

'Why should she be? Did she look like one?'

'No, but then you don't look like a private eye.'

'You've no idea who she was?'

'No, we weren't introduced; it wasn't a chummy kind of funeral. Now I recall it, not one of us spoke a single word to any of the others. Sir Ronald wore a mask of public grief, the King mourning the Crown Prince.'

'And Miss Leaming?'

'The Queen Consort; she should have had a black veil over her face.'

'I thought that her suffering was real enough,' said Sophie.

'You can't tell. No one can. Define suffering. Define real.'

Suddenly Davie Stevens spoke, rolling over on to his stomach like a playful dog.

'Miss Leaming looked pretty sick to me. Incidentally, the old lady was called Pilbeam; anyway, that was the name on the wreath.'

Sophie laughed:

'That awful cross of roses with the black-edged card? I might have guessed it came from her; but how do you know?'

'I looked, honey. The undertaker's men took the wreath off the coffin and propped it against the wall so I took a quick butcher's. The card read "With sincere sympathy from Nanny Pilbeam".'

Sophie said:

'So you did, I remember now. How beautifully feudal! Poor old nanny, it must have cost her a packet.'

'Did Mark ever talk about a Nanny Pilbeam?' Cordelia asked.

They glanced at each other quickly. Isabelle shook her head. Sophie said, 'Not to me.'

Hugo Tilling replied:

'He never talked about her, but I think I did see her once before the funeral. She called at college about six weeks ago – on Mark's twenty-first birthday actually, and asked to see him. I was in the Porter's Lodge at the time and Robbins asked me if Mark was in college. She went up to his room and they were there together for about an hour. I saw her leaving, but he never mentioned her to me either then or later.'

And soon afterwards, thought Cordelia, he gave up university. Could there be a connection? It was only a tenuous lead, but she would have to follow it.

She asked out of a curiosity that seemed both perverse and irrelevant:

'Were there any other flowers?'

It was Sophie who replied:

'A simple bunch of unwired garden flowers on the coffin. No card. Miss Leaming, I suppose. It was hardly Sir Ronald's style.'

Cordelia said:

'You were his friends. Please tell me about him.'

95

They looked at each other as if deciding who should speak. Their embarrassment was almost palpable. Sophie Tilling was picking at small blades of grass and rolling them in her hands. Without looking up, she said:

'Mark was a very private person. I'm not sure how far any of us knew him. He was quiet, gentle, self-contained, unambitious. He was intelligent without being clever. He was very kind; he cared about people, but without inflicting them with his concern. He had little self-esteem but it never seemed to worry him. I don't think there is anything else we can say about him.'

Suddenly Isabelle spoke in a voice so low that Cordelia could hardly catch it. She said:

'He was sweet.'

Hugo said with a sudden angry impatience:

'He was sweet and he is dead. There you have it. We can't tell you any more about Mark Callender than that. We none of us saw him after he chucked college. He didn't consult us before he left, and he didn't consult us before he killed himself. He was, as my sister has told you, a very private person. I suggest that you leave him his privacy.'

'Look,' said Cordelia, 'you went to the inquest, you went to the funeral. If you had stopped seeing him, if you were so unconcerned about him, why did you bother?'

'Sophie went out of affection. Davie went because Sophie did. I went out of curiosity and respect; you mustn't be seduced by my air of casual flippancy into thinking that I haven't a heart.'

Cordelia said obstinately:

'Someone visited him at the cottage on the evening he died. Someone had coffee with him. I intend to find out who that person was.'

Was it her fancy that this news surprised them? Sophie Tilling looked as if she were about to ask a question when her brother quickly broke in:

'It wasn't any of us. On the night Mark died we were all in the second row of the dress circle of the Arts Theatre watching Pinter. I don't know that I can prove it. I doubt whether the booking clerk has kept the chart for that particular night, but I booked the seats and she may remember me. If you insist on being tediously meticulous, I can probably introduce you to a friend who knew of my intention to take a party to the play; to another who saw at least some of us in the bar in the interval; and to another with whom I subsequently discussed the performance. None of this will prove anything; my friends are an accommodating bunch. It would be simpler for you to accept that I am telling the truth. Why should I lie? We were all four at the Arts Theatre on the night of 26th May.'

Davie Stevens said gently:

'Why not tell that arrogant bastard Pa Callender to go to hell and leave his son in peace, then find yourself a nice simple case of larceny?'

'Or murder,' said Hugo Tilling.

'Find yourself a nice simple case of murder.'

As if in obedience to some secret code, they began getting up, piling their books together, brushing the grass cuttings from their clothes. Cordelia followed them through the courts and out of college. Still in a silent group they made their way to a white Renault parked in the forecourt.

Cordelia came up to them and spoke directly to Isabelle.

'Did you enjoy the Pinter? Weren't you frightened by that dreadful last scene when Wyatt Gillman is gunned down by the natives?'

It was so easy that Cordelia almost despised herself. The immense violet eyes grew puzzled.

'Oh, no! I did not care about it, I was not frightened. I was with Hugo and the others, you see.'

Cordelia turned to Hugo Tilling.

'Your friend doesn't seem to know the difference between Pinter and Osborne.'

Hugo was settling himself into the driving seat of the car. He twisted round to open the back door for Sophie and Davie. He said calmly:

'My friend, as you choose to call her, is living in Cambridge, inadequately chaperoned I'm happy to say, for the purpose of learning English. So far her progress has been erratic and in some respects disappointing. One can never be certain how much my friend has understood.'

The engine purred into life. The car began to move. It was then that Sophie Tilling thrust her head out of the window and said impulsively:

'I don't mind talking about Mark if you think it will help. It won't, but you can come round to my house this afternoon if you like – 57, Norwich Street. Don't be late; Davie and I are going on the river. You can come too if you feel like it.'

The car accelerated. Cordelia watched it out of sight. Hugo raised his hand in ironic farewell but not one of them turned a head.

*

Cordelia muttered the address to herself until it was safely written down: 57, Norwich Street. Was that the address where Sophie lodged, a hostel perhaps, or did her family live in Cambridge? Well, she would find out soon enough. When ought she to arrive? Too early would look over eager; too late and they might have set out for the river. Whatever motive prompted Sophie Tilling to issue that belated invitation, she mustn't lose touch with them now.

They had some guilty knowledge; that had been obvious. Why else had they reacted so strongly to her arrival? They wanted the facts of Mark Callender's death to be left undisturbed. They would try to persuade, cajole, even to shame her into abandoning the case. Would they, she wondered, also threaten? But why? The most likely theory was that they were shielding someone. But again, why? Murder wasn't a matter of climbing late into college, a venial infringement of rules which a friend would automatically condone and conceal. Mark Callender had been their friend. Someone whom he knew and trusted had pulled a strap tight round his neck, had watched and listened to his agonized choking, had strung his body on a hook like the carcase of an animal. How could one reconcile that appalling knowledge with Davie Stevens' slightly amused and rueful glance at Sophie, with Hugo's cynical calm, with Sophie's friendly and interested eyes? If

99

they were conspirators, then they were monsters. And Isabelle? If they were shielding anyone, it was most likely to be her. But Isabelle de Lasterie couldn't have murdered Mark. Cordelia remembered those frail sloping shoulders, those ineffective hands almost transparent in the sun, the long nails painted like elegant pink talons. If Isabelle were guilty, she hadn't acted alone. Only a tall and very strong woman could have heaved that inert body onto the chair and up to the hook.

Norwich Street was a one-way thoroughfare and, initially, Cordelia approached it from the wrong direction. It took her some time to find her way back to Hills Road, past the Roman Catholic church and down the fourth turning to the right. The street was terraced with small brick houses, obviously early Victorian. Equally obviously, the road was on its way up. Most of the houses looked well cared for; the paint on the identical front doors was fresh and bright; lined curtains had replaced the draped lace at the single ground-floor windows and the bases of the walls were scarred where a damp course had been installed. Number fifty-seven had a black front door with the house number painted in white behind the glass panel above. Cordelia was relieved to see that there was space to park the Mini. There was no sign of the Renault among the almost continuous row of old cars and battered bicycles which lined the edge of the pavement.

The front door was wide open. Cordelia pressed the bell and stepped tentatively into a narrow white hall. The exterior of the house was immediately familiar to her. From her sixth birthday she had lived for two years in just such a Victorian terraced cottage with Mrs

Gibson on the outskirts of Romford. She recognized the steep and narrow staircase immediately ahead, the door on the right leading to the front parlour, the second door set aslant which led to the back parlour and through it to the kitchen and yard. She knew that there would be cupboards and a curved alcove on each side of the fireplace; she knew where to find the door under the stairs. Memory was so sharp that it imposed on this clean, sun-scented interior the strong odour of unwashed napkins, cabbage and grease which had permeated the Romford house. She could almost hear the children's voices calling her outlandish name across the rookery of the primary school playground across the road, stamping the asphalt with the ubiquitous Wellington boots which they wore in all seasons, flailing their thin jerseyed arms: 'Cor, Cor, Cor!'

The furthest door was ajar and she could glimpse a room painted bright yellow and spilling over with sunlight. Sophie's head appeared.

'Oh, it's you! Come in. Davie has gone to collect some books from college and to buy food for the picnic. Would you like tea now or shall we wait? I'm just finishing the ironing.'

'I'd rather wait, thank you.'

Cordelia sat down and watched while Sophie wound the flex round the iron and folded the cloth. She glanced around the room. It was welcoming and attractive, furnished in no particular style or period, a cosy hotchpotch of the cheap and the valuable, unpretentious and pleasing. There was a sturdy oak table against the wall; four rather ugly dining chairs; a Windsor chair with a plump yellow cushion; an elegant Victorian sofa covered with brown velvet and set under the window; three good Staffordshire figures on the mantelshelf above the hooded wrought-iron grate. One of the walls was almost covered with a notice board in dark cork which displayed posters, cards, *aides-mémoire*, and pictures cut from magazines. Two, Cordelia saw, were beautifully photographed and attractive nudes.

Outside the yellow-curtained window the small walled garden was a riot of greenery. An immense and multi-flowered hollyhock burgeoned against a tatty looking trellis; there were roses planted in Ali Baba jars and a row of pots of bright-red geraniums lined the top of the wall.

Cordelia said:

'I like this house. Is it yours?'

'Yes, I own it. Our grandmother died two years ago and left Hugo and me a small legacy. I used mine for the down payment on this house and got a local authority grant towards the cost of conversion. Hugo spent all of his laying down wine. He was ensuring a happy middle age; I was ensuring a happy present. I suppose that's the difference between us.'

She folded the ironing cloth on the end of the table and stowed it away in one of the cupboards. Sitting opposite to Cordelia, she asked abruptly:

'Do you like my brother?'

'Not very much. I thought he was rather rude to me.'

'He didn't mean to be.'

'I think that's rather worse. Rudeness should always be intentional, otherwise it's insensitivity.'

'Hugo isn't at his most agreeable when he's with Isabelle. She has that effect on him.'

'Was she in love with Mark Callender?'

'You'll have to ask her, Cordelia, but I shouldn't think so. They hardly knew each other. Mark was my lover, not hers. I thought I'd better get you here to tell you myself since someone's bound to sooner or later if you go around Cambridge ferreting out facts about him. He didn't live here with me, of course. He had rooms in college. But we were lovers for almost the whole of last year. It ended just after Christmas when I met Davie.'

'Were you in love?'

'I'm not sure. All sex is a kind of exploitation, isn't it? If you mean, did we explore our own identities through the personality of the other, then I suppose we were in love or thought that we were. Mark needed to believe himself in love. I'm not sure I know what the word means.'

Cordelia felt a surge of sympathy. She wasn't sure either. She thought of her own two lovers; Georges whom she had slept with because he was gentle and unhappy and called her Cordelia, a real name, her name, not Delia, Daddy's little fascist; and Carl who was young and angry and whom she had liked so much that it seemed churlish not to show it in the only way which seemed to him important. She had never thought of virginity as other than a temporary and inconvenient state, part of the general insecurity and vulnerability of being young. Before Georges and Carl she had been lonely and inexperienced. Afterwards she had been lonely and a little less inexperienced. Neither affair had given her the longed-for assurance in dealing with Daddy or the landladies, neither had inconveniently touched her heart. But for Carl she had felt tenderness.

It was just as well that he had left Rome before his love-making had become too pleasurable and he too important to her. It was intolerable to think that those strange gymnastics might one day become necessary. Love making, she had decided, was over-rated, not painful but surprising. The alienation between thought and action was so complete. She said:

'I suppose I only meant were you fond of each other, and did you like going to bed together?'

'Both of those things.'

'Why did it end? Did you quarrel?'

'Nothing so natural or uncivilized. One didn't quarrel with Mark. That was one of the troubles about him. I told him that I didn't want to go on with the affair and he accepted my decision as calmly as if I were just breaking a date for a play at the Arts. He didn't try to argue or dissuade me. And if you're wondering whether the break had anything to do with his death, well you're wrong. I wouldn't rank that high with anyone, particularly not Mark. I was probably fonder of him than he was of me.'

'So why did it end?'

'I felt that I was under moral scrutiny. It wasn't true; Mark wasn't a prig. But that's how I felt, or pretended to myself that I felt. I couldn't live up to him and I didn't even want to. There was Gary Webber, for example. I'd better tell you about him; it explains a lot about Mark. He's an autistic child, one of the uncontrollable, violent ones. Mark met him with his parents and their other two children on Jesus Green about a year ago; the children were playing on the swings there. Mark spoke to Gary and the boy responded to him. Children always did. He took to visiting the family and looking after Gary one evening a week so that the Webbers could get out to the pictures. During his last two vacs he stayed in the house and looked after Gary completely while the whole family went off for a holiday. The Webbers couldn't bear the boy to go to hospital; they'd tried it once and he didn't settle. But they were perfectly happy to leave him with Mark. I used to call in some evenings and see them together. Mark would hold the boy on his lap and rock him backwards and forwards for hours at a time. It was the one way to quieten him. We disagreed about Gary. I thought he would be better dead and I said so. I still think it would be better if he died, better for his parents, better for the rest of the family, better for him. Mark didn't agree. I remember saying:

' "Oh well, if you think it reasonable that children should suffer so that you can enjoy the emotional kick of relieving them—" After that the conversation became boringly metaphysical. Mark said:

' "Neither you nor I would be willing to kill Gary. He exists. His family exists. They need help which we can give. It doesn't matter what we feel. Actions are important, feelings aren't." '

Cordelia said:

'But actions arise out of feelings.'

'Oh, Cordelia, don't you start! I've had this particular conversation too many times before. Of course they do!'

They were silent for a moment. Then Cordelia, reluctant to shatter the tenuous confidence and friendship which she sensed was growing between them, made herself ask:

'Why did he kill himself – if he did kill himself?' Sophie's reply was as emphatic as a slammed door.

'He left a note.'

'A note perhaps. But, as his father pointed out, not an explanation. It's a lovely passage of prose – at least I think so – but as a justification for suicide it just isn't convincing.'

'It convinced the jury.'

'It doesn't convince me. Think, Sophie! Surely there are only two reasons for killing oneself. One is either escaping from something or to something. The first is rational. If one is in intolerable pain, despair or mental anguish and there is no reasonable chance of a cure, then it's probably sensible to prefer oblivion. But it isn't sensible to kill oneself in the hope of gaining some better existence or to extend one's sensibilities to include the experience of death. It isn't possible to experience death. I'm not even sure it's possible to experience dying. One can only experience the preparations for death, and even that seems pointless since one can't make use of the experience afterwards. If there's any sort of existence after death we shall all know soon enough. If there isn't, we shan't exist to complain that we've been cheated. People who believe in an afterlife are perfectly reasonable. They're the only ones who are safe from ultimate disillusionment.'

'You've thought it all out, haven't you? I'm not sure that suicides do. The act is probably both impulsive and irrational.'

'Was Mark impulsive and irrational?'

'I didn't know Mark.'

'But you were lovers! You slept with him!'

Sophie looked at her and cried out in angry pain.

'I didn't know him! I thought I did, but I didn't know the first thing about him!'

They sat without speaking for almost two minutes. Then Cordelia asked:

'You went to dinner at Garforth House didn't you? What was it like?'

'The food and the wine were surprisingly good, but I don't suppose that's what you had in mind. The dinner party wasn't otherwise memorable. Sir Ronald was amiable enough when he noticed I was there. Miss Leaming, when she could tear her obsessive attention from the presiding genius, looked me over like a prospective mother-in-law. Mark was rather silent. I think he'd taken me there to prove something to me, or perhaps to himself; I'm not sure what. He never talked about the evening or asked me what I thought. A month later Hugo and I both went to dinner. It was then I met Davie. He was the guest of one of the research biologists and Ronald Callender was angling to get him. Davie did a vac job there in his final year. If you want the inside dope on Garforth House, you should ask him.'

Five minutes later Hugo, Isabelle and Davie arrived. Cordelia had gone upstairs to the bathroom and heard the car stop and the jabber of voices in the hall. Footsteps passed beneath her towards the back parlour. She turned on the hot water. The gas boiler in the kitchen immediately gave forth a roar as if the little house were powered by a dynamo. Cordelia let the tap run, then stepped out of the bathroom, closing the door gently behind her. She stole to the top of the stairs. It was hard luck on Sophie to waste her hot water, she thought guiltily; but worse was the sense of treachery and shabby opportunism as she crept down the first three stairs and listened. The front door had been closed but the door to the back parlour was open. She heard Isabelle's high unemphatic voice:

'But if this man Sir Ronald is paying her to find out about Mark, why cannot I pay her to stop finding out?'

Then Hugo's voice, amused, a little contemptuous:

'Darling Isabelle, when will you learn that not everyone can be bought?'

'She can't, anyway. I like her.'

It was Sophie speaking. Her brother replied:

'We all like her. The question is, how do we get rid of her?'

Then for a few minutes there was a murmur of voices, words undistinguishable, broken by Isabelle.

'It is not, I think, a suitable job for a woman.'

There was the sound of a chair scraping against the floor, a shuffle of feet. Cordelia darted guiltily back into the bathroom and turned off the tap. She recalled Bernie's complacent admonition when she had asked whether they needed to accept a divorce case.

'You can't do our job, partner, and be a gentleman.' She stood watching at the half-open door. Hugo and Isabelle were leaving. She waited until she heard the front door close and the car drive away. Then she went down to the parlour. Sophie and Davie were together, unpacking a large carrier bag of groceries. Sophie smiled and said:

'Isabelle has a party tonight. She has a house quite close to here in Panton Street. Mark's tutor, Edward

Horsfall, will probably be there and we thought it might be useful for you to talk to him about Mark. The party's at eight o'clock but you can call for us here. Just now we're packing a picnic; we thought we'd take a punt on the river for an hour or so. Do come if you'd like to. It's really much the pleasantest way of seeing Cambridge.'

*

Afterwards, Cordelia remembered the river picnic as a series of brief but intensely clear pictures, moments in which sight and sense fused and time seemed momentarily arrested while the sunlit image was impressed on her mind. Sunlight sparkling on the river and gilding the hairs of Davie's chest and forearms; the flesh of his strong upper arms speckled like an egg; Sophie lifting her arm to wipe the sweat from her brow as she rested between thrusts of the punt pole; green-black weeds dragged by the pole from mysterious depths to writhe sinuously below the surface; a bright duck cocking its white tail before disappearing in a flurry of green water. When they had rocked under Silver Street Bridge a friend of Sophie swam alongside, sleek and snout-nosed like an otter, his black hair lying like blades across his cheeks. He rested his hands on the punt and opened his mouth to be fed chunks of sandwiches by a protesting Sophie. The punts and canoes scraped and jostled each other in the turbulence of white water racing under the bridge. The air rang with laughing voices and the green banks were peopled with half-naked bodies lying supine with their faces to the sun.

Davie punted until they reached the higher level of the river and Cordelia and Sophie stretched out on the cushions at opposite ends of the punt. Thus distanced it was impossible to carry on a private conversation; Cordelia guessed that this was precisely what Sophie had planned. From time to time, she would call out snatches of information as if to emphasize that the outing was strictly educational.

'That wedding cake is John's – we're just passing under Clare bridge, one of the prettiest, I think. Thomas Grumbald built it in 1639. They say he was only paid three shillings for the design. You know that view, of course; it's a good view of Queens', though.'

Cordelia's courage failed her at the thought of interrupting this desultory tourist's chat with the brutal demand:

'Did you and your brother kill your lover?'

Here, rocking gently on the sunlit river, the question seemed both indecent and absurd. She was in danger of beeing lulled into a gentle acceptance of defeat; viewing all her suspicions as a neurotic hankering after drama and notoriety, a need to justify her fee to Sir Ronald. She believed that Mark Callender had been murdered because she wanted to believe it. She had identified with him, with his solitariness, his self-sufficiency; his alienation from his father, his lonely childhood. She had even – most dangerous presumption of all – come to see herself as his avenger. When Sophie took over the pole, just past the Garden House Hotel, and Davie edged his way along the gently rocking punt and stretched himself out beside her, she knew that she wouldn't be able to mention Mark's name. It was out of no more than a vague, unintrusive curiosity that she found herself asking:

'Is Sir Ronald Callender a good scientist?' Davie took up a short paddle and began lazily to stir the shining water.

'His science is perfectly respectable, as my dear colleagues would say. Rather more than respectable, in fact. At present the lab is working on ways of expanding the use of biological monitors to assess pollution of the sea and estuaries; that means routine surveys of plants and animals which might serve as indicators. And they did some very useful preliminary work last year on the degradation of plastics. R.C. isn't so hot himself, but then you can't expect much original science from the over fifties. But he's a great spotter of talent and he certainly knows how to run a team if you fancy that dedicated, one for all, band of brothers approach. I don't. They even publish their papers as the Callender Research Laboratory, not under individual names. That wouldn't do for me. When I publish, it's strictly for the glory of David Forbes Stevens and, incidentally, for the gratification of Sophie. The Tillings like success.'

'Was that why you didn't want to stay on when he offered you a job?'

'That among other reasons. He pays too generously and he asks too much. I don't like being bought and I've a strong objection to dressing up every night in a dinner jacket like a performing monkey in a zoo. I'm a molecular biologist. I'm not looking for the holy grail. Dad and mum brought me up as a Methodist and I don't see why I should chuck a perfectly good religion which served me very well for twelve years just to put the great scientific principle of Ronald Callender in its place. I distrust these sacerdotal scientists. It's a bloody wonder that little lot at Garforth House aren't genuflecting three times a day in the direction of the Cavendish.'

'And what about Lunn? How does he fit in?'

'Oh, that boy's a bloody wonder! Ronald Callender found him in a children's home when he was fifteen – don't ask me how – and trained him to be a lab assistant. You couldn't find a better. There isn't an instrument made which Chris Lunn can't learn to understand and care for. He's developed one or two himself and Callender has had them patented. If anyone in that lab is indispensable it's probably Lunn. Certainly Ronald Callender cares a damn sight more for him than he did for his son. And Lunn, as you might guess, regards R.C. as God Almighty, which is very gratifying for them both. It's extraordinary really, all that violence which used to be expressed in street fights and coshing old ladies, harnessed to the service of science. You've got to hand it to Callender. He certainly knows how to pick his slaves.'

'And is Miss Leaming a slave?'

'Well, I wouldn't know just what Eliza Leaming is. She's responsible for the business management and, like Lunn, she's probably indispensable. Lunn and she seem to have a love-hate relationship, or, perhaps, a hate-hate relationship. I'm not very clever at detecting these psychological nuances.'

'But how on earth does Sir Ronald pay for it all?'

'Well that's the thousand dollar question, isn't it? It's rumoured that most of the money came from his wife and that he and Elizabeth Leaming between them invested it rather cleverly. They certainly needed to. And then he gets a certain amount from contract work.

Even so, it's an expensive hobby. While I was there they were saying that the Wolvington Trust were getting interested. If they come up with something big – and I gather it's below their dignity to come up with something small – then most of Ronald Callender's troubles should be over. Mark's death must have hit him. Mark was due to come into a pretty substantial fortune in four years' time and he told Sophie that he intended to hand most of it over to Dad.'

'Why on earth should he do that?'

'God knows. Conscience money, perhaps. Anyway, he obviously thought it was something that Sophie ought to know.'

Conscience money for what, Cordelia wondered sleepily. For not loving his father enough? For rejecting his enthusiasms? For being less than the son he had hoped for? And what would happen to Mark's fortune now? Who stood to gain by Mark's death? She supposed that she ought to consult his grandfather's will and find out. But that would mean a trip to London. Was it really worth it?

She stretched back her face to the sun and trailed one hand in the river. A splash of water from the punt pole stung her eyes. She opened them and saw that the punt was gliding close to the bank and under the shade of overhanging trees. Immediately in front of her a torn branch, cleft at the end and thick as a man's body, hung by a thread of bark and turned gently as the punt passed beneath it. She was aware of Davie's voice; he must have been talking for a long time. How odd that she couldn't remember what he'd been saying!

'You don't need reasons for killing yourself; you need reasons for not killing yourself. It was suicide, Cordelia. I should let it go at that.'

Cordelia thought that she must have briefly slept, since he seemed to be answering a question she couldn't remember having asked. But now there were other voices, louder and more insistent. Sir Ronald Callender's: 'My son is dead. *My* son. If I am in some way responsible, I'd prefer to know. If anyone else is responsible, I want to know that too.' Sergeant Maskell's: 'How would you use this to hang yourself, Miss Gray?' The feel of the belt, smooth and sinuous, slipping like a live thing through her fingers.

She sat bolt upright, hands clasped around her knees, with such suddenness that the punt rocked violently and Sophie had to clutch at an overhanging branch to keep her balance. Her dark face, intriguingly foreshortened and patterned with the shadow of leaves, looked down at Cordelia from what seemed an immense height. Their eyes met. In that moment Cordelia knew how close she had come to giving up the case. She had been suborned by the beauty of the day, by sunshine, indolence, the promise of comradeship, even friendship, into forgetting why she was here. The realization horrified her. Davie had said that Sir Ronald was a good picker. Well, he had picked her. This was her first case and nothing and no one was going to hinder her from solving it.

She said formally:

'It was good of you to let me join you, but I don't want to miss the party tonight. I ought to talk to Mark's tutor and there may be other people there who could tell me something. Isn't it time that we thought about turning back?'

Sophie turned her glance on Davie. He gave an almost imperceptible shrug. Without speaking, Sophie drove the pole hard against the bank. The punt began slowly to turn.

*

Isabelle's party was due to begin at eight o'clock but it was nearly nine when Sophie, Davie and Cordelia arrived. They walked to the house which was only five minutes from Norwich Street; Cordelia never discovered the exact address. She liked the look of the house and wondered how much it was costing Isabelle's father in rent. It was a long, white, two-storey villa with tall curved windows and green shutters, set well back from the street, with a semi-basement and a flight of steps to the front door. A similar flight led down from the sitting-room to the long garden.

The sitting-room was already fairly full. Looking at her fellow guests, Cordelia was glad that she had bought the kaftan. Most people seemed to have changed although not necessarily, she thought, into something more attractive. What was aimed at was originality; it was preferable to look spectacular, even bizarre, than to appear nondescript.

The sitting-room was elegantly but insubstantially furnished and Isabelle had impressed on it her own untidy, impractical and iconoclastic femininity. Cordelia doubted whether the owners had provided the ornate crystal chandelier, far too heavy and large for the room, which hung like a sunburst from the middle of the ceiling, or the many silken cushions and curtains which gave the room's austere proportions something of the ostentatious opulence of a courtesan's boudoir. The pictures, too, must surely be Isabelle's. No house owner letting his property would leave pictures of this quality on the walls. One, hanging above the fireplace, was of a young girl hugging a puppy. Cordelia gazed at it in excited pleasure. Surely she couldn't mistake that individual blue of the girl's dress, that marvellous painting of the cheeks and plump young arms, which simultaneously absorbed and reflected light – lovely, tangible flesh. She cried out involuntarily so that people turned to look at her:

'But that's a Renoir!'

Hugo was at her elbow. He laughed.

'Yes; but don't sound so shocked, Cordelia. It's only a small Renoir. Isabelle asked Papa for a picture for her sitting-room. You didn't expect him to provide a print of the Haywain or one of those cheap reproductions of Van Gogh's boring old chair.'

'Would Isabelle have known the difference?'

'Oh, yes. Isabelle knows an expensive object when she sees one.'

Cordelia wondered whether the bitterness, the hard edge of contempt in his voice, was for Isabelle or for himself. They looked across the room to where she stood, smiling at them. Hugo moved towards her like a man in a dream and took her hand. Cordelia watched. Isabelle had dressed her hair in a high cluster of curls, Grecian style. She was wearing an ankle-length dress of cream matt silk, with a very low square neckline and small intricately tucked sleeves. It was obviously a model and should, Cordelia felt, have looked out of place at an informal party. But it didn't. It merely made every other woman's dress look like an improvisation and reduced her own, whose colours had seemed muted and subtle when she bought it, to the status of a gaudy rag.

Cordelia was determined to get Isabelle alone some time during the evening but could see that it wasn't going to be easy. Hugo stuck tenaciously to her side, steering her among her guests with one proprietorial hand on her waist. He seemed to be drinking steadily and Isabelle's glass was always filled. Perhaps as the evening wore on they would get careless and there would be a chance to separate them. In the meantime, Cordelia decided to explore the house, and a more practical matter, to find out before she needed it where the lavatory was. It was the kind of party where guests were left to find out these things for themselves.

She went up to the first floor and making her way down the passage pushed gently open the door of the far room. The smell of whisky met her immediately; it was overpowering and Cordelia instinctively slipped into the room and closed the door behind her, afraid that it might permeate the house. The room, which was in an indescribable state of disarray, wasn't empty. On the bed and half covered by the counterpane a woman was lying; a woman with bright ginger hair splayed over the pillow and wearing a pink silk dressing-gown. Cordelia walked up to the bed and looked down at her. She was insensible with drink. She lay there emitting puffs of foul, whisky-laden breath which rose like invisible balls of smoke from the half-open mouth. Her lower lip and jaw were tense and creased, giving the face a look of stern censoriousness as if she disapproved strongly of her own condition. Her thin lips were thickly painted, the strong purple stain had seeped into the cracks around the mouth so that the body looked parched in an extremity of cold. Her hands, the gnarled fingers brown with nicotine and laden with rings, lay quietly on the counterpane. Two of the talon-like nails were broken and the brick-red varnish on the others was cracked or peeled away.

The window was obstructed by a heavy dressing-table. Averting her eyes from the mess of crumpled tissues, open bottles of face cream, spilt powder and half-drunk cups of what looked like black coffee, Cordelia squeezed behind it and pushed open the window. She gulped in lungfuls of fresh, cleansing air. Below her in the garden pale shapes moved silently over the grass and between the trees like the ghosts of long dead revellers. She left the window open and went back to the bed. There was nothing here that she could do but she placed the cold hands under the counterpane and, taking a second and warmer gown from the hook on the door, tucked it around the woman's body. That, at least, would compensate for the fresh air blowing across the bed.

That done, Cordelia slipped back into the passage, just in time to see Isabelle coming out of the room next door. She shot out an arm and half dragged the girl back into the bedroom. Isabelle gave a little cry, but Cordelia planted her back firmly against the door and said in a low, urgent whisper:

'Tell me what you know about Mark Callender.'

The violet eyes slewed from door to window as if desperate for escape.

'I wasn't there when he did it.'

'When who did what?'

Isabelle retreated towards the bed as if the inert figure, who was now groaning stertorously, could offer support. Suddenly the woman turned on her side and gave a long snort like an animal in pain. Both girls glanced at her in startled alarm. Cordelia reiterated:

'When who did what?'

'When Mark killed himself; I wasn't there.'

The woman on the bed gave a little sigh. Cordelia lowered her voice:

'But you were there some days earlier, weren't you? You called at the house and enquired for him. Miss Markland saw you. Afterwards you sat in the garden and waited until he'd finished work.'

Was it Cordelia's imagination that the girl suddenly seemed more relaxed that she was relieved at the innocuousness of the question?

'I just called to see Mark. They gave me his address at the college Lodge. I went to visit him.'

'Why?' The harsh question seemed to puzzle her. She replied simply:

'I wanted to be with him. He was my friend.'

'Was he your lover too?' asked Cordelia. This brutal frankness was surely better than asking whether they had slept together, or gone to bed together – stupid euphemisms which Isabelle might not even understand: it was hard to tell from those beautiful but frightened eyes just how much she did understand.

'No, Mark was never my lover. He was working in the garden and I had to wait for him at the cottage. He gave me a chair in the sun and a book until he was free.'

'What book?'

'I don't remember, it was very dull. I was dull too until Mark came. Then we had tea with funny mugs that had a blue band, and after tea we went for a walk and then we had supper. Mark made a salad.'

'And then?'

'I drove home.'

She was perfectly calm now. Cordelia pressed on, aware of the sound of footsteps passing up and down the stairs, of the ring of voices.

'And the time before that? When did you see him before that tea party?'

'It was a few days before Mark left college. We went for a picnic in my car to the seaside. But first we stopped at a town – St. Edmunds town, is it? – and Mark saw a doctor.'

'Why? Was he ill?'

'Oh no, he was not ill, and he did not stay long enough for what you call it – an examination. He was in the house a few minutes only. It was a very poor house. I waited for him in the car, but not just outside the house you understand.'

'Did he say why he went there?'

'No, but I do not think he got what he wanted. Afterwards he was sad for a little time, but then we went to the sea and he was happy again.'

She, too, seemed happy now. She smiled at Cordelia, her sweet, unmeaning smile. Cordelia thought: it's just the cottage that terrifies her. She doesn't mind talking about the living Mark, it's his death she can't bear to think about. And yet, this repugnance wasn't born of personal grief. He had been her friend; he was sweet; she liked him. But she was getting on very well without him.

There was a knock at the door. Cordelia stood aside and Hugo came in. He lifted an eyebrow at Isabelle and, ignoring Cordelia, said:

'It's your party, ducky; coming down?'

'Cordelia wanted to talk to me about Mark.'

'No doubt. You told her, I hope, that you spent one day with him motoring to the sea and one afternoon and evening at Summertrees and that you haven't seen him since.'

'She told me,' said Cordelia. 'She was practically word perfect. I think she's safe to be let out on her own now.'

He said easily:

'You shouldn't be sarcastic, Cordelia, it doesn't suit you. Sarcasm is all right for some women, but not for women who are beautiful in the way that you are beautiful.'

They were passing down the stairs together to meet the hubbub in the hall. The compliment irritated Cordelia. She said:

'I suppose that woman on the bed is Isabelle's chaperone. Is she often drunk?'

'Mademoiselle de Congé? Not often as drunk as that, but I admit that she is seldom absolutely sober.'

'Then oughtn't you to do something about it?'

'What should I do? Hand her over to the twentieth-century Inquisition – a psychiatrist like my father?

What has she done to us to deserve that? Besides, she is tediously conscientious on the few occasions when she's sober. It happens that her compulsions and my interest coincide.'

Cordelia said severely:

'That may be expedient but I don't think it very responsible and it isn't kind.'

He stopped in his tracks and turned towards her, smiling directly into her eyes.

'Oh, Cordelia, you talk like the child of progressive parents who has been reared by a nonconformist nanny and educated at a convent school. I do like you!'

He was still smiling as Cordelia slipped away from them and infiltrated into the party. She reflected that his diagnosis hadn't been so very far wrong.

She helped herself to a glass of wine, then moved slowly round the room listening unashamedly to scraps of conversation, hoping to hear Mark's name mentioned. She heard it only once. Two girls and a very fair, rather insipid young man were standing behind her. One of the girls said:

'Sophie Tilling seems to have recovered remarkably quickly from Mark Callender's suicide. She and Davie went to the cremation, did you know? Typical of Sophie to take her current lover to see the previous one incinerated. I suppose it gave her some kind of a kick.'

Her companion laughed.

'And little brother takes over Mark's girl. If you can't get beauty, money and brains, settle for the first two. Poor Hugo! He suffers from a sense of inferiority. Not quite handsome enough; not quite clever enough – Sophie's First must have shaken him – not quite rich enough. No wonder he has to rely on sex to give him confidence.'

'And, even there, not quite . . .'

'Darling, you should know.'

They laughed and moved away. Cordelia felt her face burning. Her hand shook almost spilling her wine. She was surprised to find how much she cared, how much she had come to like Sophie. But that, of course, was part of the plan, that was Tilling strategy. If you can't shame her into giving up the case, suborn her; take her on the river; be nice to her; get her on our side. And it was true, she was on their side, at least against malicious detractors. She comforted herself with the censorious reflection that they were as bitchy as guests at a suburban cocktail party. She had never in her life attended one of those innocuous if boring gatherings for the routine consumption of gossip, gin and canapés but, like her father who had never attended one either, she found no difficulty in believing that they were hotbeds of snobbery, spite and sexual innuendo.

A warm body was pressing against her. She turned and saw Davie. He was carrying three bottles of wine. He had obviously heard at least part of the conversation, as the girls had no doubt intended, but he grinned amiably.

'Funny how Hugo's discarded women always hate him so much. It's quite different with Sophie. Her ex-lovers clutter up Norwich Street with their beastly bicycles and broken-down cars. I'm always finding them in the sitting-room drinking my beer and confiding to her the awful trouble they're having with their present girls.'

'Do you mind?'

'Not if they don't get any further than the sitting-room. Are you enjoying yourself?'

'Not very much.'

'Come and meet a friend of mine. He's been asking who you are.'

'No thank you, Davie. I must keep myself free for Mr Horsfall. I don't want to miss him.'

He smiled at her, rather pityingly she thought, and seemed about to speak. But he changed his mind and moved away, clutching the bottles to his chest and shouting a cheerful warning as he edged himself through the throng.

Cordelia worked her way around the room, watching and listening. She was intrigued by the overt sexuality; she had thought that intellectuals breathed too rarified air to be much interested in the flesh. Obviously this was a misapprehension. Come to think of it, the comrades, who might have been supposed to live in randy promiscuity, had been remarkably staid. She had sometimes felt that their sexual activities were prompted more by duty than instinct, more a weapon of revolution or a gesture against the bourgeois mores they despised than a response to human need. Their basic energies were all devoted to politics. It was not difficult to see where most of the energies of those present were directed.

She needn't have worried about the success of the kaftan. A number of men showed themselves willing or even eager to detach themselves from their partners for the pleasure of talking to her. With one particularly, a decorative and ironically amusing young historian,

Cordelia felt that she could have spent an entertaining evening. To enjoy the sole attention of one agreeable man and no attention at all from anyone else was all she ever hoped from a party. She wasn't naturally gregarious and, alienated by the last six years from her own generation, found herself intimidated by the noise, the underlying ruthlessness and the half-understood conventions of these tribal matings. And she told herself firmly that she wasn't here to enjoy herself at Sir Ronald's expense. None of her prospective partners knew Mark Callender or showed any interest in him, dead or alive. She musn't get herself tied for the evening to people who had no information to give. When this seemed a danger and the talk became too beguiling, she would murmur her excuses and slip away to the bathroom or into the shadows of the garden where little groups were sitting on the grass smoking pot. Cordelia couldn't be mistaken in that evocative smell. They showed no disposition to chat and here, at least, she could stroll in privacy gaining courage for the next foray, for the next artfully casual question, the next inevitable response.

'Mark Callender? Sorry – we never met. Didn't he go off to sample the simple life and end by hanging himself or something?'

Once she took refuge in Mademoiselle de Congé's room, but she saw that the inert figure had been unceremoniously dumped on a cushion of pillows on the carpet and that the bed was being occupied for quite another purpose.

She wondered when Edward Horsfall would arrive or whether he would arrive at all. And if he did, would

Hugo remember or bother to introduce her? She couldn't see either of the Tillings in the hot crush of gesticulating bodies which by now had crammed the sitting-room and spilled into the hall and half-way up the stairs. She was beginning to feel that this would be a wasted evening when Hugo's hand fell on her arm. He said:

'Come and meet Edward Horsfall. Edward, this is Cordelia Gray; she wants to talk about Mark Callender.'

Edward Horsfall was another surprise. Cordelia had subconsciously conjured up the picture of an elderly don, a little distrait with the weight of his learning, a benevolent if detached mentor of the young. Horsfall could not have been much over thirty. He was very tall, his hair falling long over one eye, his lean body curved as a melon rind, a comparison reinforced by the pleated yellow shirt front under a jutting bow tie.

Any half-acknowledged, half-shameful hope which Cordelia may have nourished that he would immediately take to her and be happily ungrudging of his time so long as they were together was quickly dispersed. His eyes were restless, flicking obsessively back to the door. She suspected that he was alone by choice, deliberately keeping himself free from encumbrances until the hoped-for companion arrived. He was so fidgety that it was difficult not to be fretted by his anxiety. She said:

'You don't have to stay with me all the evening, you know, I only want some information.'

Her voice recalled him to an awareness of her and to some attempt at civility.

'That wouldn't exactly be a penance. I'm sorry. What do you want to know?'

'Anything you can tell me about Mark. You taught him history didn't you? Was he good at it?'

It wasn't a particularly relevant question but one which she felt all teachers might respond to as a start.

'He was more rewarding to teach than some students I'm afflicted with. I don't know why he chose history. He could very well have read one of the sciences. He had a lively curiosity about physical phenomena. But he decided to read history.'

'Do you think that was to disoblige his father?'

'To disoblige Sir Ronald?' He turned and stretched out an arm for a bottle. 'What are you drinking? There's one thing about Isabelle de Lasterie's parties, the drink is excellent, presumably because Hugo orders it. There's an admirable absence of beer.'

'Doesn't Hugo drink beer then?' asked Cordelia.

'He claims not to. What were we talking about? Oh, yes, disobliging Sir Ronald. Mark said that he chose history because we have no chance of understanding the present without understanding the past. That's the sort of irritating cliché people come out with at interviews, but he may have believed it. Actually, of course, the reverse is true, we interpret the past through our knowledge of the present.'

'Was he any good?' asked Cordelia. 'I mean, would he have got a First?'

A First, she naïvely believed, was the ultimate in scholastic achievement, the certificate of pronounced intelligence that the recipient carried unchallenged through life. She wanted to hear that Mark was safe for a First.

'Those are two separate and distinct questions. You seem to be confusing merit with achievement. Impossible to predict his class, hardly a First. Mark was capable of extraordinarily good and original work but he limited his material to the number of his original ideas. The result tended to be rather thin. Examiners like originality but you've got to spew up the accepted facts and orthodox opinions first if only to show that you've learnt them. An exceptional memory and fast legible handwriting; that's the secret of a First. Where are you, incidentally?' He noticed Cordelia's brief look of incomprehension.

'At what college?'

'None; I work. I'm a private detective.'

He took this information in his stride.

'My uncle employed one of those once to find out if my aunt was being screwed by their dentist. She was, but he could have found out more easily by the simple expedient of asking them. His way, he lost the services of a wife and of a dentist simultaneously and paid through the nose for information he could have got for nothing. It made quite a stir in the family at the time. I should have thought that the job was—'

Cordelia finished the sentence for him.

'An unsuitable job for a woman?'

'Not at all. Entirely suitable I should have thought, requiring, I imagine, infinite curiosity, infinite pains and a penchant for interfering with other people.' His attention was wandering again. A group near to them were talking and snatches of the conversation came to them.

'—typical of the worst kind of academic writing. Contempt for logic; a generous sprinkling of vogue names; spurious profundity and bloody awful grammar.'

The tutor gave the speakers a second's attention, dismissed their academic chat as beneath his notice and condescended to transfer his attention but not his regard back to Cordelia.

'Why are you so interested in Mark Callender?'

'His father has employed me to find out why he died. I was hoping that you might be able to help. I mean, did he ever give you a hint that he might be unhappy, unhappy enough to kill himself? Did he explain why he gave up college?'

'Not to me. I never felt that I got near him. He made a formal goodbye, thanked me for what he chose to describe as my help, and left. I made the usual noises of regret. We shook hands. I was embarrassed, but not Mark. He wasn't I think, a young man susceptible to embarrassment.'

There was a small commotion at the door and a group of new arrivals pushed themselves noisily into the throng. Among them was a tall, dark girl in a flame-coloured frock, open almost to the waist. Cordelia felt the tutor stiffen, saw his eyes fixed on the new arrival with an intense, half anxious, half supplicating look, which she had seen before. Her heart sank. She would be lucky now to get any more information. Desperately trying to recapture his attention, she said:

'I'm not sure that Mark did kill himself. I think it could have been murder.'

He spoke inattentively, his eyes on the newcomers.

'Unlikely, surely. By whom? For what reason? He was a negligible personality. He didn't even provoke a vague dislike except possibly from his father. But Ronald Callender couldn't have done it if that's what you're hoping. He was dining in Hall at High Table on the night Mark died. It was a college feast night. I sat next to him. His son telephoned him.'

Cordelia said eagerly, almost tugging at his sleeve.

'At what time?'

'Soon after the meal started, I suppose. Benskin, he's one of the College servants, came in and gave him the message. It must have been between eight and eight-fifteen. Callender disappeared for about ten minutes then returned and got on with his soup. The rest of us still hadn't reached the second course.'

'Did he say what Mark wanted? Did he seem disturbed?'

'Neither. We hardly spoke through the meal. Sir Ronald doesn't waste his conversational gifts on non-scientists. Excuse me, will you?'

He was gone, threading his way through the throng towards his prey. Cordelia put down her glass and went in search of Hugo.

'Look,' she said, 'I want to talk to Benskin, a servant at your college. Would he be there tonight?'

Hugo put down the bottle he was holding.

'He may be. He's one of the few who live in college. But I doubt whether you would winkle him out of his lair on your own. If it's all that urgent, I'd better come with you.'

*

The college porter ascertained with curiosity that Benskin was in the college and Benskin was summoned. He arrived after a wait of five minutes during which Hugo chatted to the porter and Cordelia walked outside the Lodge to amuse herself reading the college notices. Benskin arrived, unhurrying, imperturbable. He was a silver-haired, formally dressed old man, his face creased and thick skinned as an anaemic blood orange, and would, Cordelia thought, have looked like an advertisement for the ideal butler, were it not for an expression of lugubrious and sly disdain.

Cordelia gave him sight of Sir Ronald's note of authority and plunged straight into her questions. There was nothing to be gained by subtlety and since she had enlisted Hugo's help, she had little hope of shaking him off. She said:

'Sir Ronald has asked me to enquire into the circumstances of his son's death.'

'So I see, Miss.'

'I am told that Mr Mark Callender telephoned his father while Sir Ronald was dining at High Table on the night his son died and that you passed the message to Sir Ronald shortly after dinner began?'

'I was under the impression at the time that it was Mr Callender who was ringing, Miss, but I was mistaken.'

'How can you be sure of that, Mr Benskin?'

'Sir Ronald himself told me, Miss, when I saw him in college some few days after his son's death. I've known Sir Ronald since he was an undergraduate and I made bold to express my condolences. During our brief conversation I made reference to the telephone call of 26th May and Sir Ronald told me that I was mistaken, that it was not Mr Callender who had called.'

'Did he say who it was?'

'Sir Ronald informed me that it was his laboratory assistant, Mr Chris Lunn.'

'Did that surprise you – that you were wrong, I mean?'

'I confess that I was somewhat surprised, Miss, but the mistake was perhaps excusable. My subsequent reference to the incident was fortuitous and in the circumstances regrettable.'

'Do you really believe that you misheard the name?'

The obstinate old face did not relax.

'Sir Ronald could have been in no doubt about the person who telephoned him.'

'Was it usual for Mr Callender to ring his father while he was dining in College?'

'I had never previously taken a call from him, but then answering the telephone is not part of my normal duties. It is possible that some of the other college servants may be able to help but I hardly think that an enquiry would be productive or that the news that college servants had been questioned would be gratifying to Sir Ronald.'

'Any enquiry which can help ascertain the truth is likely to be gratifying to Sir Ronald,' said Cordelia. Really, she thought, Benskin's prose style is becoming infectious. She added more naturally:

'Sir Ronald is very anxious to find out everything possible about his son's death. Is there anything that you can tell me, any help that you can give me, Mr Benskin?'

This was perilously close to an appeal but it met with no response.

'Nothing, Miss. Mr Callender was a quiet and pleasant young gentleman who seemed, as far as I was able to observe him, to be in good health and spirits up to the time he left us. His death has been very much felt in the college. Is there anything else, Miss?'

He stood patiently waiting to be dismissed and Cordelia let him go. As she and Hugo left college together and walked back into Trumpington Street she said bitterly:

'He doesn't care, does he?'

'Why should he? Benskin's an old phoney but he's been at college for seventy years and he's seen it all before. A thousand ages in his sight are but an evening gone. I've only known Benskin distressed once over the suicide of an undergraduate and that was a Duke's son. Benskin thought that there were some things that college shouldn't permit to happen.'

'But he wasn't mistaken about Mark's call. You could tell that from his whole manner, at least I could. He knows what he heard. He isn't going to admit it, of course, but he knows in his heart he wasn't mistaken.'

Hugo said lightly:

'He was being the old college servant, very correct, very proper; that's Benskin all over. "The young gentlemen aren't what they were when I first came to college." I should bloody well hope not! They wore side whiskers then and noblemen sported fancy gowns to distinguish them from the plebs. Benskin would bring all that back if he could. He's an anachronism, pottering through the court hand in hand with a statelier past.'

'But he isn't deaf. I deliberately spoke in a soft voice and he heard me perfectly. Do you really believe that he was mistaken?'

'Chris Lunn and his son are very similar sounds.'

'But Lunn doesn't announce himself that way. All the time I was with Sir Ronald and Miss Leaming they just called him Lunn.'

'Look, Cordelia, you can't possibly suspect Ronald Callender of having a hand in his son's death! Be logical. You accept, I suppose, that a rational murderer hopes not to be found out. You admit, no doubt, that Ronald Callender, although a disagreeable bastard, is a rational being. Mark is dead and his body cremated. No one except you has mentioned murder. Then Sir Ronald employs you to stir things up. Why should he if he's got something to hide? He doesn't even need to divert suspicion, there is no suspicion.'

'Of course I don't suspect him of killing his son. He doesn't know how Mark died and he desperately needs to know. That's why he's taken me on. I could tell that at our interview; I couldn't be wrong about that. But I don't understand why he should have lied about the telephone call.'

'If he is lying there could be half a dozen innocent explanations. If Mark did ring the college it must have been something pretty urgent, perhaps something which his father didn't want to make public, something which gives a clue to his son's suicide.'

'Then why employ me to find out why he killed himself?'

'True, wise Cordelia; I'll try again. Mark asked for help, perhaps an urgent visit which Dad refused. You can imagine his reaction. "Don't be ridiculous, Mark, I'm dining at High Table with the Master. Obviously I can't leave the cutlets and claret just because you telephone me in this hysterical way and demand to see me. Pull yourself together." That sort of thing wouldn't sound so good in open court; coroners are notoriously censorious. Hugo's voice took on a deep magisterial tone. '"It is not for me to add to Sir Ronald's distress, but it is, perhaps, unfortunate that he chose to ignore what was obviously a cry for help. Had he left his meal immediately and gone to his son's side this brilliant young student might have been saved." Cambridge suicides, so I've noticed, are always brilliant; I'm still waiting to read the report of an inquest where the college authorities testify that the student only just killed himself in time before they kicked him out.'

'But Mark died between seven and nine p.m. That telephone call is Sir Ronald's alibi!'

'He wouldn't see it like that. He doesn't need an alibi. If you know you're not involved and the question of foul play never arises, you don't think in terms of alibis. It's only the guilty who do that.'

'But how did Mark know where to find his father? In his evidence Sir Ronald said that he hadn't spoken to his son for over two weeks.'

'I can see you have a point there. Ask Miss Leaming. Better still, ask Lunn if it was, in fact, he who rang the college. If you're looking for a villain Lunn should suit admirably. I find him absolutely sinister.'

'I didn't know that you knew him.'

'Oh, he's pretty well known in Cambridge. He drives that horrid little closed van around with ferocious dedication as if he were transporting recalcitrant students to the gas chambers. Everyone knows Lunn. Seldom he smiles and smiles in such a way as if he mocked himself and scorned his spirit that could be moved to smile at anything. I should concentrate on Lunn.'

They walked on in silence through the warm scented night while the waters sang in the runnels of Trumpington Street. Lights were shining now in college doorways and in porters' lodges and the far gardens and interconnecting courts, glimpsed as they passed, looked remote and ethereal as in a dream. Cordelia was suddenly oppressed with loneliness and melancholy. If Bernie were alive they would be discussing the case, cosily ensconced in the furthest corner of some Cambridge pub, insulated by noise and smoke and anonymity from the curiosity of their neighbours; talking low voiced in their own particular jargon. They would be speculating on the personality of a young man who slept under that gentle and intellectual painting, yet who had bought a vulgar magazine of salacious nudes. Or had he? And if not, how had it come to be in the cottage garden? They would be discussing a father who lied about his son's last telephone call; speculating in happy complicity about an uncleaned spade, a row of earth half dug, an unwashed coffee mug, a quotation from Blake meticulously typed. They would be talking about Isabelle who was terrified and Sophie who was surely honest and Hugo who certainly knew something about Mark's death and who was clever but not as clever as he needed to be. For the first time since the case began Cordelia doubted her ability to solve it alone. If only there were someone reliable in whom she could confide, someone who would reinforce her confidence. She thought again of Sophie, but Sophie had been Mark's mistress and was Hugo's sister. They were both involved. She was on her own and that, when she came to think about it, was no different from how essentially it had always been. Ironically, the realization brought her comfort and a return of hope.

At the corner of Panton Street they paused and he said:

'You're coming back to the party?'

'No, thank you, Hugo; I've got work to do.'

'Are you staying in Cambridge?'

Cordelia wondered whether the question was prompted by more than polite interest. Suddenly cautious, she said:

'Only for the next day or two. I've found a very dull but cheap bed and breakfast place near the station.'

He accepted the lie without comment and they said goodnight. She made her way back to Norwich Street. The little car was still outside number fifty-seven, but the house was dark and quiet as if to emphasize her exclusion and the three windows were as blank as dead rejecting eyes.

*

She was tired by the time she got back to the cottage and had parked the Mini on the edge of the copse. The garden gate creaked at her hand. The night was dark and she felt in her bag for her torch and followed its bright pool round the side of the cottage and to the back door. By its light she fitted the key into the lock. She turned it and, dazed with tiredness, stepped into the sitting-room. The torch, still switched on, hung loosely from her hand, making erratic patterns of light on the tiled floor. Then in one involuntary movement it jerked upwards and shone full on the thing that hung from the centre hook of the ceiling. Cordelia gave a cry and clutched at the table. It was the bolster from her bed, the bolster with a cord drawn tight about one end making a grotesque and bulbous head, and the other end stuffed into a pair of Mark's trousers. The legs hung pathetically flat and empty, one lower than the other. As she stared at it in fascinated horror, her heart hammering, a slight breeze wafted in from the open door and it swung slowly round as if twisted by a living hand.

She must have stood there rooted with fear and staring wild-eyed at the bolster for seconds only, yet it seemed minutes before she found the strength to pull out a chair from the table and take the thing down. Even in the moment of repulsion and terror she remembered to look closely at the knot. The cord was attached to the hook by a simple loop and two half-hitches. So, either her secret visitor had chosen not to repeat his former tactics, or he hadn't known how the first knot had been tied. She laid the bolster on the chair and went outside for the gun. In her tiredness she had forgotten it, but now she longed for the reassurance of the hard cold metal in her hand. She stood at the back door and listened. The garden seemed suddenly full of noises, mysterious rustlings, leaves moving in the slight breeze like human sighs, furtive scurryings in the undergrowth, the bat-like squeak of an animal disconcertingly close at hand. The night seemed to be holding its breath as she crept out towards the elder bush. She waited, listening to her own heart, before she found courage to turn her back and stretch up her hand to feel for the gun. It was still there. She sighed audibly with relief and immediately felt better. The gun wasn't loaded but that hardly seemed to matter. She hurried back to the cottage, her terror assuaged.

It was nearly an hour before she finally went to bed. She lit the lamp and, gun in hand, made a search of the whole cottage. Next she examined the window. It was obvious enough how he had got in. The window had no catch and was easy to push open from outside. Cordelia fetched a roll of Scotch tape from her scene-of-crime kit and, as Bernie had shown her, cut two very narrow strips and pasted them across the base of the pane and the wooden frame. She doubted whether the front windows could be opened but she took no chances and sealed them in the same way. It wouldn't stop an intruder but at least she would know next morning that he had gained access. Finally, having washed in the kitchen, she went upstairs to bed. There was no lock on her door but she wedged it slightly open and balanced a saucepan lid on the top or the frame. It anyone did succeed in getting in, he wouldn't take her by surprise. She loaded the gun and placed it on her bedside table, remembering that she was dealing with a killer. She examined the cord. It was a four-foot length of ordinary strong string, obviously not new, and frayed at one end. Her heart sank at the hopelessness of trying to identify it. But she labelled it carefully, as Bernie had taught her, and packed it in her scene-of-crime kit. She did the same with the curled strap and the typed passage of Blake, transferring them from the bottom of her shoulder bag to plastic exhibit envelopes. She was so weary that even this routine chore cost her an effort of will. Then she placed the bolster back on the bed, resisting an impulse to sling it on the floor and sleep without it. But, by then, nothing – neither fear nor discomfort could have kept her awake. She lay for only a few minutes listening to the ticking of her watch before tiredness overcame her and bore her unresisting down the dark tide of sleep.

CHAPTER FOUR

Cordelia was awakened early next morning by the discordant chattering of the birds and the strong clear light of another fine day. She lay for several minutes stretching herself within her sleeping-bag, savouring the smell of a country morning, that subtle and evocative fusion of earth, sweet wet grass and stronger farmyard smell. She washed in the kitchen as Mark had obviously done, standing in the tin bath from the shed and gasping as she poured saucepans of cold tap water over her naked body. There was something about the simple life which disposed one to these austerities. Cordelia thought it unlikely that, in any circumstances, she would willingly have bathed in cold water in London or so much relished the smell of the paraffin stove superimposed on the appetizing sizzle of frying bacon, or the flavour of her first strong mug of tea.

The cottage was filled with sunlight, a warm friendly sanctum from which she could safely venture out to whatever the day held. In the calm peace of a summer morning the little sitting-room seemed untouched by the tragedy of Mark Callender's death. The hook in the ceiling looked as innocuous as if it had never served its dreadful purpose. The horror of that moment when her torch had first picked out the dark swollen shadow of the bolster moving in the night breeze now had the unreality of a dream. Even the memory of the precautions of the night before were embarrassing viewed in the unambiguous light of day. She felt rather foolish as she unloaded the gun, secreted the ammunition among her underclothes, and hid the pistol in the elder bush, watching carefully to see that she wasn't observed. When the washing-up was done and the one teacloth washed through and hung out to dry, she picked a small posy of pansies, cowslips and meadow-sweet from the far end of the garden and set them on the table in one of the ribbed mugs.

She had decided that her first task must be to try to trace Nanny Pilbeam. Even if the woman had nothing to tell her about Mark's death or his reason for leaving college, she would be able to speak about his childhood and boyhood; she, probably better than anyone, would know what his essential nature had been. She had cared enough about him to attend the funeral and to send an expensive wreath. She had called on him in college on his twenty-first birthday. He had probably kept in touch with her, might even have confided in her. He had no mother and Nanny Pilbeam could have been, in some sense, a substitute.

As she drove into Cambridge Cordelia considered tactics. The probability was that Miss Pilbeam lived somewhere in the district. It was unlikely that she actually lived in the city since Hugo Tilling had only seen her once. From his brief account of her, it sounded as if she were old and probably poor. It was unlikely, therefore, that she would travel far to attend the funeral. It was apparent that she hadn't been one of the official mourners from Garforth House, hadn't been invited by Sir Ronald. According to Hugo, none of the party had even spoken to each other. This hardly suggested that Miss Pilbeam was the elderly and valued retainer of tradition, almost one of the family. Sir Ronald's neglect of her on such an occasion intrigued Cordelia. She wondered just what Miss Pilbeam's position in the family had been.

If the old lady lived near Cambridge, she had probably ordered the wreath at one of the city florists. Villages were very unlikely to provide this kind of service. It had been an ostentatious wreath, which suggested that Miss Pilbeam had been prepared to spend lavishly and had probably gone to one of the larger florists. The likelihood was that she had ordered it personally. Elderly ladies, apart from the fact that they were seldom on the telephone, like to attend to these matters direct, having, Cordelia suspected, a well-founded suspicion that only face-to-face confrontation and the meticulous recital of one's precise requirements extracted the best service. If Miss Pilbeam had come in from her village by train or by bus, she had probably selected a shop somewhere near the centre of the city. Cordelia decided to begin her search by enquiring of passers-by if they could recommend the name of a good florist.

She had already learned that Cambridge was not a city for the cruising motorist. She drew up and consulted the folding map at the back of her guide book and decided to leave the Mini on the car park next to Parker's Piece. Her search might take some time and would be best done on foot. She daren't risk a parking fine nor the impounding of the car. She checked her watch. It was still only a few minutes after nine o'clock. She had made a good start to the day.

The first hour was disappointing. The people of whom she enquired were anxious to be helpful but their ideas of what constituted a reliable florist somewhere near the centre of the city were peculiar. Cordelia was directed to small greengrocer's selling a few bunches of cut flowers as a side line, to the supplier of gardening equipment who dealt in plants but not in wreaths, and once to a funeral director. The two florists' shops which at first sight seemed possible had never heard of Miss Pilbeam and had provided no wreaths for the Mark Callender funeral. A little weary with much walking and beginning to feel despondent, Cordelia decided that the whole quest had been unreasonably sanguine. Probably Miss Pilbeam had come in from Bury St. Edmunds or Newmarket and had bought the wreath in her own town.

But the visit to the undertakers was not wasted. In reply to her enquiry, they recommended the name of a firm which 'provided a very nice class of wreath, Miss, really very nice indeed'. The shop was further from the centre of the city than Cordelia had expected. Even from the pavement it smelt of weddings or funerals, as one's mood dictated, and as she pushed open the door Cordelia was welcomed by a gush of warm air which caught at the throat. There were flowers everywhere. Large green buckets lined the walls holding clumps of lilies, irises and lupins; smaller containers were packed tight with wallflowers and marigolds and stocks; there were frigid bundles of tight budded roses on thornless stems, each flower identical in size and colour and looking as if it had been cultivated in a test tube. Pots of indoor plants, decorated with variegated ribbon, lined the path to the counter like a floral guard of honour.

There was a room at the back of the shop where two assistants were working. Through the open door Cordelia watched them. The younger, a languid blonde with a spotted skin, was assistant executioner, laying open roses and freesias, predestined victims, graded according to type and colour. Her senior, whose status was denoted by a better fitting overall and an air of authority, was twisting off the flower heads, piercing each mutilated bloom with wire and threading them closely on to a huge bed of moss in the shape of a heart. Cordelia averted her eyes from this horror.

A buxom lady in a pink smock appeared behind the counter apparently from nowhere. She was as pungently scented as the shop, but had obviously decided that no ordinary floral perfume could compete and that she had better rely on the exotic. She smelt of curry powder and pine so strongly that the effect was practically anaesthetizing.

Cordelia said her prepared speech:

'I'm from Sir Robert Callender of Garforth House. I wonder whether you can help us? His son was cremated on 3rd of June and their old nurse very kindly sent a wreath, a cross of red roses. Sir Ronald has lost her address and very much wants to write to her. The name is Pilbeam.'

'Oh, I don't think we executed any orders of that type for 3rd June.'

'If you would be kind enough to just look in the book—'

Suddenly the young blonde looked up from her work and called out:

'It's Goddard.'

'I beg your pardon, Shirley?' said the buxom lady repressively.

'The name's Goddard. The card on the wreath said Nanny Pilbeam, but the customer was a Mrs Goddard. Another lady came to enquire from Sir Ronald Callender and that was the name she gave. I looked it up for her. Mrs Goddard, Lavender Cottage, Ickleton. One cross, four foot long in red roses. Six pounds. It's there in the book.'

'Thank you very much,' said Cordelia fervently. She smiled her thanks impartially at the three of them and left quickly in case she got embroiled in an argument about the other enquirer from Garforth House. It must have looked odd, she knew, but the three of them would no doubt enjoy themselves discussing it after she had left. Lavender Cottage, Ickleton. She kept repeating the address to herself until she was at a safe distance from the shop and could pause to write it down.

Her tiredness seemed miraculously to have left her as she sped back to the car park. She consulted her map. Ickleton was a village near the Essex border about ten miles from Cambridge. It wasn't far from Duxford so that she would be retracing her steps. She could be there in less than half an hour.

But it took longer than she had expected to thread her way through the Cambridge traffic and it wasn't until thirty-five minutes later that she came to Ickleton's fine flint and pebble church with its broach spire, and drove the Mini close to the church gate. It was a temptation to take a brief look inside, but she resisted it. Mrs Goddard might even now be preparing to catch the Cambridge bus. She went in search of Lavender Cottage.

It wasn't, in fact, a cottage at all but a small semi-detached house of hideous red brick at the end of the High Street. There was only a narrow strip of grass between the front door and the road and neither smell nor sight of lavender. The iron knocker, in the form of a lion's head, fell heavily, shaking the door. The response came, not from Lavender Cottage, but from the next house. An elderly woman appeared, thin, almost toothless and swathed in an immense apron patterned with roses. She had carpet slippers on her feet, a woollen cap decorated with a bobble on her head and an air of lively interest in the world in general.

'You'll be wanting Mrs Goddard, I daresay?'

'Yes. Could you tell me where I could find her?'

'She'll be over at the graveyard, I don't doubt. She usually is this time of a fine morning.'

'I've just come from the church. I didn't see anyone.'

'Bless you, Miss, she's not at the church! They haven't been burying us there for many a year now. Her old man is where they'll be putting her in time, in the cemetery on Hinxton Road. You can't miss it. Just keep straight on.'

'I'll have to go back to the church for my car,' said Cordelia. It was obvious that she was going to be watched out of sight and it seemed necessary to explain why she was departing in the opposite direction to the one indicated. The old woman smiled and nodded and came out to lean on her gate for a better view of Cordelia's progress down the High Street, nodding her head like a marionette so that the bright bobble danced in the sun.

*

The cemetery was easily found. Cordelia parked the Mini on a convenient patch of grass where a signpost pointed the footpath to Duxford and walked the few yards back to the iron gates. There was a small flint chapel of rest with an apse at the east end and beside it an ancient wooden seat green with lichen and spattered with bird lime which gave a view of the whole burial ground. A wide swathe of turf ran straight down the middle and on each side were the graves, variously marked with white marble crosses, grey headstones, small rusted circles of iron heeling over towards the smooth turf and bright splashes of flowers patchworked over the newly dug earth. It was very peaceful. The burial ground was surrounded by trees, their leaves scarcely stirring in the calm, hot air. There was little sound except the chirruping of crickets in the grass and from time to time the nearby ringing of a railway level-crossing bell and the swooping horn of a diesel train.

There was only one other person in the graveyard, an elderly woman bending over one of the far graves. Cordelia sat quietly on the seat, arms folded in her lap, before making her way silently down the grass path towards her. She knew with certainty that this interview was going to be crucial yet paradoxically she was in no hurry to begin. She came up to the woman and stood, still unnoticed, at the foot of the grave.

She was a small woman dressed in black, whose old-fashioned straw hat, its brim wreathed with faded net, was screwed to her hair with an immense black bobbed hat pin. She knelt with her back to Cordelia showing the soles of a pair of mis-shapen shoes from which her thin legs stuck out like sticks. She was weeding the grave; her fingers, darting like a reptile's tongue over the grass, plucked at small, almost undetectable weeds. At her side was a punnet holding a folded newspaper and a gardening trowel. From time to time, she dropped into the punnet her little mush of weeds.

After a couple of minutes, during which Cordelia watched her in silence, she paused satisfied and began smoothing the surface of the grass as if comforting the bones underneath. Cordelia read the inscription carved deep on the headstone. 'Sacred to the memory of Charles Albert Goddard beloved husband of Annie who departed this life 27th August 1962, aged 70 years. At rest.' At rest; the commonest epitaph of a generation to whom rest must have seemed the ultimate luxury, the supreme benediction.

The woman rested back for a second on her heels and contemplated the grave with satisfaction. It was then that she became aware of Cordelia. She turned a bright much wrinkled face towards her and said without curiosity or resentment at her presence:

'It's a nice stone, isn't it?'

'Yes, it is. I was admiring the lettering.'

'Cut deep that is. It cost a mint of money but it was worth it. That'll last, you see. Half the lettering here won't it's that shallow. It takes the pleasure out of a cemetery. I like to read the grave stones, like to know who people were and when they died and how long the women lived after they buried their men. It sets you wondering how they managed and whether they were lonely. There's no use in a stone if you can't read the lettering. Of course, this stone looks a bit top-heavy at present. That's because I asked them to leave space for me: "Also to Annie his wife, departed this life, . . ." and then the date: that'll even it up nicely. I've left the money to pay for it.'

'What text were you thinking of having?' enquired Cordelia.

'Oh, no text! At rest will be good enough for the both of us. We shan't be asking more of the good Lord than that.'

Cordelia said:

'That cross of roses you sent to Mark Callender's funeral was beautiful.'

'Oh, did you see it? You weren't at the funeral, were you? Yes, I was pleased with it. They made a nice job of it, I thought. Poor boy, he hadn't much else, had he?'

She looked at Cordelia with benign interest:

'So you knew Mr Mark? Would you be his young lady perhaps?'

'No, not that, but I cared about him. It's odd that he never talked about you, his old nurse.'

'But I wasn't his nurse, my dear, or at least, only for a month or two. He was a baby then, it meant nothing to him. No, I was nurse to his dear mother.'

'But you visited Mark on his twenty-first birthday?'

'So he told you that, did he? I was glad to see him again after all those years, but I wouldn't have pushed myself on him. It wouldn't have been right, his father feeling as he did. No, I went to give him something from his mother, to do something she had asked me to

149

do when she was dying. Do you know, I hadn't seen Mr Mark for over twenty years – odd, really, considering that we didn't live that far apart – but I knew him at once. He had a great look of his mother about him, poor boy.'

'Could you tell me about it? It's not just curiosity; it's important for me to know.'

Leaning for support on the handle of her basket, Mrs Goddard got laboriously to her feet. She picked at a few short blades of grass adhering to her skirt, felt in her pocket for a pair of grey cotton gloves and put them on. Together they made their way slowly down the path.

'Important, is it? I don't know why it should be. It's all in the past now. She's dead, poor lady, and so is he. All that hope and promise come to nothing. I haven't spoken to anyone else about it, but then who would care to know?'

'Perhaps we could sit on this bench and talk together for a time?'

'I don't see why we shouldn't. There's nothing to hurry home for now. Do you know, my dear, I didn't marry my husband until I was fifty-three and yet I miss him as if we had been childhood sweethearts. People said I was a fool to take on a man at that age but you see I had known his wife for thirty years, we were at school together, and I knew him. If a man's good to one woman, he'll be good to another. That's what I reckoned and I was right.'

They sat side by side on the bench gazing over the green swathe towards the grave. Cordelia said:

'Tell me about Mark's mother.'

'She was a Miss Bottley, Evelyn Bottley. I went to her mother as under-nursemaid before she was born. There was only little Harry then. He was killed in the war on his first raid over Germany. His Dad took it very hard; there was never anyone to match Harry, the sun shone out of his eyes. The master never really cared for Miss Evie, it was all the boy with him. Mrs Bottley died when Evie was born and that may have made a difference. People say that it does, but I've never believed it. I've known fathers who loved a baby even more – poor innocent things, how can they be blamed? If you ask me, it was just an excuse for not taking to the child, that she killed her mother.'

'Yes, I know a father who made it an excuse too. But it isn't their fault. We can't make ourselves love someone just because we want to.'

'More's the pity, my dear, or the world would be an easier place. But his own child, that's not natural!'

'Did she love him?'

'How could she? You won't get love from a child if you don't give love. But she never had the trick of pleasing him, of humouring him – he was a big man, fierce, loud talking, frightening to a child. He would have done better with a pretty, pert little thing, who wouldn't have been afraid of him.'

'What happened to her? How did she meet Sir Ronald Callender?'

'He wasn't Sir Ronald then, my dear. Oh, dear no! He was Ronny Callender the gardener's son. They lived at Harrowgate you see. Oh, such a lovely house they had! When I first went into service there they had three gardeners. That was before the war, of course. Mr Bottley worked in Bradford; he was in the wool trade. Well, you were asking about Ronny Callender. I remember him well, a pugnacious, good-looking lad but one who kept his thoughts to himself. He was clever that one, oh he was clever! He got a scholarship to the grammar school and did very well.'

'And Evelyn Bottley fell in love?'

'She may have done, my dear. What there was between them when they were young, who can tell. But then the war came and he went away. She was wild to do something useful and they took her on as a V.A.D., though how she passed the medical I'll never know. And then they met again in London as people did in the war – and the next thing we knew they were married.'

'And came to live here outside Cambridge?'

'Not until after the war. At first she kept on with her nursing and he was sent overseas. He had what the men call a good war; we'd call it a bad war I daresay, a lot of killing and fighting, imprisonment and escaping. It ought to have made Mr Bottley proud of him and reconciled to the marriage but it didn't. I think he thought that Ronny had his eye on the money, because there was money to come, no doubt about that. He may have been right, but who's to blame the boy? My mother used to say, "Don't marry for money, but marry where money is!" There's no harm in looking for money as long as there's kindness as well.'

'And do you think there was kindness?'

'There was never unkindness that I could see, and she was mad about him. After the war he went up to Cambridge. He'd always wanted to be a scientist and he got a grant because he was ex-service. She had some money from her father and they bought the house he lives in now so that he could live at home when he was studying. It didn't look the same then, of course. He's done a lot to it since. They were quite poor then and Miss Evie managed with practically no one to help, only me. Mr Bottley used to come and stay from time to time. She used to dread his visits, poor darling. He was looking for a grandchild, you see, and one didn't come. And then Mr Callender finished at the university and got a job teaching. He wanted to stay on at college to be a Don or something like that, but they wouldn't have him. He used to say it was because he hadn't influence, but I think he may not have been quite clever enough. In Harrogate we thought he was the cleverest boy in the grammar school. But then, Cambridge is full of clever men.'

'And then Mark was born?'

'Yes, on the 25th April 1951, nine years after they were married. He was born in Italy. Mr Bottley was that pleased when she became pregnant that he increased the allowance and they used to spend a lot of holidays in Tuscany. My lady loved Italy, always had, and I think she wanted the child to be born there. Otherwise she wouldn't have gone on holiday in the last month of her pregnancy. I went to visit her about a month after she came home with the baby and I've never seen a woman so happy. Oh, he was a lovely little boy!'

'But why did you visit her; weren't you living and working there?'

'No, my dear. Not for some months. She wasn't well in the early days of her pregnancy. I could see that she was strained and unhappy and then one day Mr Callender sent for me and told me that she had taken against me and that I'd have to leave. I wouldn't have believed it, but when I went to her she just put out her hand and said: "I'm sorry, Nanny, I think it would be better if you went."

'Pregnant women have strange fancies, I know, and the baby was so important to them both. I thought she might have asked me to come back afterwards and so she did, but not living in. I took a bedsitting room in the village with the postmistress and used to give four mornings a week to my lady and the rest to other ladies in the village. It worked very well, really, but I missed the baby when I wasn't with him. I hadn't seen her often during her pregnancy but once we met in Cambridge. She must have been near the end of her time. She was very heavy, poor dear, dragging herself along. At first she pretended that she hadn't noticed me and then she thought better of it and came across the road. "We're off to Italy next week, Nanny," she said. "Isn't it lovely?" I said: "If you're not careful, my dear, that baby will be a little Italian," and she laughed. It seemed as though she couldn't wait to get back to the sun.'

'And what happened after she came home?'

'She died after nine months, my dear. She was never strong, as I said, and she caught influenza. I helped look after her and I'd have done more but Mr Callender took over the nursing himself. He couldn't bear anyone else to be near her. We only had a few minutes together just before she died and it was then that she asked me to give her prayer book to Mark on his twenty-first birthday. I can hear her now: "Give it to Mark when he's twenty-one, Nanny. Wrap it up carefully and take it to

him when he comes of age. You won't forget, will you?"
I said: "I'll not forget, my darling, you know that."
Then she said a strange thing. 'If you do, or if you die
before then, or if he doesn't understand, it won't really
matter. It will mean that God wants it that way." '

'What do you think she meant?'

'Who's to say, my dear? She was very religious was
Miss Evie, too religious for her own good, I sometimes
thought. I believe we should accept our own responsibilities, solve our own problems, not leave it all to God
as if He hadn't enough to be thinking about with the
world in the state it is. But that's what she said not three
hours before she died and that's what I promised. So
when Mr Mark was twenty-one, I found out what
college he was at and went to see him.'

'What happened?'

'Oh, we had a very happy time together. Do you know,
his father had never spoken about his mother. That sometimes happens when a wife dies but I think a son ought to
know about his mother. He was full of questions, things
that I thought his father would have told him.

'He was glad to get the prayer book. It was a few
days later that he came to see me. He asked the name of
the doctor who had treated his mother. I told him that
it was old Dr Gladwin. Mr Callender and she had
never had any other doctor. I used to think it a pity
sometimes, Miss Evie being so frail. Dr Gladwin must
have been seventy then, and although there were people
who wouldn't say a word against him, I never thought
much of him myself. Drink, you know, my dear; he was
never really reliable. But I expect he's gone to his rest
long since, poor man. Anyway, I told Mr Mark the

name and he wrote it down. Then we had tea and a little chat and he left. I never saw him again.'

'And no one else knows about the prayer book?'

'No one in the world, my dear. Miss Leaming saw the florist's name on my card and asked them for my address. She came here the day after the funeral to thank me for attending but I could see it was only curiosity. If she and Sir Ronald were so pleased to see me, what was to stop them from coming over and shaking hands? She as good as suggested that I was there without an invitation. An invitation to a funeral! Who ever heard of such a thing?'

'So you told her nothing?' asked Cordelia.

'I've told no one but you, my dear, and I'm not sure why I've told you. But no, I didn't tell her. I never liked her, to tell you the truth. I'm not saying there was anything between her and Sir Ronald, not while Miss Evie was alive anyway. There was never any gossip and she lived in a flat in Cambridge and kept herself to herself, I'll give her that. Mr Callender met her when he was teaching science at one of the village schools. She was the English mistress. It wasn't until after Miss Evie died that he set up his own laboratory.'

'Do you mean that Miss Leaming has a degree in English?'

'Oh, yes, my dear! She wasn't trained as a secretary. Of course she gave up the teaching when she started working for Mr Callender.'

'So you left Garforth House after Mrs Callender died? You didn't stay on to care for the baby?'

'I wasn't wanted. Mr Callender employed one of those new college-trained girls and then, when Mark was still only a baby, he was sent away to school. His father made it plain that he didn't like me to see the child and after all, a father has his rights. I wouldn't have gone on seeing Mr Mark knowing that his father didn't approve. It would have only put the boy in a false position. But now he's dead and we've all lost him. The coroner said that he killed himself, and he may have been right.'

Cordelia said:

'I don't think he killed himself.'

'Don't you, my dear? That's kind of you. But he's dead, isn't he, so what does it matter now? I think it's time for me to go home. If you don't mind, I won't ask you to tea, my dear, I'm a little tired today. But you know where to find me, and if ever you want to see me again, you'll always be welcome.'

They made their way out of the burial ground together. At the gates, they parted. Mrs Goddard patted Cordelia on the shoulder with the clumsy affection she might have shown to an animal, then walked off slowly towards the village.

As Cordelia drove round the curve of the road, the level-crossing came into sight. A train had just passed and the barriers were being raised. Three vehicles had been caught at the crossing and the last in line was quickest away, accelerating past the first two cars as they bumped slowly over the rails. Cordelia saw that it was a small black van.

*

Later Cordelia remembered little of the journey back to the cottage. She drove fast, concentrating on the road ahead, trying to control her rising excitement by meticulous attention to gears and brakes. She drove the Mini hard against the front hedge, careless of whether it were seen. The cottage looked and smelt just as she had left it. She had almost expected to find it ransacked and the prayer book gone. Sighing with relief, she saw that the white spine was still there among the taller and darker covers. Cordelia opened it. She hardly knew what she expected to find; an inscription perhaps, or a message, cryptic or plain, a letter folded between the leaves. But the only inscription could have no possible relevance to the case. It was written in a shaky, old-fashioned hand; the steel nib had crawled spider-like over the page. 'To Evelyn Mary on the occasion of her confirmation, with love from her Godmother, 5th August 1934.'

Cordelia shook the book. No slip of paper fluttered out. She skimmed through the pages. Nothing.

She sat on the bed drooping with disappointment. Had it been unreasonable to imagine that there was something significant in the bequest of the prayer book; had she fabricated a promising edifice of conjecture and mystery on an old woman's confused recollections of a perfectly ordinary and understandable action – a devout and dying mother leaving a prayer book to her son? And even if she hadn't been wrong, why should the message still be there? If Mark had found a note from his mother, placed between the leaves, he might well have destroyed it after reading. And if he hadn't destroyed it, someone else might have done so. The note, if it ever existed, was now probably part of the shifting heap of white ash and charred debris in the cottage grate.

She shook herself out of her despondency. There was still a line of enquiry to pursue; she would try to trace Dr Gladwin. After a second's thought she put the prayer book in her bag. Looking at her watch, she saw that it was nearly one o'clock. She decided to have a picnic lunch of cheese and fruit in the garden and then set off again for Cambridge to visit the central library and consult a medical directory.

Less than an hour later she found the information she wanted. There was only one Dr Gladwin still on the register who could have attended Mrs Callender as an old man of over seventy, twenty years ago. He was Emlyn Thomas Gladwin who had qualified at St. Thomas's Hospital in 1904. She wrote down the address in her notebook: 4 Pratts Way, Ixworth Road, Bury St. Edmunds. Edmunds town! The town which Isabelle had said that she and Mark had visited on their way to the sea.

So the day hadn't been wasted after all – she was following in Mark Callender's footsteps. Impatient to consult a map she went over to the atlas section of the library. It was now two-fifteen. If she took the A45 road direct through Newmarket she could be in Bury St. Edmunds in about an hour. Allow an hour for the visit to the doctor and another for the return journey. She could be home at the cottage before half past five.

She was driving through the gentle unemphatic countryside just outside Newmarket when she noticed the black van following her. It was too far away to see who was driving but she thought it was Lunn and that he was alone. She accelerated, trying to keep the distance between them, but the van drew a little nearer. There was no reason, of course, why Lunn shouldn't be driving to Newmarket on Sir Ronald Callender's business, but the sight of the squat little van perpetually in her driving mirror was disconcerting. Cordelia decided to throw him off. There were few side turns on the road she was travelling and the country was unfamiliar to her. She decided to wait until she reached Newmarket and seize what opportunity offered.

The main through street of the town was a tangle of traffic and every turn seemed to be blocked. It was only at the second set of traffic lights that Cordelia saw her chance. The black van was caught at the intersection about fifty yards behind. As the light turned green, she accelerated quickly and swung round to the left. There was another turn to the left and she took it, then one to the right. She drove on through unfamiliar streets, then after about five minutes, stopped at an intersection and waited. The black van did not appear. It looked as if she had succeeded in shaking him off. She waited for another five minutes, then made her way slowly back to the main road and joined in the flow of eastward traffic. Half an hour later she had passed through Bury St. Edmunds and was driving very slowly down the Ixworth Road, watching for Pratts Way. Fifty yards farther on she came to it, a row of six small stucco houses standing back from a lay-by. She stopped the car outside number four remembering Isabelle, biddable and docile, who had obviously been told to drive further on and wait in the car. Was that because Mark thought the white Renault too conspicuous? Even the arrival of the Mini had provoked interest. There were faces at upper windows and a small group of children had mysteriously appeared, clustered around a neighbouring gate and watching her with wide and expressionless eyes.

Number four was a depressing house; the front garden was unweeded and the fence had gaps where the planks had rotted or been wrenched apart. The external paint had flaked away to the bare wood and the brown front door had peeled and blistered in the sun. But Cordelia saw that the bottom windows were shining and that the white net curtains were clean. Mrs Gladwin was probably a careful housewife, struggling to keep up her standards but too old for the heavy work and too poor to afford help. Cordelia felt benevolent towards her. But the woman, who, after some minutes, finally opened to her knock – the bell was out of order – was a disconcerting antidote to her sentimental pity. Compassion died before those hard distrustful eyes, that mouth tight as a trap, the thin arms clasped in a bony barrier across her chest as if to repel human contact. It was difficult to guess her age. Her hair, screwed back into a small tight bun, was still black but her face was deeply lined and the sinews and veins stood out in the thin neck like cords. She was wearing carpet slippers and a gaudy cotton overall. Cordelia said:

'My name is Cordelia Gray. I wondered if I could talk to Dr Gladwin, if he's in. It's about an old patient.'

'He's in, where else would he be? He's in the garden. You'd better go through.'

The house smelt horrible, an amalgam of extreme old age, the sour taint of excreta and stale food, with an overlay of strong disinfectant. Cordelia went through to the garden, carefully avoiding looking at the hall or kitchen since curiosity might seem impertinent.

Dr Gladwin was sitting in a high Windsor chair placed in the sun. Cordelia had never seen a man so old. He seemed to be wearing a woollen track suit, his swollen legs were encased in immense felt slippers and there was a knitted patchwork shawl across his knees. His two hands hung over the arms of the chair as if too heavy for the frail wrists, hands stained and brittle as autumn leaves which trembled with a gentle insistence. The high-domed skull, spiked with a few grey bristles, looked as small and vulnerable as a child's. The eyes were pale yolks swimming in their glutinous blue-veined whites.

Cordelia went to him and called him gently by his name. There was no response. She knelt on the grass at his feet and looked up into his face.

'Dr Gladwin, I wanted to talk to you about a patient. It was a long time ago. Mrs Callender. Do you remember Mrs Callender of Garforth House?'

There was no reply. Cordelia knew that there wouldn't be. Even to ask again seemed an outrage. Mrs Gladwin was standing beside him as if displaying him to a wondering world.

'Go on, ask him! It's all in his head, you know. That's what he used to tell me. "I'm not one for records and notes. It's all in my head." '

Cordelia said:

'What happened to his medical records when he gave up practice? Did anyone take them over?'

'That's what I've just told you. There never were any records. And it's no use asking me. I told the boy that too. The doctor was glad enough to marry me when he wanted a nurse, but he didn't discuss his patients. Oh, dear no! He was drinking all the practice profits away, but he could still talk about medical ethics.'

The bitterness in her voice was horrible. Cordelia could not meet her eyes. Just then she thought she saw the old man's lips move. She bent down her head and caught the one word. 'Cold.'

'I think he's trying to say that he's cold. Is there another shawl perhaps that he could have round his shoulders?'

'Cold! In this sun! He's always cold.'

'But perhaps another blanket would help. Shall I fetch it for you?'

'You let him be, Miss. If you want to look after him, then look after him. See how you enjoy keeping him clean like a baby, washing his nappies, changing the bed every morning. I'll get him another shawl, but in two minutes he'll be pushing it off. He doesn't know what he wants.'

'I'm sorry,' said Cordelia helplessly. She wondered whether Mrs Gladwin was getting all the help available, whether the District Nurse called, whether she had asked her doctor to try to find a hospital bed. But these were useless questions. Even she could recognize the hopeless rejection of help, the despair which no longer had energy even to look for relief. She said:

'I'm sorry; I won't trouble either of you any further.'

They walked back together through the house. But there was one question Cordelia had to ask. When they reached the front gate she said:

'You talked about a boy who visited. Was his name Mark?'

'Mark Callender. He was asking about his mother. And then about ten days later we get the other one calling.'

'What other one?'

'He was a gentleman all right. Walked in as if he owned the place. He wouldn't give a name but I've seen his face somewhere. He asked to see Dr Gladwin and I showed him in. We were sitting in the back parlour that day as there was a breeze. He went up to the doctor and said "Good afternoon, Gladwin" loudly as if talking to a servant. Then he bent down and looked at him. Eye to eye they were. Then he straightened up, wished me good day and left. Oh, we're getting popular, we are! Any more of you and I'll have to charge for the show.'

They stood together at the gate. Cordelia wondered whether to hold out her hand but sensed that Mrs Gladwin was willing her not to go. Suddenly the woman spoke in a loud and gruff voice, looking straight ahead.

'That friend of yours, the boy who came here. He left his address. He said he wouldn't mind sitting with the doctor on a Sunday if I wanted a break; he said he could get them both a bit of dinner. I have a fancy to see my sister at Haverhill this Sunday. Tell him he can come over if he wants to.'

The capitulation was ungracious, the invitation grudging. Cordelia could guess what it had cost her to give it. She said impulsively:

'I could come on Sunday instead. I've got a car, I could get here sooner.'

It would be a day lost to Sir Ronald Callender, but she wouldn't charge him. And even a private eye was surely entitled to a day off on Sundays.

'He won't want a slip of a girl. There's things to do for him that need a man. He took to that boy. I could see that. Tell him he can come.'

Cordelia turned to her.

'He would have come, I know he would. But he can't. He's dead.'

Mrs Gladwin did not speak. Cordelia put out a tentative hand and touched her sleeve. There was no response. She whispered:

'I'm sorry. I'll go now.' She nearly added: 'If there's nothing I can do for you,' but stopped herself in time. There was nothing she or anyone could do.

She looked back once as the road bent towards Bury and saw the rigid figure still at the gate.

Cordelia wasn't sure what made her decide to stop at Bury and walk for ten minutes in the Abbey gardens. But she felt she couldn't face the drive back to Cambridge without calming her spirits and the glimpse of grass and flowers through the great Norman doorway was irresistible. She parked the Mini on Angel Hill, then walked through the gardens to the river bank. There she sat for five minutes in the sun. She remembered that there was money spent on petrol to be recorded in her notebook and felt for it in her bag. Her hand brought out the white prayer book. She sat quietly thinking. Suppose she had been Mrs Callender and had wanted to leave a message, a message which Mark would find and other searchers might miss. Where would she place it? The answer now seemed childishly simple. Surely somewhere on the page with the collect, gospel and epistle for St. Mark's Day. He had been born on April 25th. He had been named after the Saint. Quickly she found the place. In the bright sunlight reflected from the water she saw what a quick rustle through the pages had missed. There against Cranmer's gentle petition for grace to withstand the blasts of false doctrine was a small pattern of hieroglyphics so faint that the mark on the paper was little more than a smudge. She saw that it was a group of letters and figures.

E M C
A A
14.1.52

The first three letters, of course, were his mother's initials. The date must be that on which she wrote the message. Hadn't Mrs Goddard said that Mrs Callender had died when her son was about nine months old? But the double A? Cordelia's mind chased after motoring associations before she remembered the card in Mark's wallet. Surely these two letters under an initial could only show one thing, the blood group. Mark had been B. His mother was AA. There was only one reason why she should have wanted him to have that information. The next step was to discover Sir Ronald Callender's group.

She almost cried out with triumph as she ran through the gardens and turned the Mini again towards Cambridge. She hadn't thought out the implications of this discovery, or even whether her arguments were valid. But at least she had something to do, at least she had a lead. She drove fast, desperate to get to the city before the post office closed. There, she seemed to remember, it was possible to get a copy of the Executive Council's list of local doctors. It was handed over. And now for a telephone. She knew only one house in Cambridge where there was a chance of being left in peace to telephone for up to an hour. She drove to 57, Norwich Street.

Sophie and Davie were at home playing chess in the sitting-room, fair head and dark almost touching over the board. They showed no surprise at Cordelia's plea to use the telephone for a series of calls.

'I'll pay, of course. I'll make a note of how many.'

'You'll want the room to yourself, I expect?' said Sophie. 'We'll finish the game in the garden, Davie.'

Blessedly incurious they carried the chess board with care through the kitchen and set it up on the garden table. Cordelia drew a chair to the table and settled down with her list. It was formidably long. There was no clue where to begin but perhaps those doctors with group practices and addresses near the centre of the city would be the best bet. She would start with them, ticking off their names after each call. She remembered another reported pearl of the Superintendent's wisdom: 'Detection requires a patient persistence which amounts to obstinacy.' She thought of him as she dialled the first number. What an intolerably demanding and irritating boss he must have been! But he was almost certainly old now – forty-five at least. He had probably eased up a bit by now.

But an hour's obstinacy was unfruitful. Her calls were invariably answered; one advantage of ringing a doctor's surgery was that the telephone was at least manned. But the replies, given politely, curtly or in tones of harassed haste by a variety of respondents from the doctors themselves to obliging daily women prepared to convey a message, were the same. Sir Ronald Callender was not a patient of this practice. Cordelia repeated her formula. 'I'm so sorry to have troubled you. I must have misheard the name.'

But after nearly seventy minutes of patient dialling she struck lucky. The doctor's wife answered.

'I'm afraid you've got the wrong practice. Dr Venables looks after Sir Ronald Callender's household.'

This was luck indeed! Dr Venables wasn't on her preliminary list and she wouldn't have reached the V's for at least another hour. She ran her finger down the names and dialled for the last time.

It was Dr Venables' nurse who answered. Cordelia spoke her prepared piece:

'I'm ringing for Miss Leaming from Garforth House. I'm sorry to trouble you but could you please remind us of Sir Ronald Callender's blood group? He wants to know it before the Helsinki Conference next month.'

'Just a minute, please.' There was a brief wait; the sound of footsteps returning.

'Sir Ronald is Group A. I should make a careful note of it if I were you. His son had to ring a month or so ago with the same enquiry.'

'Thank you! Thank you! I'll be careful to make a note.' Cordelia decided to take a risk.

'I'm new here, assisting Miss Leaming, and she did tell me to note it down last time but stupidly I forgot. If she should happen to call, please don't tell her that I had to trouble you again.'

The voice laughed, indulgent to the inefficiency of the young. After all, it wasn't likely to inconvenience her much.

'Don't worry, I shan't tell her. I'm glad she's got herself some help at last. Everyone's well, I hope?'

'Oh, yes! Everyone's fine.'

Cordelia put down the receiver. She looked out of the window and saw that Sophie and Davie were just finishing their game and were putting the pieces back in the box. She had just finished in time. She knew the answer to her query but she still had to verify it. The information was too important to leave to her own vague recollection of the Mendelian rules of inheritance gleaned from the chapter on blood and identity in Bernie's book on forensic medicine. Davie would know, of course. The quickest way would be to ask him now. But she couldn't ask Davie. It would mean going back to the public library, and she would have to hurry if she were to be there before it closed.

But she got there just in time. The librarian, who by now had got used to seeing her, was as helpful as ever. The necessary reference book was quickly produced. Cordelia verified what she had already known. A man and wife both of whose bloods were A could not produce a B group child.

*

Cordelia was very tired by the time she got back to the cottage. So much had happened during one day; so much had been discovered. It seemed impossible that less than twelve hours previously she had started out on her search for Nanny Pilbeam with only a vague hope that the woman, if she could be found, might provide a clue to Mark Callender's personality, might tell her something about his formative years. She was exhilarated by the success of the day, restless with excitement, but too mentally exhausted to tease out the tangle of conjecture which lay knotted at the back of her mind.

At present the facts were disordered; there was no clear pattern, no theory which would at once explain the mystery of Mark's birth, Isabelle's terror, Hugo and Sophie's secret knowledge, Miss Markland's obsessive interest in the cottage, Sergeant Maskell's almost reluctant suspicions, the oddities and unexplained inconsistencies which surrounded Mark's death.

She busied herself about the cottage with the energy of mental overtiredness. She washed the kitchen floor, laid a fire on top of the heap of ash in case the next evening should be chilly, weeded the back flower patch, then made herself a mushroom omelette and ate it sitting, as he must have done, at the simple table. Last of all, she fetched the gun from its hiding pace and set it on the table beside the bed. She locked the back door carefully and drew the curtains across the window, checking once more that the seals were intact. But she didn't balance a saucepan on the top of her door. Tonight that particular precaution seemed childish and unnecessary. She lit her bedside candle then went to the window to choose a book. The night was balmy and windless; the flame of the candle burned steadily in the still air. Outside, darkness had not yet fallen but the garden was very quiet, the peace broken only by the distant crescendo of a car on the main road or the cry of a night bird. And then, seen dimly through the gloaming, she glimpsed a figure at the gate. It was Miss Markland. The woman hesitated, hand on the latch, as if wondering whether to enter the garden. Cordelia slipped to one side, back pressed against the wall. The shadowy figure was so still that it seemed as if she sensed a watching presence and had frozen like an animal surprised. Then, after two minutes, she moved away and was lost among the trees of the orchard. Cordelia relaxed, took a copy of *The Warden* from Mark's row of books, and wriggled into her sleeping-bag. Half an hour later, she blew out the candle and stretched her body comfortably for the slow acquiescent descent into sleep.

She stirred in the early hours and was instantly awake, eyes wide open in the half darkness. Time lay suspended; the still air was expectant as if the day had been taken by surprise. She could hear the ticking of her wrist watch on the bedside table and could see beside it the crooked, comforting outline of the pistol, the black cylinder of her torch. She lay and listened to the night. One lived so seldom in these still hours, the time most often slept or dreamt away, that one came to them tentative and unpractised like a creature newly born. She wasn't aware of fear, only of an all-embracing peace, a gentle lassitude. Her breathing filled the room, and the still, uncontaminated air seemed to be breathing in unity with her.

Suddenly, she realized what had woken her. Visitors were coming to the cottage. She must subconsciously in some brief phase of uneasy sleep have recognized the sound of a car. Now there was the whine of the gate, the rustle of feet, furtive as an animal in undergrowth, a faint, broken murmur of voices. She wriggled out of her sleeping-bag and stole to the window. Mark hadn't attempted to clean the glass of the front windows; perhaps he hadn't had time, perhaps he welcomed their occluding dirt. Cordelia rubbed her fingers with desperate haste against the gritty accretion of years. But, at last, she felt the cold smooth glass. It squeaked with the friction of her fingers, high and thin like an animal's squeal so that she thought the noise must betray her. She peered through the narrow strip of clear pane into the garden below.

The Renault was almost hidden by the high hedge but she could see the front of the bonnet gleaming by the gate and the two pools of light from the side lamps shining like twin moons on the lane. Isabelle was wearing something long and clinging; her pale figure trembled like a wave against the dark of the hedge. Hugo was only a black shadow at her side. But then he turned and Cordelia saw the flash of a white shirt-front. They were both in evening dress. They came together quietly up the path and conferred briefly at the front door, then moved towards the corner of the cottage.

Snatching up her torch, Cordelia rushed on silent, naked feet down the stairs and threw herself across the sitting-room to unlock the back door. The key turned easily and silently. Hardly daring to breathe she retreated back into the shadows at the foot of the stairs. She was just in time. The door opened, letting in a shaft of paler light. She heard Hugo's voice:

'Just a minute, I'll strike a match.'

The match flared, illuminating in a gentle, momentary light the two grave anticipatory faces, Isabelle's immense and terrified eyes. Then it went out. She heard Hugo's muttered curse followed by the scratch of the second match striking against the box. This time he held it high. It shone on the table, on the mute accusing hook; on the silent watcher at the foot of the stairs. Hugo gasped; his hand jerked and the match went out. Immediately, Isabelle began to scream.

Hugo's voice was sharp.

'What the hell—'

Cordelia switched on her torch and came forward.

'It's only me; Cordelia.'

But Isabelle was beyond hearing. The screams rang out with such piercing intensity that Cordelia half feared that the Marklands must hear. The sound was inhuman, the shriek of animal terror. It was cut short by the swing of Hugo's arm; the sound of a slap; a gasp. It was succeeded by a second of absolute silence, then Isabelle collapsed against Hugo sobbing quietly.

He turned harshly on Cordelia:

'What the hell did you do that for?'

'Do what?'

'You terrified her, lurking there. What are you doing here anyway?'

'I could ask you that.'

'We came to collect the Antonello which Isabelle lent to Mark when she came to supper with him, and to cure her of a certain morbid obsession with this place. We've been to the Pitt Club Ball. It seemed a good idea to call here on our way home. Obviously, it was a bloody stupid idea. Is there any drink in the cottage?'

'Only beer.'

'Oh God, Cordelia, there would be! She needs something stronger.'

'There isn't anything stronger, but I'll make coffee. You set a light to the fire. It's laid.'

She stood the torch upright on the table and lit the table lamp, turning the wick low, then helped Isabelle into one of the fireside chairs.

The girl was trembling. Cordelia fetched one of Mark's heavy sweaters and placed it round her shoulders. The kindling began to flame under Hugo's careful hands. Cordelia went into the kitchen to make coffee, laying her torch on its side at the edge of the window sill so that it shone on the oil stove. She lit the stronger of the two burners and took from the shelf a brown earthenware jug, the two blue-rimmed mugs and a cup for herself. A second and chipped cup held the sugar. It took only a couple of minutes to boil half a kettle of water and to pour it over the coffee grains. She could hear Hugo's voice from the sitting-room, low, urgent, consolatory, interposed with Isabelle's monosyllabic replies. Without waiting for the coffee to brew she placed it on the only tray, a bent tin one patterned with a chipped picture of Edinburgh castle, and carried it into the sitting-room, setting it down in the hearth. The faggots spluttered and blazed, shooting out a falling shower of bright sparks which patterned Isabelle's dress with stars. Then a stouter brand caught flame and the fire glowed with a stronger, more mellow, heart.

As she bent forward to stir the coffee Cordelia saw a small beetle scurrying in desperate haste along the ridges of one of the small logs. She picked up a twig from the kindling still in the hearth and held it out as a way of escape. But it confused the beetle still more. It turned in panic and raced back towards the flame, then doubled in its tracks and fell finally into a split in the wood. Cordelia wondered whether it briefly comprehended its dreadful end. Putting a match to a fire was such a trivial act to cause such agony, such terror.

She handed Isabelle and Hugo their mugs and took her own. The comforting smell of fresh coffee mingled with the resinous tang of the burning wood. The fire threw long shadows over the tiled floor and the oil lamp cast its gentle glow over their faces. Surely, thought Cordelia, no murder suspects could have been interrogated in a cosier setting. Even Isabelle had lost her fears. Whether it was the reassurance of Hugo's arm across her shoulders, the stimulus of the coffee or the homely warmth and crackle of the fire, she seemed almost at ease.

Cordelia said to Hugo:

'You said that Isabelle was morbidly obsessed by this place. Why should she be?'

'Isabelle's very sensitive; she isn't tough like you.'

Cordelia privately thought that all beautiful women were tough – how else could they survive? – and that Isabelle's fibres could compare well for resilience with her own. But nothing would be gained by challenging Hugo's illusions. Beauty was fragile, transitory, vulnerable. Isabelle's sensitivities must be protected. The toughies could look after themselves. She said:

'According to you, she's only been here once before. I know that Mark Callender died in this room, but you hardly expect me to believe that she's grieving over Mark. There's something that both of you know and it would be better if you told me now. If you don't I shall have to report to Sir Ronald Callender that Isabelle, your sister and you are somehow concerned in his son's death and it will be up to him to decide whether to call in the police. I can't see Isabelle standing up to even the mildest police questioning, can you?'

Even to Cordelia it sounded a stilted, sententious little speech, an unsubstantiated accusation backed up by an empty threat. She half expected Hugo to counter it with amused contempt. But he looked at her for a minute as if assessing more than the reality of the danger. Then he said quietly:

'Can't you accept my word that Mark died by his own hand and that if you do call in the police it will cause unhappiness and distress to his father, to his friends and be absolutely no help to anyone?'

'No, Hugo, I can't.'

'Then if we do tell you what we know, will you promise that it won't go any further?'

'How can I, any more than I can promise to believe you?'

Suddenly Isabelle cried:

'Oh, tell her, Hugo! What does it matter?'

Cordelia said:

'I think that you must. I don't think you've any choice.'

'So it seems. All right.' He put his coffee mug down in the hearth and looked into the fire.

'I told you that we went – Sophie, Isabelle, Davie and I – to the Arts Theatre on the night Mark died but that, as you've probably guessed, was only three-quarters true. They had only three seats left when I booked so we allocated them to the three people mostly likely to enjoy the play. Isabelle goes to the theatre to be seen rather than to see and is bored by any show with a cast of less than fifty so she was the one left out. Thus neglected by her current lover, she very reasonably decided to seek consolation with the next.'

Isabelle said with a secret, anticipatory smile:

'Mark was not my lover, Hugo.'

She spoke without rancour or resentment. It was a matter of putting the record straight.

'I know. Mark was a romantic. He never took a girl to bed – or anywhere else that I could see – until he judged that there was an adequate depth of inter-personal communication, or whatever jargon he used, between them. Actually, that's unfair. It's my father who uses bloody awful meaningless phrases like that. But Mark agreed with the general idea. I doubt whether he could enjoy sex until he'd convinced himself that he and the girl were in love. It was a necessary preliminary – like undressing. I gather that with Isabelle the relation-ship hadn't reached the necessary depths, hadn't achieved the essential emotional rapport. It was only a matter of time, of course. Where Isabelle was con-cerned, Mark was as capable of self-deception as the rest of us.'

The high, slightly hesitant voice was edged with jealousy.

Isabelle said, slowly and patiently, like a mother explaining to a wilfully obtuse child:

'Mark never made love to me, Hugo.'

'That's what I'm saying. Poor Mark! He exchanged the substance for the shadow and now he has neither.'

'But what happened that night?'

Cordelia spoke to Isabelle, but it was Hugo who replied.

'Isabelle drove here and arrived shortly after half past seven. The curtains were drawn across the back win-dow, the front one is impenetrable anyway, but the door was open. She came in. Mark was already dead. His body was hanging by the strap from that hook. But he didn't look as he did when Miss Markland found him next morning.'

He turned to Isabelle:

'You tell her.' She hesitated. Hugo bent forward and kissed her lightly on the lips.

'Go on, tell. There are some unpleasantnesses which all Papa's money can't entirely shield from you and this, darling, is one.'

*

Isabelle turned her head and looked intently into the four corners of the room as if satisfying herself that the three of them were really alone. The irises of her remarkable eyes were purple in the firelight. She leaned towards Cordelia with something of the confiding relish of a village gossip about to relate the latest scandal. Cordelia saw that her panic had left her. Isabelle's agonies were elemental, violent but short lived, easily comforted. She would have kept her secret while Hugo instructed her to keep it, but she was glad of his order of release. Probably her instinct told her that the story, once told, would lose the sting of terror. She said:

'I thought I would call to see Mark and, perhaps, that we would have supper together. Mademoiselle de Congé was not well and Hugo and Sophie were at the theatre and I was bored. I came to the back door because Mark had told me that the front door would not open. I thought that I might see him in the garden, but he was not there, only the garden fork in the ground and his shoes at the door. So I pushed open the door. I did not knock because I thought that I would be a surprise for Mark.'

She hesitated and looked down into the mug of coffee, twisting it between her hands.

178

'And then?' prompted Cordelia.

'And then I saw him. He was hanging there by the belt from that hook in the ceiling and I knew he was dead. Cordelia, it was horrible! He was dressed like a woman in a black bra and black lace panties. Nothing else. And his face! He had painted his lips, all over his lips, Cordelia, like a clown! It was terrible but it was funny too. I wanted to laugh and scream at the same time. He didn't look like Mark. He didn't look like a human being at all. And on the table there were three pictures. Not nice pictures, Cordelia. Pictures of naked women.'

Her wide eyes stared into Cordelia's, dismayed, uncomprehending. Hugo said:

'Don't look like that, Cordelia. It was horrible for Isabelle at the time and disagreeable to think about now. But it isn't so very uncommon. It does happen. It's probably one of the more innocuous of sexual deviations. He wasn't involving anyone but himself. And he didn't mean to kill himself; that was just bad luck. I imagine that the buckle of the belt slipped and he never had a chance.' Cordelia said:

'I don't believe it.'

'I thought you might not. But it's true, Cordelia. Why not come with us now and ring Sophie? She'll confirm it.'

'I don't need confirmation of Isabelle's story. I already have that. I mean I still don't believe that Mark killed himself.'

As soon as she spoke she knew that it had been a mistake. She shouldn't have revealed her suspicions. But it was too late now and there were questions she had to ask. She saw Hugo's face, his quick impatient frown at her obtuseness, her obstinacy. And then she detected a subtle change of mood; was it irritation, fear, disappointment? She spoke directly to Isabelle.

'You said that the door was open. Did you notice the key?'

'It was in this side of the door. I saw it when I went out.'

'What about the curtains?'

'They were like now, across the window.'

'And where was the lipstick?'

'What lipstick, Cordelia?'

'The one used to paint Mark's lips. It wasn't in the pockets of his jeans or the police would have found it, so where was it? Did you see it on the table?'

'There was nothing on the table except the pictures.'

'What colour was the lipstick?'

'Purple. An old lady's colour. No one would choose such a colour I think.'

'And the underclothes, could you describe them?'

'Oh, yes! They were from M & S. I recognized them.'

'You mean that you recognized those particular ones, that they were yours?'

'Oh, no Cordelia! They were not mine. I never wear black underclothes. I only like white next to my skin. But they were the kind I usually buy; I always get my underclothes from M & S.'

Cordelia reflected that Isabelle was hardly one of the store's best customers, but that no other witness would have been as reliable when it came to details, particularly of clothes. Even in that moment of absolute terror and revulsion, Isabelle had noticed the type of underclothes. And if she said that she hadn't seen the lipstick, then it was because the lipstick hadn't been there to see.

Cordelia went on inexorably:

'Did you touch anything, Mark's body perhaps, to see if he was dead?'

Isabelle was shocked. The facts of life she could take in her stride, but not the facts of death.

'I couldn't touch Mark! I touched nothing. And I knew that he was dead.'

Hugo said: 'A respectable, sensible law-abiding citizen would have found the nearest telephone and rung the police. Luckily Isabelle is none of these things. Her instinct was to come to me. She waited until the play ended, and then met us outside the theatre. When we came out she was pacing up and down the pavement on the other side of the road. Davie, Sophie and I came back here with her in the Renault. We only stopped briefly at Norwich Street to collect Davie's camera and flash.'

'Why?'

'That was my idea. Obviously, we had no intention of letting the fuzz and Ronald Callender know how Mark had died. Our idea was to fake a suicide. We planned to dress him in his own clothes, clean his face and then leave him for someone else to find. We hadn't it in mind to fake a suicide note; that was a refinement somewhat outside our powers. We collected the camera so that we could photograph him as he was. We didn't know what particular law we were breaking in faking a suicide, but there must have been one. You can't do the simplest service for your friends these days without it being liable to misconstruction by the fuzz. If there were trouble we wanted some evidence of the truth. We were all fond of Mark in our different ways, but not fond enough to risk a murder charge. However, our good intentions were frustrated. Someone else had got here first.'

'Tell me about it.'

'There's nothing to tell. We told the two girls to wait in the car, Isabelle because she had already seen enough and Sophie because Isabelle was too frightened to be left alone. Besides, it seemed only fair to Mark to keep Sophie out of it, to prevent her from seeing him. Don't you find it odd, Cordelia, this concern one has for the susceptibilities of the dead?'

Thinking of her father and Bernie, Cordelia said:

'Perhaps it's only when people are dead that we can safely show how much we cared about them. We know that it's too late for them to do anything about it.'

'Cynical but true. Anyway, there was nothing for us to do here. We found Mark's body and this room as Miss Markland described them at the inquest. The door was open, the curtains drawn across. Mark was naked except for his blue jeans. There were no magazine pictures on the table and no lipstick on his face. But there was a suicide note in the typewriter and a mound of ash in the grate. It looked as if the visitor had made a thorough job of it. We didn't linger. Someone else – perhaps someone from the house – might have turned up at any minute. Admittedly, it was very late by then but it seemed an evening for people to pop in. Mark must have had more visitors that night than during his whole time at the cottage; first Isabelle; then the unknown samaritan; then us.'

Cordelia thought that there had been someone before Isabelle. Mark's murderer had been there first. She asked suddenly:

'Someone played a stupid trick on me last night. When I got back here from the party there was a bolster slung from that hook. Did you do that?'

If his surprise were not genuine, then Hugo was a better actor than Cordelia thought possible.

'Of course I didn't! I thought you were living in Cambridge not here. And why on earth should I?'

'To warn me off.'

'But that would be crazy! It wouldn't warn you off, would it? It might scare some women, but not you. We wanted to convince you that there was nothing to investigate about Mark's death. That sort of trick would only convince you that there was. Someone else was trying to scare you. The most likely person is the one who came here after us.'

'I know. Someone took a risk for Mark. He – or she – won't want me ferreting around. But he would have got rid of me more sensibly by telling me the truth.'

'How could he know whether to trust you? What will you do now, Cordelia? Go back to town?'

He was trying to keep his voice casual but she thought she detected the underlying anxiety. She replied:

'I expect so. I'll have to see Sir Ronald first.'

'What will you tell him?'

'I'll think of something. Don't worry.'

Dawn was staining the eastern sky and the first chorus of birds was noisily contradicting the new day before Hugo and Isabelle left. They took the Antonello with them. Cordelia saw it taken down with a pang of regret as if something of Mark was leaving the cottage. Isabelle examined the picture closely with a grave professional eye before tucking it under her arm. Cordelia thought that she was probably generous enough with her possessions, both people and pictures, provided they were on loan only, to be returned promptly on demand and in the same condition as when she parted with them. Cordelia watched from the front gate as the Renault, with Hugo driving, moved out of the shadow of the hedge. She lifted her hand in a formal gesture of farewell like a weary hostess speeding her final guests, then turned back to the cottage.

The sitting-room seemed empty and cold without them. The fire was dying and she hastily pushed in the few remaining sticks from the hearth and blew on them to kindle the flame. She moved restlessly about the little room. She was too lively to go back to bed, but her short and disturbed night had left her edgy with tiredness. But her mind was tormented by something more fundamental than lack of sleep. For the first time she knew that she was afraid. Evil existed – it hadn't needed a convent education to convince her of that reality – and it had been present in this room. Something here had been stronger than wickedness, ruthlessness, cruelty or expedience. Evil. She had no doubt that Mark had been murdered, but with what diabolical cleverness it had been done! If Isabelle told her story, who now would ever believe that he hadn't died accidentally, but by his own hand? Cordelia had no need to refer to her book on forensic medicine to know how it would appear to the police. As Hugo had said, these cases weren't so very uncommon. He, as a psychiatrist's son, would have heard or read of them. Who else would know? Probably any reasonably sophisticated person. But it couldn't have been Hugo. Hugo had an alibi. Her mind revolted at the thought that Davie or Sophie could have participated in such a horror. But how typical that they should have collected the camera. Even their compassion had been overlaid with self concern. Would Hugo and Davie have stood here, under Mark's grotesque body, calmly discussing distance and exposure before taking the photograph which would, if necessary, exonerate them at his expense?

She went into the kitchen to make tea, glad to be free of the malignant fascination of that hook in the ceiling. Previously it had hardly worried her, now it was as obtrusive as a fetish. It seemed to have grown since the previous night, to be growing still as it drew her eyes compulsively upwards. And the sitting-room itself had surely shrunk; no longer a sanctum but a claustrophobic cell, tawdry and shameful as an execution shed. Even the bright morning air was redolent with evil.

Waiting for the kettle to boil she made herself contemplate the day's activities. It was still too early to theorize; her mind was too preoccupied with horror to deal rationally with its new knowledge. Isabelle's story had complicated, not illumined the case. But there were still relevant facts to be discovered. She would go on with the programme she had already planned. Today she would go to London to examine Mark's grandfather's will.

But there were still two hours to get through before it was time to start out. She had decided to travel to London by train and to leave the car at Cambridge station since this would be both quicker and easier. It was irritating to have to spend a day in town when the heart of the mystery so obviously lay in Cambridgeshire, but for once she wasn't sorry at the prospect of leaving the cottage. Shocked and restless, she wandered aimlessly from room to room and prowled around the garden, fretting to be away. Finally in desperation she took hold of the garden fork and completed the digging of Mark's unfinished row. She wasn't sure that this was wise: Mark's interrupted work was part of the evidence for his murder. But other people, including Sergeant Maskell, had seen it and could testify if necessary, and the sight of the partly-completed job, of the fork still askew in the soil, was unbearably irritating. When the row was completed she felt calmer and she dug on without pausing for another hour before carefully cleaning the fork and placing it with the other tools in the garden shed.

At last it was time to go. The seven o'clock weather forecast had prophesied thundery storms in the south-east so she put on her suit, the heaviest protection she had brought with her. She hadn't worn it since Bernie's death and she discovered that the waist band was uncomfortably loose. She had lost some weight. After a moment's thought, she took Mark's belt from the scene-of-crime kit and wound it twice round her waist. She felt no repugnance as the leather tightened against her. It was impossible to believe that anything he had ever touched or owned could frighten or distress her. The strength and heaviness of the leather so close to her skin was even obscurely comforting and reassuring as if the belt were a talisman.

CHAPTER FIVE

The storm broke just as Cordelia alighted from the number 11 bus outside Somerset House. There was a jagged flash of lightning and, almost instantaneously, the thunder crashed like a barrage round her ears and she raced across the inner courtyard between the ranks of parked cars through a wall of water while the rain spouted around her ankles as if the paving stones were being raked with bullets. She pushed open the door and stood draining pools of water on the mat and laughing aloud with relief. One or two of the people present glanced up from their perusal of wills and smiled at her, while a motherly looking woman behind the counter tut-tutted her concern. Cordelia shook her jacket over the mat then hung it on the back of one of the chairs and tried ineffectually to dry her hair with her handkerchief before approaching the counter.

The motherly woman was helpful. Consulted by Cordelia on the correct procedure, she indicated the shelves of heavy, bound volumes in the middle of the hall and explained that the wills were indexed under the surname of the testator and the year in which the document was lodged with Somerset House. It was for Cordelia to trace the catalogue number and bring the volume to the desk. The original will would then be sent for and she could consult it for a fee of 20 pence.

Not knowing when George Bottley had died, Cordelia was in some perplexity where to begin her search. But she deduced that the will must have been made after the birth, or at least the conception, of Mark, since he had been left a fortune by his grandfather. But Mr Bottley had also left money to his daughter and this part of his fortune had come on her death to her husband. The strong probability was that he had died before her, since otherwise he would surely have made a new will. Cordelia decided to begin her search with the year of Mark's birth, 1951.

Her deductions proved correct. George Albert Bottley of Stonegate Lodge, Harrogate, had died on 26th July 1951, exactly three months and one day after the birth of his grandson and only three weeks after making his will. Cordelia wondered whether his death had been sudden and unexpected or whether this was the will of a dying man. She saw that he had left an estate of nearly three quarters of a million pounds. How had he made this, she wondered? Surely not all from wool. She heaved the heavy book across to the counter, the clerk wrote the details on a white form and pointed out the way to the cashier's office. Within a surprisingly few minutes of paying what seemed to her a modest fee, Cordelia was seated under the light at one of the desks near the window with the will in her hands.

She hadn't liked what she had heard about George Bottley from Nanny Pilbeam and she didn't like him any better after reading his will. She had feared that the document might be long, complicated and difficult to understand; it was surprisingly short, simple and intelligible. Mr Bottley directed that all his possessions should be sold, 'since I wish to prevent the usual unseemly wrangling over bric-à-brac'. He left modest sums to servants in his employ at the time of his death but there was no mention, Cordelia noticed, of his gardener. He bequeathed half of the residue of his fortune to his daughter, absolutely, 'now that she has demonstrated that she has at least one of the normal attributes of a woman'. The remaining half he left to his beloved grandson Mark Callender on attaining his twenty-fifth birthday, 'by which date, if he hasn't learned the value of money, he will at least be of an age to avoid exploitation'. The income from the capital was left to six Bottley relations, some of them, apparently, only distant kinsmen. The will recreated a residual trust; as each beneficiary died his share would be distributed among the survivors. The testator was confident that this arrangement would promote in the beneficiaries a lively interest in each other's health and survival while encouraging them to achieve the distinction of longevity, no other distinction being within their reach. If Mark died before his twenty-fifth birthday the family trust would continue until all the beneficiaries were dead and the capital would then be distributed among a formidable list of charities chosen, as far as Cordelia could see, because they were well known and successful rather than because they represented any personal concern or sympathy on the part of the testator. It was as if he had asked his lawyers for a list of the more reliable charities, having no real interest in what happened to his fortune if his own issue were not alive to inherit it.

It was a strange will. Mr Bottley had left nothing to his son-in-law yet had apparently been unworried by the possibility that his daughter, whom he knew not to be strong, might die and leave her fortune to her husband. In some respects it was a gambler's will and Cordelia wondered again how George Bottley had made his fortune. But, despite the cynical unkindness of its comments, the will was neither unfair nor ungenerous. Unlike some very rich men he hadn't attempted to control his great fortune from beyond the grave, obsessively determined that not one penny should ever get into unfavoured hands. His daughter and his grandson had both been left their fortunes absolutely. It was impossible to like Mr Bottley but difficult not to respect him. And the implications of his will were very clear. No one stood to gain by Mark's death except a long list of highly respectable charities.

Cordelia made a note of the main clauses of the will, more because of Bernie's insistence on meticulous documentation than from any fear of forgetting them; slipped the receipt for 20p into the expenses page of her notebook; added the cost of her cheap day return ticket from Cambridge and her bus fare, and returned the will to the counter. The storm had been as short as it was violent. The hot sun was already drying the windows and the puddles lay bright on the rain-washed courtyard. Cordelia decided that she ought to charge Sir Ronald for half a day only and spend the rest of her time in London at the office. There might be post to collect. There might even be another case awaiting her.

But the decision was a mistake. The office seemed even more sordid than when she had left it and the air smelt sour in contrast to the rain-washed streets outside. There was a thick film of dust over the furniture and the blood stain on the rug had deepened into a brick-brown which looked even more sinister than the original bright red. There was nothing in the letterbox but a final demand from the electricity board and a bill from the stationer. Bernie had paid dearly – or rather, had not paid – for the despised writing paper.

Cordelia wrote a cheque for the electricity bill, dusted the furniture, made one last and unsuccessful attempt to clean the rug. Then she locked the office and set off to walk to Trafalgar Square. She would seek consolation in the National Gallery.

*

She caught the eighteen-sixteen train from Liverpool Street and it was nearly eight o'clock before she arrived back at the cottage. She parked the Mini in its usual place in the shelter of the copse and made her way round the side of the cottage. She hesitated for a moment wondering whether to collect the gun from its hiding place but decided that this could wait until later. She was hungry and the first priority was to get a meal. She had carefully locked the back door and had stuck a thin strip of Scotch tape across the window sill before leaving that morning. If there were any more secret visitors she wanted to be warned. But the tape was still intact. She felt in her shoulder bag for the key and, bending down, fitted it into the lock. She wasn't expecting trouble outside the cottage and the attack took her completely by surprise. There was the half-second of pre-knowledge before the blanket fell but that was too late. There was a cord around her neck pulling the mask of hot stifling wool taut against her mouth and nostrils. She gasped for breath and tasted the dry strong-smelling fibres on her tongue. Then a sharp pain exploded in her chest and she remembered nothing.

The moment of liberation was a miracle and a horror. The blanket was whipped off. She never saw her assailant. There was a second of sweet reviving air, a glimpse, so brief that it was barely comprehended, of blinding sky seen through greenness and then she felt herself falling, falling in helpless astonishment into cold darkness. The fall was a confusion of old nightmares, unbelievable seconds of childhood terrors recalled. Then her body hit the water. Ice-cold hands dragged her into a vortex of horror. Instinctively, she had closed her mouth at the moment of impact and she struggled to the surface through what seemed an eternity of cold encompassing blackness. She shook her head and, through her stinging eyes, she looked up. The black tunnel that stretched above her ended in a moon of blue light. Even as she looked, the well lid was dragged slowly back like the shutter of a camera. The moon became a half moon; then a crescent. At last there was nothing but eight thin slits of light.

Desperately she trod water, reaching tentatively for the bottom. There was no bottom. Frantically moving hands and feet, willing herself not to panic, she felt around the walls of the well for a possible foothold. There was none. The funnel of bricks, smooth, sweating with moisture, stretched around and above her like a circular tomb. As she gazed upwards they writhed, expanded, swayed and reeled like the belly of a monstrous snake.

And then she felt a saving anger. She wouldn't let herself drown, wouldn't die in this horrible place, alone and terrified. The well was deep but small, the diameter barely three feet. If she kept her head and took time, she could brace her legs and shoulders against the bricks and work her way upwards.

She hadn't bruised or stunned herself against the walls as she fell. Miraculously she was uninjured. The fall had been clean. She was alive and capable of thought. She had always been a survivor. She would survive.

She floated on her back, bracing her shoulders against the cold walls, spreading her arms and digging her elbows into the interstices of the bricks to get a better grip. Shuffling off her shoes, she planted both feet against the opposite wall. Just beneath the surface of the water, she could feel that one of the bricks was slightly un-aligned. She curved her toes around it. It gave her a precarious but welcome foothold for the start of the climb. By means of it, she could lift her body out of the water and could relieve for a moment the strain on the muscles of her back and thighs.

Then slowly she began to climb, first shifting her feet, one after the other in tiny sliding steps, then humping up her body inch by painful inch. She kept her eyes fixed on the opposite curve of the wall, willing herself not to look down, nor up, counting progress by the width of each brick. Time passed. She couldn't see Bernie's watch, although its ticking seemed unnaturally loud, a regular obtrusive metronome to the thumping of her heart and the fierce gasping of her breath. The pain in her legs was intense and her shirt was sticking to her back with a warm, almost comforting effusion, which she knew must be blood. She willed herself not to think of the water beneath her or of the thin, but widen-ing clefts of light above. If she were to survive, all her energy must be harnessed for the next painful inch.

Once, her legs slipped and she slithered back several yards before her feet, scrabbling ineffectually against the slimy walls, at last found a purchase. The fall had grazed her injured back and left her whimpering with self-pity and disappointment. She scourged her mind into courage and began climbing again. Once she was gripped by cramp and lay stretched as if on a rack until the agony passed and her fixed muscles could move. From time to time her feet found another small foot-hold and she was able to stretch her legs and rest. The temptation to stay in comparative safety and ease was almost irresistible and she had to will herself to start again on the slow tortuous climb.

It seemed that she had been climbing for hours, moving in a parody of a difficult labour towards some desperate birth. Darkness was falling. The light from the well top was wider now but less strong. She told herself that the climb wasn't really difficult. It was only the darkness and loneliness which made it seem so. If this were a fabricated obstacle race, an exercise in the school gymnasium, surely she could have done it easily enough. She filled her mind with the comforting images of rib stools and vaulting horses, of the fifth form shouting their encouragement. Sister Perpetua was there. But why wasn't she looking at Cordelia? Why had she turned away? Cordelia called her and the figure turned slowly and smiled at her. But it wasn't Sister after all. It was Miss Leaming, the lean pale face sardonic under the white veil.

And now when she knew that, unaided, she could get no further, Cordelia saw salvation. A few feet above her was the bottom rung of a short wooden ladder fixed to the last few feet of the well. At first she thought that it was an illusion, a phantasm born of exhaustion and despair. She shut her eyes for a few minutes; her lips moved. Then she opened her eyes again. The ladder was still there, seen dimly but comfortingly solid in the fading light. She lifted impotent hands towards it knowing, even as she did so, that it was out of reach. It could save her life and she knew that she hadn't the strength to reach it.

It was then, without conscious thought or scheming, that she remembered the belt. Her hand dropped to her waist feeling for the heavy brass buckle. She undid it and drew the long snake of leather from her body. Carefully she threw the buckled end towards the bottom rung of the ladder. The first three times the metal struck the wood with a sharp crack but didn't fall over the rung, the fourth time it did. She pushed the other end of the belt gently upwards and the buckle dropped towards her until she could reach out her hand and grasp it. She fastened it to the other end to form a strong loop. Then she pulled, at first very gently and then harder until most of her weight was on the strap. The relief was indescribable. She braced herself against the brickwork, gathering strength for the final triumphant effort. Then it happened. The rung, rotted at its joints, broke loose with a harsh tearing sound and spun past her into darkness, just missing her head. It seemed minutes rather than seconds before the distant splash reverberated round the wall.

She unbuckled the belt and tried again. The next rung was a foot higher and the throw more difficult. Even this small effort was exhausting in her present state and she made herself take time. Every unsuccessful throw made the next more difficult. She didn't count the number of attempts, but at last the buckle fell over the rung and dropped towards her. When it snaked within reach she found that she could only just buckle the strap. The next rung would be too high. If this one broke, it would be the end.

But the rung held. She had no clear memory of the last half hour of the climb but at last she reached the ladder and strapped herself firmly to the uprights. For the first time she was physically safe. As long as the ladder held she needn't fear falling. She let herself relax into brief unconsciousness. But then the wheels of the mind which had been spinning blissfully free, took hold again and she began to think. She knew that she had no hope of moving the heavy wooden cover unaided. She stretched out both hands and pushed against it but it didn't shift, and the high concave dome made it impossible for her to brace her shoulders against the wood. She would have to rely on outside help and that wouldn't come till daylight. It might not come even then, but she pushed the thought away. Sooner or later someone would come. She could hope to hold on, thus strapped, for several days. Even if she lost consciousness there was a chance that she would be rescued alive. Miss Markland knew that she was at the cottage; her things were still there. Miss Markland would come.

She gave thought to how she could attract attention. There was room to push something between the boards of wood if only she had something sufficiently stiff to push. The edge of the buckle was possible provided she strapped herself more tightly. But she must wait until the morning. There was nothing she could do now. She would relax and sleep and await rescue.

And then the final horror burst upon her. There would be no rescue. Someone would be coming to the well, coming on quiet and stealthy feet under the cover of darkness. But it would be her murderer. He had to return; it was part of his plan. The attack, which at the time had seemed so astonishingly, so brutally stupid, hadn't been stupid at all. It was intended to look like an accident. He would come back that night and remove the well cover again. Then, some time next day or within the next few days, Miss Markland would blunder through the garden and discover what had happened. No one would ever be able to prove that Cordelia's death wasn't an accident. She recalled the words of Sergeant Maskell: 'It isn't what you suspect; it's what you can prove.' But this time would there even be suspicion? Here was a young, impulsive, over-curious young woman living at the cottage without the owner's authority. She had obviously decided to explore the well. She had smashed the padlock, drawn back the lid with the coil of rope which the killer would leave ready to be found, and tempted by the ladder, had let herself down those few steps until the final rung broke beneath her. Her prints and no one else's would be found on the ladder, if they took the trouble to look. The cottage was utterly deserted; the chance that her murderer would be seen returning was remote. There was nothing she could do but wait until she heard his footsteps, his heavy breathing, and the lid was drawn slowly back to reveal his face.

After the first intensity of terror, Cordelia waited for death without hope and without further struggle. There was even a kind of peace in resignation. Strapped like a victim to the uprights of the ladder she drifted mercifully into brief oblivion and prayed that it might be so when her killer returned, that she might not be conscious at the moment of the final blow. She had no longer any interest in seeing her murderer's face. She wouldn't humiliate herself by pleading for her life, wouldn't beg for mercy from a man who had strung up Mark. She knew that there would be no mercy.

But she was conscious when the well lid began slowly to move. The light came in above her bowed head. The gap widened. And then she heard a voice, a woman's voice, low, urgent and sharp with terror.

'Cordelia!'

She looked up.

Kneeling at the rim of the well, her pale face immense and seeming to float disembodied in space like the phantasm of a nightmare, was Miss Markland. And the eyes which stared into Cordelia's face were as wild with terror as her own.

Ten minutes later Cordelia was lying slumped in the fireside chair. Her whole body ached and she was powerless to control her violent shivering. Her thin shirt was stuck to her wounded back and every shift of movement was pain. Miss Markland had put a light to the kindling and was now making coffee. Cordelia could hear her moving to and fro in the little kitchen and could smell the stove as it was turned high and, soon, the evocative aroma of coffee. These familiar sights and sounds would normally have been reassuring and comforting, but now she was desperate to be alone. The killer would still return. He had to return, and when he did, she wanted to be there to meet him. Miss Markland brought in the two mugs and pressed one into Cordelia's shivering hands. She stumped upstairs and came down with one of Mark's jumpers which she wound round the girl's neck. Her terror had left her, but she was as agitated as a young girl sharing her first half-shameful adventure. Her eyes were wild, her whole body trembled with excitement. She sat down directly in front of Cordelia and fixed her with her sharp inquisitive eyes.

'How did it happen? You must tell me.'

Cordelia had not forgotten how to think.

'I don't know. I can't remember anything that happened before I hit the water. I must have decided to explore the well and lost my balance.'

'But the well lid! The lid was in place!'

'I know. Someone must have replaced it.'

'But why? Who would have come this way?'

'I don't know. But someone must have seen it. Someone must have dragged it back.'

She said more gently:

'You saved my life. How did you notice what had happened?'

'I came to the cottage to see if you were still here. I came earlier today but there was no sign of you. There was a coil of rope – the one that you used, I expect – left in the path and I stumbled over it. Then I noticed that the lid wasn't quite in place and that the padlock had been smashed.'

'You saved my life,' said Cordelia again, 'but please go now. Please go. I'm all right, really I am.'

'But you aren't fit to be left alone! And that man – the one who replaced the lid – he might return. I don't like to think of strangers snooping around the cottage and you here alone.'

'I'm perfectly safe. Besides, I have a gun. I only want to be left in peace to rest. Please don't worry about me!'

Cordelia could detect the note of desperation, almost of hysteria, in her own voice.

But Miss Markland seemed not to hear. Suddenly she was on her knees in front of Cordelia and pouring out a spate of high, excited chatter. Without thought and without compassion, she was confiding to the girl her terrible story, a story of her son, the four-year-old child of herself and her lover, who had broken his way through the cottage hedge and fallen into the well to his death. Cordelia tried to shake herself free from the wild eyes. It was surely all a fantasy. The woman must be mad. And if it were true, it was horrible and unthinkable and she could not bear to hear it. Sometime later she would remember it, remember every word, and think of the child, of his last terror, his desperate cry for his mother, the cold suffocating water dragging him to his death. She would live his agony in nightmares as she would relive her own. But not now. Through the spate of words, the self-accusations, the terror recalled, Cordelia recognized the note of liberation. What to her had been horror, to Miss Markland had been release. A life for a life. Suddenly Cordelia could bear it no longer. She said violently:

'I'm sorry! I'm sorry! You've saved my life and I'm grateful. But I can't bear to listen. I don't want you here. For God's sake go!'

All her life she would remember the woman's hurt face, her silent withdrawal. Cordelia didn't hear her go, didn't remember the soft closing of the door. All she knew was that she was alone. The shaking was over now although she still felt very cold. She went upstairs and pulled on her slacks and then unwound Mark's jumper from her neck and put it on. It would cover the blood stains on her shirt and the warmth was immediately comforting. She was moving very quickly. She felt for the ammunition, took her torch and let herself out of the back door of the cottage. The gun was where she had left it, in the fold of the tree. She loaded it and felt its familiar shape and heaviness in her hand. Then she stood back among the bushes and waited.

It was too dark to see the dial of her wrist watch but Cordelia reckoned that she must have waited there immobile in the shadows for nearly half an hour before her ears caught the sound for which she was waiting. A car was approaching down the lane. Cordelia held her breath. The sound of the engine reached a brief crescendo and then faded away. The car had driven on without stopping. It was unusual for a car to pass down the lane after dark and she wondered who it could be. Again she waited, moving deeper into the shelter of the elder bush so that she could rest her back against the bark. She had been clutching the gun so tightly that her right wrist ached and she moved the pistol to her other hand and rotated the wrist slowly, stretching the cramped fingers.

Again she waited. The slow minutes passed. The silence was broken only by the furtive scuffling of some small night prowler in the grass and the sudden wild hoot of an owl. And then once more she heard the sound of an engine. This time the noise was faint and it came no closer. Someone had stopped a car further up the road.

She took the gun in her right hand, cradling the muzzle with her left. Her heart was pounding so loudly that she felt its wild hammering must betray her. She imagined rather than heard the thin whine of the front gate but the sound of feet moving round the cottage was unmistakable and clear. And now he was in sight, a stocky, broad-shouldered figure, black against the light. He moved towards her and she could see her shoulder bag hanging from his left shoulder. The discovery disconcerted her. She had completely forgotten the bag. But now she had realized why he had seized it. He had wanted to search it for evidence, but it was important that, finally, it should be discovered with her body in the well.

He came forward gently on tip-toe, his long simian arms held stiffly away from his body like a caricature of a film cowboy ready for the draw. When he got to the rim of the well he waited and the moon struck the white of his eyes as he gazed slowly round. Then he bent down and felt in the grass for the coil of rope. Cordelia had laid it where Miss Markland had found it, but something about it, some slight difference perhaps in the way it was coiled, seemed to strike him. He rose uncertainly and stood for a moment with the rope dangling from his hand. Cordelia tried to control her breathing. It seemed impossible that he should not hear, smell or see her, that he should be so like a predator yet without the beast's instinct for the enemy in the dark. He moved forward. Now he was at the well. He bent and threaded one end of the rope through the iron hoop.

Cordelia moved with one step out of the darkness. She held the gun firmly and straight as Bernie had shown her. This time the target was very close. She knew that she wouldn't fire but, in that moment, she knew too what it was that could make a man kill. She said loudly:

'Good evening, Mr Lunn.'

She never knew whether he saw the gun. But for one unforgettable second, as the clouded moon sailed into the open sky, she saw his face clearly; saw the hate, the despair, the agony and the rictus of terror. He gave one hoarse cry, threw down the shoulder bag and the rope and rushed through the garden in a blind panic. She gave chase, hardly knowing why, or what she hoped to achieve, determined only that he shouldn't get back to Garforth House before her. And still she didn't fire the gun.

But he had an advantage. As she threw herself through the gate she saw that he had parked the van some fifty yards up the road and left the engine running. She chased after him but could see that it was hopeless. Her only hope of catching up with him was to get the Mini. She tore down the lane feeling in her shoulder bag as she ran. The prayer book and her notebook were both gone but her fingers found the car keys. She unlocked the Mini, threw herself in and reversed it violently onto the road. The rear lights of the van were about a hundred yards ahead of her. She didn't know what speed it could do, but doubted whether it could out-pace the Mini. She trod on the accelerator and gave pursuit. She turned left out of the lane on to the subsidiary road and now she could see the van still ahead.

He was driving fast and was holding the distance. Now the road turned and for a few seconds he was out of sight. He must be getting very close now to the junction with the Cambridge road.

She heard the crash just before she herself reached the junction, an instantaneous explosion of sound which shook the hedges and made the little car tremble. Cordelia's hands tightened momentarily on the wheel and the Mini jerked to a stop. She ran forward round the corner and saw before her the gleaming, headlamp-lit surface of the main Cambridge road. It was peopled with running shapes. The transporter, still upright, was an immense oblong mass blocking the sky line, a barricade slewed across the road. The van had crumpled under its front wheels like a child's toy. There was a smell of petrol, a woman's harsh scream, the squeal of braking tyres. Cordelia walked slowly up to the transporter. The driver was still in his seat, gazing rigidly ahead, his face a mask of dedicated concentration. People were shouting at him, stretching out their arms. He didn't move. Someone – a man in a heavy leather coat and goggles – said:

'It's shock. We'd better drag him clear.'

Three figures moved between Cordelia and the driver. Shoulders heaved in unison. There was a grunt of effort. The driver was lifted out, rigid as a manikin, his knees bent, his clenched hands held out as if still grasping the immense wheel. The shoulders bent over him in secret conclave.

There were other figures standing round the crushed van. Cordelia joined the ring of anonymous faces. Cigarette ends glowed and faded like signals, casting a momentary glow on the shaking hands, the wide, horrified eyes. She asked:

'Is he dead?' The man in goggles replied laconically:
'What do you think?'

There was a girl's voice, tentative, breathless.

'Has anyone called the ambulance?'

'Yeah. Yeah. That chap in the Cortina's gone off to phone.'

The group stood irresolute. The girl and the young man to whom she was clinging began to back away. Another car stopped. A tall figure was pushing his way through the crowd. Cordelia heard a high, authoritative voice.

'I'm a doctor. Has anyone called the ambulance?'

'Yes, sir.'

The reply was deferential. They stood aside to let the expert through. He turned to Cordelia, perhaps because she was nearest.

'If you didn't witness the accident, young woman, you'd better get on your way. And stand back, the rest of you. There's nothing that you can do. And put out those cigarettes!'

Cordelia walked slowly back to the Mini, placing each foot carefully before the other like a convalescent trying her first painful steps. She drove carefully round the accident, bumping the Mini on the grass verge. There was the wail of approaching sirens. As she turned off the main road, her driving mirror glowed suddenly red and she heard a whoosh of sound followed by a low, concerted groan which was broken by a woman's high, single scream. There was a wall of flame across the road. The doctor's warning had been too late. The van was on fire. There was no hope now for Lunn; but then, there never had been.

Cordelia knew that she was driving erratically. Passing cars hooted at her and flashed their lights and one motorist slowed down and shouted angrily. She saw a gate and drew in off the road and switched off the engine. The silence was absolute. Her hands were moist and shaking. She wiped them on her handkerchief and laid them in her lap feeling that they were separate from the rest of her body. She was hardly aware of a car passing and then slowing to a halt. A face appeared at the window. The voice was slurred and nervous but horribly ingratiating. She could smell the drink on his breath.

'Anything wrong, Miss?'

'Nothing. I've just stopped for a rest.'

'No point in resting alone – a pretty girl like you.'

His hand was on the door handle. Cordelia felt in her shoulder bag and drew out the gun. She pushed it into his face.

'It's loaded. Go away at once or I'll shoot.'

The menace in her voice struck cold even to her own ears. The pale, moist face disintegrated with surprise, the jaw fell. He backed away.

'Sorry, Miss, I'm sure. My mistake. No offence.'

Cordelia waited until his car was out of sight. Then she turned on the engine. But she knew that she couldn't go on. She turned off the engine again. Waves of tiredness flowed over her, an irresistible tide, gentle as a blessing, which neither her exhausted mind nor body had the will to resist. Her head fell forward and Cordelia slept.

CHAPTER SIX

Cordelia slept soundly but briefly. She didn't know what woke her, whether the blinding light of a passing car sweeping across her closed eyes or her own subconscious knowledge that rest must be rationed to a brief half hour, the minimum necessary to enable her to do what had to be done before she could give herself over to sleep. She eased her body upright, feeling the stab of pain in her strained muscles and the half-pleasurable itch of dried blood on her back. The night air was heavy and odorous with the heat and scents of the day; even the road winding ahead looked tacky in the glare of her headlights. But Cordelia's chilled and aching body was still grateful for the warmth of Mark's jersey. For the first time since she had pulled it over her head she saw that it was dark green. How odd that she hadn't noticed its colour before!

She drove the rest of the journey like a novice, sitting bolt upright, eyes rigidly ahead, hands and feet tense on the controls. And here at last were the gates of Garforth House. They loomed in her headlights far taller and more ornamental than she remembered them, and they were closed. She ran from the Mini praying that they wouldn't be locked. But the iron latch, although heavy, rose to her desperate hands. The gates swung soundlessly back.

There were no other cars in the drive and she parked the Mini some little way from the house. The windows were dark and the only light, gentle and inviting, shone through the open front door. Cordelia took the pistol in her hand and, without ringing, stepped into the hall. She was more exhausted in body than when she had first come to Garforth House, but tonight she saw it with a new intensity, her nerves sensitive to every detail. The hall was empty, the air expectant. It seemed as if the house had waited for her. The same smell met her of roses and lavender, but tonight she saw that the lavender came from a huge Chinese bowl set on a side table. She recalled the insistent ticking of a clock, but now she noticed for the first time the delicate carving on the clock case, the intricate scrolls and whirls on the face. She stood in the middle of the hall, swaying slightly, the pistol held lightly in her drooping right hand, and looked down. The carpet was a formal geometrical design in rich olive greens, pale blues and crimson, each pattern shaped like the shadow of a kneeling man. It seemed to draw her to her knees. Was it perhaps an eastern prayer mat?

She was aware of Miss Leaming coming quietly down the stairs towards her, her long red dressing-gown sweeping round her ankles. The pistol was taken suddenly but firmly from Cordelia's unresisting hand. She knew that it had gone because her hand felt suddenly lighter. It made no difference. She could never defend herself with it, never kill a man. She had learnt that about herself when Lunn had run from her in terror. Miss Leaming said:

'There is no one here you need defend yourself against, Miss Gray.'

Cordelia said:

'I've come to report to Sir Ronald. Where is he?'

'Where he was the last time you came here, in his study.'

As before, he was sitting at his desk. He had been dictating and the machine was at his right hand. When he saw Cordelia, he switched it off, then walked to the wall and pulled the plug from the socket. He walked back to the desk and they sat down opposite each other He folded his hands in the pool of light from the desk lamp and looked at Cordelia. She almost cried out with shock. His face reminded her of faces seen grotesquely reflected in grubby train windows at night – cavernous, the bones stripped of flesh, eyes set in fathomless sockets – faces resurrected from the dead.

When he spoke his voice was low, reminiscent.

'Half an hour ago I learned that Chris Lunn was dead. He was the best lab assistant I ever had. I took him out of an orphanage fifteen years ago. He never knew his parents. He was an ugly, difficult boy, already on proba-tion. School had done nothing for him. But Lunn was one of the best natural scientists I've ever known. If he'd had the education, he'd have been as good as I am.'

'Then why didn't you give him his chance, why didn't you educate him?'

'Because he was more useful to me as a lab assistant. I said that he could have been as good as I am. That isn't quite good enough. I can find plenty of scientists as good. I couldn't have found another lab assistant to equal Lunn. He had a marvellous hand with instru-ments.'

He looked up at Cordelia, but without curiosity, apparently without interest.

'You've come to report, of course. It's very late, Miss Gray, and, as you see, I'm tired. Can't it wait until tomorrow?'

Cordelia thought that this was as close to an appeal as he could ever bring himself. She said:

'No, I'm tired too. But I want to finish the case tonight, now.' He picked up an ebony paper-knife from the desk and, without looking at Cordelia, balanced it on his forefinger.

'Then tell me, why did my son kill himself? I take it that you do have news for me? You would hardly have burst in here at this hour without something to report.'

'Your son didn't kill himself. He was murdered. He was murdered by someone he knew very well, someone he didn't hesitate to let into the cottage, someone who came prepared. He was strangled or suffocated, then slung up on that hook by his own belt. Last of all, his murderer painted his lips, dressed him in a woman's underclothes and spread out pictures of nudes on the table in front of him. It was meant to look like accidental death during sexual experiment; such cases aren't so very uncommon.'

There was half a minute of silence. Then he said with perfect calmness:

'And who was responsible, Miss Gray?'

'You were. You killed your son.'

'For what reason?' He might have been an examiner, putting his inexorable questions.

'Because he discovered that your wife wasn't his mother, that the money left to her and to him by his grandfather had come by fraud. Because he had no intention of benefiting by it a moment longer, nor of accepting his legacy in four years' time. You were afraid that he might make this knowledge public. And what about the Wolvington Trust? If the truth came out, that would be the end of their promised grant. The future of your laboratory was at stake. You couldn't take the risk.'

'And who undressed him again, typed out that suicide note, washed the lipstick from his face?'

'I think I know, but I shan't tell you. That's really what you employed me to discover, isn't it? That's what you couldn't bear not to know. But you killed Mark. You even prepared an alibi just in case it was needed. You got Lunn to ring you at college and announce himself as your son. He was the one person you could rely on absolutely. I don't suppose you told him the truth. He was only your lab assistant. He didn't require explanations, he did what you told him. And even if he did guess the truth, he was safe, wasn't he? You prepared an alibi which you dared not use, because you didn't know when Mark's body was first discovered. If someone had found him and faked that suicide before you had claimed to have spoken to him on the telephone, your alibi would have been broken, and a broken alibi is damning. So you made a chance to talk to Benskin and put matters right. You told him the truth; that it was Lunn who had rung you. You could rely on Lunn to back up your story. But it wouldn't really matter, would it, even if he did talk? No one would believe him.'

'No, any more than they will believe you. You've been determined to earn your fee, Miss Gray. Your explanation is ingenious; there is even a certain plausibility about some of the details. But you know, and I know, that no police officer in the world would take it seriously. It's unfortunate for you that you couldn't question Lunn. But Lunn, as I said, is dead. He burnt to death in a road accident.'

'I know, I saw. He tried to kill me tonight. Did you know that? And earlier, he tried to scare me into dropping the case. Was that because he had begun to suspect the truth?'

'If he did try to kill you, he exceeded his instructions. I merely asked him to keep an eye on you. I had contracted for your sole and whole-time services, if you remember; I wanted to be sure I was getting value. I am getting value of a kind. But you mustn't indulge your imagination outside this room. Neither the police nor the courts are sympathetic to slander nor to hysterical nonsense. And what proof have you? None. My wife was cremated There is nothing alive or dead on this earth to prove that Mark was not her son.'

Cordelia said:

'You visited Dr Gladwin to satisfy yourself that he was too senile to give evidence against you. You needn't have worried. He never did suspect, did he? You chose him as your wife's doctor because he was old and incompetent. But I have one small piece of evidence. Lunn was bringing it to you.'

'Then you should have looked after it better. Nothing of Lunn except his bones has survived that crash.'

'There are still the female clothes, the black pants and the bra. Someone might remember who bought them, particularly if that person was a man.'

'Men do buy underclothes for their women. But if I were planning such a murder, I don't think buying the accessories would worry me. Would any harassed shop girl at the cash desk of a popular multiple store remember a particular purchase, a purchase paid for with cash, one of a number of innocuous items, all presented together at the busiest time of the day? The man might even have worn a simple disguise. I doubt whether she would even notice his face. Would you really expect her to remember, weeks afterwards, to identify one of thousands of customers and identify him with sufficient certainty to satisfy a jury? And if she did, what would it prove unless you have the clothes in question? Be sure of one thing, Miss Gray, if I needed to kill I should do it efficiently. I should not be found out. If the police ever learn how my son was found, as they well may do since, apparently, someone other than yourself knows it, they will only believe with greater certainty that he killed himself. Mark's death was necessary and, unlike most deaths, it served a purpose. Human beings have an irresistible urge towards self-sacrifice. They die for any reason or none at all, for meaningless abstractions like patriotism, justice, peace; for other men's ideals, for other men's power, for a few feet of earth. You, no doubt, would give your life to save a child or if you were convinced that the sacrifice would find a cure for cancer.'

'I might. I like to think that I would. But I should want the decision to be mine, not yours.'

'Of course. That would provide you with the necessary emotional satisfaction. But it wouldn't alter the fact of your dying nor the result of your death. And don't say that what I'm doing here isn't worth one single human life. Spare me that hypocrisy. You don't know and you're incapable of understanding the value of what I'm doing here. What difference will Mark's death make to you? You'd never heard of him until you came to Garforth House.'

Cordelia said:

'It will make a difference to Gary Webber.'

'Am I expected to lose everything I've worked for here because Gary Webber wants someone to play squash or discuss history with?'

Suddenly he looked Cordelia full in the face. He said sharply:

'What is the matter? Are you ill?'

'No I'm not ill. I knew that I must be right. I knew that what I had reasoned was true. But I can't believe it. I can't believe that a human being could be so evil.'

'If you are capable of imagining it, then I'm capable of doing it. Haven't you yet discovered that about human beings, Miss Gray? It's the key to what you would call the wickedness of man.'

Suddenly Cordelia could no longer bear this cynical antiphony. She cried out in passionate protest.

'But what is the use of making the world more beautiful if the people who live in it can't love one another?'

She had stung him at last into anger.

'Love! The most overused word in the language. Has it any meaning except the particular connotation which you choose to give it? What do you mean by love? That human beings must learn to live together with a decent concern for each other's welfare? The law enforces that. The greatest good of the greatest number. Beside that fundamental declaration of common sense all other philosophies are metaphysical abstractions. Or do you define love in the Christian sense, caritas? Read history,

Miss Gray. See to what horrors, to what violence, hatred and repression the religion of love has led mankind. But perhaps you prefer a more feminine, more individual definition; love as a passionate commitment to another's personality. Intense personal commitment always ends in jealousy and enslavement. Love is more destructive than hate. If you must dedicate your life to something, dedicate it to an idea.'

'I mean love, as a parent loves a child.'

'The worse for them both, perhaps. But if he doesn't love, there is no power on earth which can stimulate or compel him to. And where there is no love, there can be none of the obligations of love.'

'You could have let him live! The money wasn't important to him. He would have understood your needs and kept silent.'

'Would he? How could he – or I – have explained his rejection of a great fortune in four years' time? People at the mercy of what they call their conscience are never safe. My son was a self-righteous prig. How could I put myself and my work in his hands?'

'You are in mine, Sir Ronald.'

'You are mistaken. I am in no one's hands. Unfortunately for you that tape recorder is not working. We have no witnesses. You will repeat nothing that has been said in this room to anyone outside. If you do I shall have to ruin you. I shall make you unemployable, Miss Gray. And first of all I shall bankrupt that pathetic business of yours. From what Miss Leaming told me it shouldn't be difficult. Slander can be a highly expensive indulgence. Remember that if you are ever tempted to talk. Remember this too. You will harm yourself; you will harm Mark's memory; you will not harm me.'

*

Cordelia never knew how long the tall figure in the red dressing-gown had been watching and listening in the shadow of the door. She never knew how much Miss Leaming had heard or at what moment she had stolen quietly away. But now she was aware of the red shadow moving soundlessly over the carpet, eyes on the figure behind the desk, the gun held closely against her breast. Cordelia watched in fascinated horror, not breathing. She knew exactly what was going to happen. It must have taken less than three seconds but they passed as slowly as minutes. Surely there had been time to cry out, time to warn, time to leap forward and wrench the gun from that steady hand? Surely there had been time for him to cry out? But he made no sound. He half rose, incredulous, and gazed at the muzzle in blind disbelief. Then he turned his head towards Cordelia as if in sup-plication. She would never forget that last look. It was beyond terror, beyond hope. It held nothing but the blank acceptance of defeat.

It was an execution, neat, unhurried, ritually precise. The bullet went in behind the right ear. The body leapt into the air, shoulders humped, softened before Cordelia's eyes as if the bones were melting into wax, and lay discarded at last over the desk. A thing; like Bernie; like her father.

Miss Leaming said:

'He killed my son.'

'Your son?'

'Of course. Mark was my son. His son and mine. I thought you might have guessed.'

She stood with the gun in her hand gazing with expressionless eyes through the open window to the lawn. There was no sound. Nothing moved. Miss Leaming said:

'He was right when he said that no one could touch him. There was no proof.'

Cordelia cried out appalled:

'Then how could you kill him? How could you be so sure?'

Without releasing her hold on the pistol, Miss Leaming put her hand into the pocket of her dressing-gown. The hand moved over the desk top. A small gilt cylinder rolled over the polished wood towards Cordelia, then rocked into stillness. Miss Leaming said:

'The lipstick was mine. I found it a minute ago in the pocket of his dress suit. He hadn't worn that suit since he last dined in Hall on Feast night. He was always a magpie. He put small objects instinctively into his pockets.'

Cordelia had never doubted Sir Ronald's guilt but now every nerve was desperate for reassurance.

'But it could have been planted there! Lunn could have put it there to incriminate him.'

'Lunn didn't kill Mark. He was in bed with me at the time Mark died. He only left my side for five minutes and that was to make a telephone call shortly after eight o'clock.'

'You were in love with Lunn!'

'Don't look at me like that! I only loved one man in my life and he's the one I've just killed. Talk about things you understand. Love had nothing to do with what Lunn and I needed from each other.'

There was a moment's silence. Then Cordelia said:

'Is there anyone in the house?'

'No. The servants are in London. No one is working late at the lab tonight.'

And Lunn was dead. Miss Leaming said with weary resignation:

'Hadn't you better phone the police?'

'Do you want me to?'

'What does it matter?'

'Prison matters. Losing your freedom matters. And do you really want the truth to come out in open court? Do you want everyone to know how your son died and who killed him? Is that what Mark himself would want?'

'No. Mark never believed in punishment. Tell me what I have to do.'

'We've got to work quickly and plan carefully. We have to trust each other and we have to be intelligent.'

'We are intelligent. What must we do?'

Cordelia took out her handkerchief and dropping it over the gun, took the weapon from Miss Leaming and placed it on the desk. She grasped the woman's thin wrist and pushed her protesting hand against Sir Ronald's palm, pulling against the instinctive recoil, forcing the stiff but living fingers against the soft unresisting hand of the dead.

'There may be firing residue. I don't really know much about that, but the police may test for it. Now wash your hands and get me a pair of thin gloves. Quickly.'

She went without a word. Left alone, Cordelia looked down at the dead scientist. He had fallen with his chin against the desk top and his arms swinging loosely at his sides, an awkward, uncomfortable-looking pose which gave him the appearance of peering malevolently over his desk. Cordelia could not look at his eyes, but she was conscious of feeling nothing, not hatred, or anger, or pity. Between her eyes and the sprawled figure swung an elongated shape, head hideously crooked, toes pathetically pointed. She walked over to the open window and looked out over the garden with the casual curiosity of a guest kept waiting in a strange room. The air was warm and very still. The scent of roses came in waves through the open window, alternately sickeningly sweet and then as elusive as a half-caught memory.

This curious hiatus of peace and timelessness must have lasted less than half a minute. Then Cordelia began to plan. She thought about the Clandon case. Memory pictured herself and Bernie, sitting astride a fallen log in Epping Forest and eating their picnic lunch. It brought back the yeasty smell of fresh rolls, butter and tangy cheese, the heavy fungoid smell of summer woods. He had rested the pistol on the bark between them and had mumbled at her through the bread and cheese. 'How would you shoot yourself behind the right ear? Go on, Cordelia – show.'

Cordelia had taken the pistol in her right hand, index finger lightly resting on the trigger, and with some difficulty had strained back her arm to place the muzzle of the gun against the base of the skull. 'Like that?' 'You wouldn't, you know. Not if you were used to a gun. That's the little mistake Mrs Clandon made and it nearly hanged her. She shot her husband behind the right ear with his service revolver and then tried to fake a suicide. But she pressed the wrong finger on the trigger. If he'd really shot himself behind the right ear he'd have pressed the trigger with his thumb and held the revolver with his palm round the back of the butt. I remember that case well. It was the first murder I worked on with the Super – Inspector Dalgliesh, as he was then. Mrs Clandon confessed in the end.' 'What happened to her, Bernie?' 'Life. She'd probably have got away with manslaughter if she hadn't tried to fake a suicide. The jury didn't much like what they heard about Major Clandon's little habits.'

But Miss Leaming couldn't get away with manslaughter; not unless she told the whole story of Mark's death.

She was back in the room now. She handed Cordelia a pair of thin cotton gloves. Cordelia said:

'I think you'd better wait outside. What you don't see you won't have the trouble of forgetting. What were you doing when you met me in the hall?'

'I was getting myself a nightcap, a whisky.'

'Then you would have met me again coming out of the study as you took it up to your room. Get it now and leave the glass on the side table in the hall. That's the kind of detail the police are trained to notice.'

Alone again, Cordelia took up the gun. It was astonishing how repulsive she found this inert weight of metal now. How odd that she should ever have seen it as a harmless toy! She rubbed it thoroughly with the handkerchief erasing Miss Leaming's prints. Then she handled it. It was her gun. They would expect to find some of her prints on the butt together with those of the dead man. She placed it again on the desk top and drew on the gloves. This was the more difficult part. She handled the pistol gingerly and took it over to the inert right hand. She pressed his thumb firmly against the trigger, then wound the cold, unresisting hand round the back of the butt. Then she released his fingers and let the gun fall. It struck the carpet with a dull thud. She peeled off the gloves and went out to Miss Leaming in the hall, closing the study door quietly behind her.

'Here, you'd better put these back where you found them. We mustn't leave them lying around for the police to find.'

She was gone only a few seconds. When she returned, Cordelia said:

'Now we must act the rest just as it would have happened. You meet me as I come out of the room. I have been with Sir Ronald about two minutes. You put down your glass of whisky on the hall table and walk with me to the front door. You say – what would you say?'

'Has he paid you?'

'No, I'm to come in the morning for my money. I'm sorry it wasn't a success. I've told Sir Ronald that I don't want to go on with the case.'

'That's your concern, Miss Gray. It was a foolish business in the first place.'

They were walking out of the front door now. Suddenly Miss Leaming turned to Cordelia and said urgently and in her normal voice:

'There's one thing you had better know. It was I who found Mark first and faked the suicide. He'd rung me earlier in the day and asked me to call. I couldn't get away until after nine because of Lunn. I didn't want him to be suspicious.'

'But didn't it occur to you when you found Mark that there might be something odd about the death? The door was unlocked although the curtains were drawn. The lipstick was missing.'

'I suspected nothing until tonight when I stood in the shadows and heard you talking. We're all sexually sophisticated these days. I believed what I saw. It was all horror but I knew what I had to do. I worked quickly, terrified that someone would come. I cleaned his face with my handkerchief dampened with water from the kitchen sink. It seemed that the lipstick would never come off. I undressed him and pulled on his jeans which had been thrown over the back of a chair. I didn't wait to put on his shoes, that didn't seem important. Typing the note was the worst part. I knew that he would have his Blake with him somewhere in the cottage and that the passage I chose might be more convincing than an ordinary suicide note. The clattering of the typewriter keys sounded unnaturally loud in the quietness; I was terrified that someone would hear. He had been keeping a kind of journal. There wasn't time to read it but I burnt the typescript in the sitting-room grate. Last of all, I bundled up the clothes and the pictures and brought them back here to be burnt in the lab incinerator.'

'You dropped one of the pictures in the garden. And you didn't quite succeed in cleaning the lipstick from his face.'

'So that's how you guessed?'

Cordelia didn't reply immediately. Whatever happened she must keep Isabelle de Lasterie out of the case.

'I wasn't sure if it was you who had been there first but I thought it must have been. There were four things. You didn't want me to investigate Mark's death; you read English at Cambridge and could have known where to find that Blake quotation; you are an experienced typist and I didn't think that the note had been typed by an amateur despite the late attempt to make it look like Mark's work; when I was first at Garforth House and asked about the suicide note you spoke the whole of the Blake quotation; the typed version was ten words short. I first noticed that when I visited the police station and was shown the note. It pointed direct to you. That was the strongest evidence I had.'

They had reached the car now and paused together. Cordelia said:

'We mustn't waste any more time before ringing the police. Someone may have heard the shot.'

'It's not likely. We're some distance from the village. Do we hear it now?'

'Yes. We hear it now.' There was a second's pause then Cordelia said:

'What was that? It sounded like a shot.'

'It couldn't have been. It was probably a car back-firing.'

Miss Leaming spoke like a bad actress, the words were stilted, unconvincing. But she spoke them; she would remember them.

'But there isn't a car passing. And it came from the house.'

They glanced at each other, then ran back together through the open door into the hall. Miss Leaming paused for a moment and looked Cordelia in the face before she opened the study door. Cordelia came in behind her. Miss Leaming said:

'He's been shot! I'd better phone the police.'

Cordelia said:

'You wouldn't say that! Don't ever think like that! You'd go up to the body first and then you'd say:

' "He's shot himself. I'd better phone the police." '

Miss Leaming looked unemotionally at her lover's body, then glanced round the room. Forgetting her role, she asked:

'What have you done in here? What about finger prints?'

'Never mind. I've looked after that. All you have to remember is that you didn't know I had a gun when I first came to Garforth House; you didn't know Sir Ronald took it from me. You haven't seen that gun until this moment. When I arrived tonight you showed me into the study and met me again when I came out two minutes later. We walked together to the car and spoke as we have just spoken. We heard the shot. We did what we have just done. Forget everything else that has happened. When they question you, don't embroider, don't invent, don't be afraid to say you can't remember. And now – ring the Cambridge police.'

*

Three minutes later they were standing together at the open door waiting for the police to arrive. Miss Leaming said:

'We mustn't talk together once they're here. And, afterwards, we mustn't meet or show any particular interest in each other. They'll know that this can't be

224

murder unless we two are in it together. And why should we conspire together when we've only met once before, when we don't even like each other?'

She was right, thought Cordelia. They didn't even like each other. She didn't really care if Elizabeth Leaming went to prison; she did care if Mark's mother went to prison. She cared, too, that the truth of his death should never be known. The strength of that determination struck her as irrational. It could make no difference to him now and he wasn't a boy who had cared over much what people thought of him. But Ronald Callender had desecrated his body after death; had planned to make him an object, at worse of contempt, at best of pity. She had set her face against Ronald Callender. She hadn't wanted him to die; wouldn't have been capable herself of pressing the trigger. But he was dead and she couldn't feel regret, nor could she be an instrument of retribution for his murderer. It was expedient, no more than that, that Miss Leaming shouldn't be punished. Gazing out into the summer night and waiting for the sound of the police cars, Cordelia accepted once and for all the enormity and the justification of what she had done and was still planning to do. She was never afterwards to feel the least tinge of regret or of remorse.

Miss Leaming said:

'There are things you probably want to ask me, things I suppose you've a right to know. We can meet in King's College Chapel after Evensong on the first Sunday after the inquest. I'll go through the screen into the chancel, you stay in the nave. It will seem natural enough for us to meet by chance there, that is if we are both still free.'

Cordelia was interested to see that Miss Leaming was taking charge again. She said:

'We shall be. If we keep our heads this can't go wrong.'

There was a moment's silence. Miss Leaming said:

'They're taking their time. Surely they should be here by now?'

'They won't be much longer.'

Miss Leaming suddenly laughed and said with revealing bitterness:

'What is there to be frightened of? We shall be dealing only with men.'

So they waited quietly together. They heard the approaching cars before the headlamps swept over the drive, illuminating every pebble, picking out the small plants at the edge of the beds, bathing the blue haze of the wisteria with light, dazzling the watchers' eyes. Then the lights were dimmed as the cars rocked gently to a stop in front of the house. Dark shapes emerged and came unhurriedly but resolutely forward. The hall was suddenly filled with large, calm men, some in plain clothes. Cordelia effaced herself against the wall and it was Miss Leaming who stepped forward, spoke to them in a low voice and led them into the study.

Two uniformed men were left in the hall. They stood talking together, taking no notice of Cordelia. Their colleagues were taking their time. They must have used the telephone in the study because more cars and men began to arrive. First the police surgeon, identified by his bag even if he hadn't been greeted with:

'Good evening Doc. In here, please.'

How often he must have heard that phrase! He glanced with brief curiosity at Cordelia as he trotted

226

through the hall, a fat, dishevelled little man, his face crumpled and petulant as a child when forcibly woken from sleep. Next came a civilian photographer carrying his camera, tripod and box of equipment; a fingerprint expert; two other civilians whom Cordelia, instructed in procedure by Bernie, guessed were scene-of-crime officers. So they were treating this as a suspicious death. And why not? It was suspicious.

The head of the household lay dead, but the house itself seemed to have come alive. The police talked, not in whispers, but in confident normal voices unsubdued by death. They were professionals doing their job, working easily to the prescribed routine. They had been initiated into the mysteries of violent death; its victims held no awe for them. They had seen too many bodies: bodies scraped off motorways; loaded piecemeal into ambulances; dragged by hook and net from the depths of rivers; dug putrefying from the clogging earth. Like doctors, they were kind and condescendingly gentle to the uninstructed, keeping inviolate their awful knowledge. This body, while it breathed, had been more important than others. It wasn't important now, but it could still make trouble for them. They would be that much more meticulous, that much more tactful. But it was still only a case.

Cordelia sat alone and waited. She was suddenly overcome with tiredness. She longed for nothing but to put down her head on the hall table and sleep. She was hardly aware of Miss Leaming passing through the hall on her way to the drawing room, of the tall officer talking to her as they passed. Neither took any notice of the small figure in its immense woollen jersey, sitting against the wall. Cordelia willed herself to stay awake. She knew what she had to say; it was all clear enough in her mind. If only they would come to question her and let her sleep.

It wasn't until the photographer and the print man had finished their work that one of the senior officers came out to her. She was never afterwards able to recall his face but she remembered his voice, a careful, unemphatic voice from which every tinge of emotion had been excluded. He held out the gun towards her. It was resting on his open palm, protected by a handkerchief from the contamination of his hand.

'Do you recognize this weapon, Miss Gray?'

Cordelia thought it odd that he should use the word weapon. Why not just say gun?

'I think so. I think it must be mine.'

'You aren't sure?'

'It must be mine, unless Sir Ronald owned one of the same make. He took it from me when I first came here four or five days ago. He promised to let me have it back when I called tomorrow morning for my pay.'

'So this is only the second time you've been in this house?'

'Yes.'

'Have you ever met Sir Ronald Callender or Miss Leaming before?'

'No. Not until Sir Ronald sent for me to undertake this case.'

He went away. Cordelia rested her head back against the wall and took short snatches of sleep. Another officer came. This time he had a uniformed man with him, taking notes. There were more questions. Cordelia told her prepared story. They wrote it down without comment and went away.

She must have dozed. She awoke to find a tall, uniformed officer standing over her. He said:

'Miss Leaming is making tea in the kitchen, Miss. Perhaps you would like to give her a hand. It's something to do, isn't it?'

Cordelia thought; they're going to take away the body. She said:

'I don't know where the kitchen is.'

She saw his eyes flicker.

'Oh, don't you, Miss? You're a stranger here, are you? Well, it's this way.'

The kitchen was at the back of the house. It smelt of spice, oil and tomato sauce, bringing back memories of meals in Italy with her father. Miss Leaming was taking down cups from a vast dresser. An electric kettle was already hissing steam. The police officer stayed. So they weren't to be left alone. Cordelia said:

'Can I help?' Miss Leaming did not look at her.

'There are some biscuits in that tin. You can put them out on a tray. The milk is in the fridge.'

Cordelia moved like an automaton. The milk bottle was an icy column in her hands, the biscuit tin lid resisted her tired fingers and she broke a nail prising it off. She noticed the details of the kitchen – a wall calendar of St. Theresa of Avila, the saint's face unnaturally elongated and pale so that she looked like a hallowed Miss Leaming; a china donkey with two panniers of artificial flowers, its melancholy head crowned with a miniature straw hat; an immense blue bowl of brown eggs.

There were two trays. The police constable took the larger from Miss Leaming and led the way into the hall. Cordelia followed with the second tray, holding it high against her chest like a child, permitted as a privilege to help mother. Police officers gathered round. She took a cup herself and returned to her usual chair.

And now there was the sound of yet another car. A middle-aged woman came in with a uniformed chauffeur at her shoulder. Through the fog of her tiredness, Cordelia heard a high, didactic voice.

'My dear Eliza, this is appalling! You must come back to the Lodge tonight. No, I insist. Is the Chief Constable here?'

'No, Marjorie, but these officers have been very kind.'

'Leave them the key. They'll lock up the house when they've finished. You can't possibly stay here alone tonight.'

There were introductions, hurried consultations with the detectives in which the newcomer's voice was dominant. Miss Leaming went upstairs with her visitor and reappeared five minutes later with a small case, her coat over her arm. They went off together, escorted to the car by the chauffeur and one of the detectives. None of the little party glanced at Cordelia.

Five minutes later the Inspector came up to Cordelia, key in hand.

'We shall lock up the house tonight, Miss Gray. It's time you were getting home. Are you thinking of staying at the cottage?'

'Just for the next few days, if Major Markland will let me.'

'You look very tired. One of my men will drive you in your own car. I should like a written statement from you tomorrow. Can you come to the station as soon as possible after breakfast? You know where it is?'

'Yes, I know.'

One of the police panda cars drove off first and the Mini followed. The police driver drove fast, lurching the little car around the corners. Cordelia's head lolled against the back of the seat and, from time to time, was thrown against the driver's arm. He was wearing shirt sleeves and she was vaguely conscious of the comfort of the warm flesh through the cotton. The car window was open and she was aware of hot night air rushing against her face, of the scudding clouds, of the first unbelievable colours of the day staining the eastern sky. The route seemed strange to her and time itself disjointed; she wondered why the car had suddenly stopped and it took a minute for her to recognize the tall hedge bending over the lane like a menacing shadow, the ramshackle gate. She was home. The driver said:

'Is this the place, Miss?'

'Yes, this is it. But I usually leave the Mini further down the lane on the right. There's a copse there where you can drive it off the road.'

'Right, Miss.'

He got out of the car to consult the other driver. They moved on slowly for the last few yards of the journey. And now, at last, the police car had driven away and she was alone at the gate. It was an effort to push it open against the weight of the weeds and she lurched round the cottage to the back door like a drunken creature. It took some little time to fit the key into the lock, but that was the last problem. There was no longer a gun to hide; there was no longer need to check the tape sealing the windows. Lunn was dead and she was alive. Every night that she had slept at the cottage Cordelia had come home tired, but never before had she been as tired as this. She made her way upstairs as if sleepwalking and, too exhausted even to zip herself into her sleeping-bag, crept underneath it and knew nothing more.

*

And at last – it seemed to Cordelia after months, not days, of waiting – there was another inquest. It was as unhurried, as unostentatiously formal, as Bernie's had been, but there was a difference. Here, instead of a handful of pathetic casuals who had sneaked into the warmth of the back benches to hear Bernie's obsequies, were grave-faced colleagues and friends, muted voices, the whispered preliminaries of lawyers and police, an indefinable sense of occasion. Cordelia guessed that the grey-haired man escorting Miss Leaming must be her lawyer. She watched him at work, affable but not deferential to the senior police, quietly solicitous for his client, exuding a confidence that they were all engaged in a necessary if tedious formality, a ritual as unworrying as Sunday Matins.

Miss Leaming looked very pale. She was wearing the grey suit she had worn when Cordelia first met her but with a small black hat, black gloves and a black chiffon scarf knotted at her throat. The two women did not look at each other. Cordelia found a seat at the end of a bench and sat there, unrepresented and alone. One or two of the younger policemen smiled at her with a reassuring but pitying kindness.

Miss Leaming gave her evidence first in a low, composed voice. She affirmed instead of taking the oath, a decision which caused a brief spasm of distress to pass over her lawyer's face. But she gave him no further cause for concern. She testified that Sir Ronald had been depressed at his son's death and, she thought, had blamed himself for not knowing that something was worrying Mark. He had told her that he intended to call in a private detective, and it had been she who had originally interviewed Miss Gray and had brought her back to Garforth House. Miss Leaming said that she had opposed the suggestion; she had seen no useful purpose in it, and thought that this futile and fruitless enquiry would only remind Sir Ronald of the tragedy. She had not known that Miss Gray possessed a gun nor that Sir Ronald had taken it from her. She had not been present during the whole of their preliminary interview. Sir Ronald had escorted Miss Gray to view his son's room while she, Miss Leaming, had gone in search of a photograph of Mr Callender for which Miss Gray had asked.

The coroner asked her gently about the night of Sir Ronald's death.

Miss Leaming said that Miss Gray had arrived to give her first report shortly after half past ten. She herself had been passing through the front hall when the girl appeared. Miss Leaming had pointed out that it was late, but Miss Gray had said that she wanted to abandon the case and get back to town. She had shown Miss Gray into the study where Sir Ronald was working.

They had been together, she thought, for less than two minutes. Miss Gray had then come out of the study and she had walked with her to her car; they had only talked briefly. Miss Gray said that Sir Ronald had asked her to call back in the morning for her pay. She had made no mention of a gun.

Sir Ronald had, only half an hour before that, received a telephone call from the police to say that his laboratory assistant, Christopher Lunn, had been killed in a road accident. She had not told Miss Gray the news about Lunn before her interview with Sir Ronald; it hadn't occurred to her to do so. The girl had gone almost immediately into the study to see Sir Ronald. Miss Leaming said that they were standing together at the car talking when they heard the shot. At first she had thought it was a car backfiring but then she had realized that it had come from the house. They had both rushed into the study and found Sir Ronald lying slumped over his desk. The gun had dropped from his hand to the floor.

No, Sir Ronald had never given her any idea that he contemplated suicide. She thought that he was very distressed about the death of Mr Lunn but it was difficult to tell. Sir Ronald was not a man to show emotion. He had been working very hard recently and had not seemed himself since the death of his son. But Miss Leaming had never for a moment thought that Sir Ronald was a man who might put an end to his life.

She was followed by the police witnesses, deferential, professional, but managing to give an impression that none of this was new to them; they had seen it all before and would see it again.

They were followed by the doctors, including the pathologist, who testified in what the court obviously thought was unnecessary detail to the effect of firing a jacketed hollow-cavity bullet of ninety grains into the human brain. The coroner asked:

'You have heard the police evidence that there was the print of Sir Ronald Callender's thumb on the trigger of the gun and a palm mark smudged around the butt. What would you deduce from that?'

The pathologist looked slightly surprised at being asked to deduce anything but said that it was apparent that Sir Ronald had held the gun with his thumb on the trigger when pointing it against his head The pathologist thought that it was probably the most comfortable way, having regard to the position of the wound of entry.

Lastly, Cordelia was called to the witness box and took the oath. She had given some thought to the propriety of this and had wondered whether to follow Miss Leaming's example. There were moments, usually on a sunny Easter morning, when she wished that she could with sincerity call herself a Christian; but for the rest of the year she knew herself to be what she was – incurably agnostic but prone to unpredictable relapses into faith. This seemed to her, however, a moment when religious scrupulosity was an indulgence which she couldn't afford. The lies she was about to tell would not be the more heinous because they were tinged with blasphemy.

The coroner let her tell her story without interruption. She sensed that the court was puzzled by her but not unsympathetic. For once, the carefully modulated middle-class accent, which in her six years at the convent she had unconsciously acquired, and which in other people often irritated her as much as her own voice had irritated her father, was proving an advantage. She wore her suit and had bought a black chiffon scarf to cover her head. She remembered that she must call the coroner 'sir'.

After she had briefly confirmed Miss Leaming's story of how she had been called to the case, the coroner said:

'And now, Miss Gray, will you explain to the court what happened on the night Sir Ronald Callender died?'

'I had decided, sir, that I didn't want to go on with the case. I hadn't discovered anything useful and I didn't think there was anything to discover. I had been living in the cottage where Mark Callender had spent the last weeks of his life and I had come to think that what I was doing was wrong, that I was taking money for prying into his private life. I decided on impulse to tell Sir Ronald that I wanted to finish the case. I drove to Garforth House. I got there about ten-thirty. I knew it was late but I was anxious to get back to London the next morning. I saw Miss Leaming as she was crossing the hall and she showed me straight into the study.'

'Will you please describe to the court how you found Sir Ronald?'

'He seemed to be tired and distracted. I tried to explain why I wanted to give up the case but I'm not sure that he heard me. He said I was to come back next morning for my money and I said that I had only proposed to charge expenses, but that I would like to have my gun. He just waved a hand in dismissal and said, "Tomorrow morning, Miss Gray. Tomorrow morning."'

'And then you left him?'

236

'Yes, sir. Miss Leaming accompanied me back to the car and I was just about to drive away when we heard the shot.'

'You didn't see the gun in Sir Ronald's possession while you were in the study with him?'

'No, sir.'

'He didn't talk to you about Mr Lunn's death or give you any idea that he was contemplating suicide?'

'No, sir.'

The coroner doodled on the pad before him. Without looking at Cordelia, he said:

'And now, Miss Gray, will you please explain to the court how Sir Ronald came to have your gun.'

This was the difficult part, but Cordelia had rehearsed it. The Cambridge police had been very thorough. They had asked the same questions over and over again. She knew exactly how Sir Ronald had come to have the gun. She remembered a piece of Dalgliesh dogma, reported by Bernie, which had seemed to her at the time more appropriate advice for a criminal than a detective. 'Never tell an unnecessary lie; the truth has great authority. The cleverest murderers have been caught, not because they told the one essential lie, but because they continued to lie about unimportant detail when the truth could have done them no harm.'

She said:

'My partner, Mr Pryde, owned the gun and was very proud of it. When he killed himself I knew that he meant me to have it. That was why he cut his wrists instead of shooting himself, which would have been quicker and easier.'

The Coroner looked up sharply.

'And were you there when he killed himself?'

'No, sir. But I found the body.'

There was a murmur of sympathy from the court; she could feel their concern.

'Did you know that the gun wasn't licensed?'

'No, sir, but I think I suspected that it might not have been. I brought it with me on this case because I didn't want to leave it in the office and because I found it a comfort. I meant to check up on the licence as soon as I got back. I didn't expect ever to use the gun. I didn't really think of it as a lethal weapon. It's just that this was my first case and Bernie had left it to me and I felt happier having it with me.'

'I see,' said the coroner.

Cordelia thought that he probably did see and so did the court. They were having no difficulty in believing her because she was telling the somewhat improbable truth. Now that she was about to lie, they would go on believing her.

'And now will you please tell the court how Sir Ronald came to take the gun from you?'

'It was on my first visit to Garforth House when Sir Ronald was showing me his son's bedroom. He knew that I was the sole owner of the Agency, and he asked me if it wasn't a difficult and rather frightening job for a woman. I said that I wasn't frightened but that I had Bernie's gun. When he found that I had it with me in my bag he made me hand it over to him. He said that he didn't propose to engage someone who might be a danger to other people or herself. He said that he wouldn't take the responsibility. He took the gun and the ammunition.'

'And what did he do with the gun?'

Cordelia had thought this one out carefully. Obviously he hadn't carried it downstairs in his hand or Miss Leaming would have seen it. She would have liked to have said that he put it into a drawer in Mark's room but she couldn't remember whether the bedside table had had any drawers. She said:

'He took it out of the room with him; he didn't tell me where. He was only away for a moment and then we went downstairs together.'

'And you didn't set eyes on the gun again until you saw it on the floor close to Sir Ronald's hand when you and Miss Leaming found his body?'

'No, sir.'

Cordelia was the last witness. The verdict was quickly given, one that the court obviously felt would have been agreeable to Sir Ronald's scrupulously exact and scientific brain. It was that the deceased had taken his own life but that there was no evidence as to the state of his mind. The coroner delivered at length the obligatory warning about the danger of guns. Guns, the court was informed, could kill people. He managed to convey that unlicensed guns were particularly prone to this danger. He pronounced no strictures on Cordelia personally although it was apparent that this restraint cost him an effort. He rose and the court rose with him.

After the coroner had left the bench the court broke up into little whispering groups. Miss Leaming was quickly surrounded. Cordelia saw her shaking hands, receiving condolences, listening with grave assenting face to the first tentative proposals for a memorial service. Cordelia wondered how she could ever have feared that Miss Leaming would be suspected. She herself stood a little apart, delinquent. She knew that the police would charge her with illegal possession of the gun. They could do no less. True, she would be lightly punished, if punished at all. But for the rest of her life she would be the girl whose carelessness and naïveté had lost England one of her foremost scientists.

As Hugo had said, all Cambridge suicides were brilliant. But about this one there could be little doubt. Sir Ronald's death would probably raise him to the status of genius.

Almost unnoticed, she came alone out of the courtroom on to Market Hill. Hugo must have been waiting, now he fell into step with her.

'How did it go? I must say death seems to follow you around, doesn't it?'

'It went all right. I seem to follow death.'

'I suppose he did shoot himself?'

'Yes. He shot himself.'

'And with your gun?'

'As you will know if you were in court. I didn't see you.'

'I wasn't there, I had a tutorial, but the news did get around. I shouldn't let it worry you. Ronald Callender wasn't as important as some people in Cambridge may choose to believe.'

'You know nothing about him. He was a human being and he's dead. The fact is always important.'

'It isn't, you know, Cordelia. Death is the least important thing about us. Comfort yourself with Joseph Hall. "Death borders upon our birth and our cradle stands in the grave." And he did choose his own weapon, his own time. He'd had enough of himself. Plenty of people had had enough of him.'

They walked together down St. Edward's Passage towards King's Parade. Cordelia wasn't sure where they were making for. Her need at present was just to walk, but she didn't find her companion disagreeable.

She asked:

'Where's Isabelle?'

'Isabelle is home in Lyons. Papa turned up unexpectedly yesterday and found that mademoiselle wasn't exactly earning her wages. Papa decided that dear Isabelle was getting less – or it may have been more – out of her Cambridge education than he had expected. I don't think you need worry about her. Isabelle is safe enough now. Even if the police do decide that it's worthwhile going to France to question her – and why on earth should they? – it won't help them. Papa will surround her with a barrage of lawyers. He's not in a mood to stand any nonsense from Englishmen at present.'

'And what about you? If anyone asks you how Mark died, you'll never tell them the truth?'

'What do you think? Sophie, Davie and I are safe enough. I'm reliable when it comes to essentials.'

For a moment Cordelia wished that he were reliable in less essential matters. She asked:

'Are you sorry about Isabelle leaving?'

'I am rather. Beauty is intellectually confusing; it sabotages common sense. I could never quite accept that Isabelle was what she is: a generous, indolent, over-affectionate and stupid young woman. I thought that any woman as beautiful as she must have an instinct about life, access to some secret wisdom which is beyond cleverness. Every time she opened that delicious mouth I was expecting her to illumine life. I think I could have spent all my life just looking at her and waiting for the oracle. And all she could talk about was clothes.'

'Poor Hugo.'

'Never poor Hugo. I'm not unhappy. The secret of contentment is never to allow yourself to want anything which reason tells you you haven't a chance of getting.'

Cordelia thought that he was young, well-off, clever, even if not clever enough, handsome; there wasn't much that he would have to forgo on that or any other criteria.

She heard him speaking:

'Why not stay in Cambridge for a week or so and let me show you the city? Sophie would let you have her spare room.'

'No thank you, Hugo. I have to get back to town.'

There was nothing in town for her, but with Hugo there would be nothing in Cambridge for her either. There was only one reason for staying in this city. She would remain at the cottage until Sunday and her meeting with Miss Leaming. After that, as far as she was concerned, the case of Mark Callender would be finished for good.

Sunday afternoon Evensong was over and the congregation, who had listened in respectful silence to the singing of responses, psalms and anthem by one of the finest choirs in the world, rose and joined with joyous abandon in the final hymn. Cordelia rose and sang with them. She had seated herself at the end of the row close to the richly carved screen. From here she could see into the chancel. The robes of the choristers gleamed scarlet and white; the candles flickered in patterned rows and high circles of golden light; two tall and slender candles stood each side of the softly illuminated Rubens above the high altar, seen dimly as a distant smudge of crimson, blue and gold. The blessing was pronounced, the final amen impeccably sung and the choir began to file decorously out of the chancel. The south door was opened and sunlight flooded into the chapel. The members of the college who had attended divine service strolled out after the Provost and Fellows in casual disarray, their regulation surplices dingy and limp over a cheerful incongruity of corduroy and tweed. The great organ snuffled and groaned like an animal gathering breath, before giving forth its magnificent voice in a Bach fugue. Cordelia sat quietly in her chair, listening and waiting. Now the congregation was moving down the main aisle – small groups in bright summer cottons whispering discreetly, serious young men in sober Sunday black, tourists clutching their illustrated guides and half-embarrassed by their obtrusive cameras, a group of nuns with calm and cheerful faces.

Miss Leaming was one of the last, a tall figure in a grey linen dress and white gloves, her head bare, a white cardigan slung carelessly around her shoulders against the chill of the chapel. She was obviously alone and unwatched and her careful pretence of surprise at recognizing Cordelia was probably an unnecessary precaution. They passed out of the chapel together.

The gravel path outside the doorway was thronged with people. A little party of Japanese, festooned with cameras and accessories, added their high staccato jabber to the muted Sunday afternoon chat. From here the silver stream of the Cam was invisible but the truncated bodies of punters glided against the far bank like puppets in a show, raising their arms above the pole and turning to thrust it backwards as if participating in some ritual dance. The great lawn lay unshadowed in the sun, a quintessence of greenness staining the scented air. A frail and elderly Don in gown and mortarboard was limping across the grass; the sleeves of his gown caught a stray breeze and billowed out so that he looked like a winged and monstrous crow struggling to rise. Miss Leaming said, as if Cordelia had asked for an explanation:

'He's a Fellow. The sacred turf is, therefore, uncontaminated by his feet.'

They walked in silence by Gibbs Building. Cordelia wondered when Miss Leaming would speak. When she did, her first question was unexpected.

'Do you think you'll make a success of it?'

Sensing Cordelia's surprise, she added impatiently:

'The Detective Agency. Do you think you'll be be able to cope?'

'I shall have to try. It's the only job I know.'

She had no intention of justifying to Miss Leaming her affection and loyalty to Bernie; she would have had some difficulty in explaining it to herself.

'Your overheads are too high.'

It was a pronouncement made with all the authority of a verdict.

'Do you mean the office and the Mini?' asked Cordelia.

'Yes. In your job I don't see how one person in the field can bring in sufficient income to cover expenses. You can't be sitting in the office taking orders and typing letters and be out solving cases at the same time. On the other hand, I don't suppose you can afford help.'

'Not yet. I've been thinking that I might rent a telephone answering service. That will take care of the orders although, of course, clients much prefer to come to the office and discuss their case. If I can only make enough in expenses just to live, then any fees can cover the overheads.'

'If there are any fees.'

There seemed nothing to say to this and they walked on in silence for a few seconds. Then Miss Leaming said:

'There'll be the expenses from this case anyway. That at least should help towards your fine for illegal possession of the gun. I've put the matter in the hands of my solicitors. You should be getting a cheque fairly soon.'

'I don't want to take any money for this case.'

'I can understand that. As you pointed out to Ronald, it falls under your fair deal clause. Strictly speaking you aren't entitled to any. All the same, I think it would look less suspicious if you took your expenses. Would thirty pounds strike you as reasonable?'

'Perfectly, thank you.'

They had reached the corner of the lawn and had turned to walk towards King's Bridge. Miss Leaming said:

'I shall have to be grateful to you for the rest of my life. That for me is an unaccustomed humility and I'm not sure that I like it.'

'Then don't feel it. I was thinking of Mark, not of you.'

'I thought you might have acted in the service of justice or some such abstraction.'

'I wasn't thinking about any abstraction. I was thinking about a person.'

They had reached the bridge now and leaned over it side by side to look down into the bright water. The paths leading up to the bridge were, for a few minutes, empty of people. Miss Leaming said:

'Pregnancy isn't difficult to fake, you know. It only needs a loose corset and judicious stuffing. It's humiliating for the woman, of course, almost indecent if she happens to be barren. But it isn't difficult, particularly if she isn't closely watched. Evelyn wasn't. She had always been a shy, self-contained woman. People expected her to be excessively modest about her pregnancy. Garforth House wasn't filled with friends and relations swapping horror stories about the ante-natal clinic and patting her stomach. We had to get rid of that tedious fool Nanny Pilbeam, of course. Ronald regarded her departure as one of the subsidiary benefits of the pseudo pregnancy. He was tired of being spoken to as if he were still Ronnie Callender, the bright grammar school boy from Harrogate.'

Cordelia said:

'Mrs Goddard told me that Mark had a great look of his mother.'

'She would. She was sentimental as well as stupid.'

Cordelia did not speak. After a few moments' silence Miss Leaming went on:

'I discovered that I was carrying Ronald's child at about the same time as a London specialist confirmed what the three of us already guessed, that Evelyn was most unlikely to conceive. I wanted to have the baby; Ronald desperately wanted a son; Evelyn's father was obsessional about his need for a grandson and was willing to part with half a million to prove it. It was all so easy. I resigned from my teaching job and went off to the safe anonymity of London and Evelyn told her father she was pregnant at last. Neither Ronald nor I had any conscience about defrauding George Bottley. He was an arrogant, brutal, self-satisfied fool who couldn't imagine how the world would continue without his issue to supervise it. He even subsidized his own deceit. The cheques for Evelyn began to arrive, each with a note imploring her to look after her health, to consult the best London doctors, to rest, to take a holiday in the sun. She had always loved Italy, and Italy became part of the plan. The three of us would meet in London every two months and fly together to Pisa. Ronald would rent a small villa outside Florence and, once there, I became Mrs Callender and Evelyn became me. We had only daily servants and there was no need for them to look at our passports. They got used to our visits and so did the local doctor who was called in to supervise my health. The locals thought it flattering that the English lady should be so fond of Italy that she came back month after month, so close to her confinement.'

Cordelia asked:

'But how could she do it, how could she bear to be there with you in the house, watching you with her husband, knowing that you were going to have his child?'

'She did it because she loved Ronald and couldn't bear to lose him. She hadn't been much success as a woman. If she lost her husband, what else was there for her? She couldn't have gone back to her father. Besides, we had a bribe for her. She was to have the child. If she refused, then Ronald would leave her and seek a divorce to marry me.'

'I would rather have left him and gone off to scrub doorsteps.'

'Not everyone has a talent for scrubbing doorsteps and not everyone has your capacity for moral indignation. Evelyn was religious. She was, therefore, practised in self-deception. She convinced herself that what we were doing was best for the child.'

'And her father? Didn't he ever suspect?'

'He despised her for her piety. He always had. Psychologically he could hardly indulge that dislike and at the same time think her capable of deceit. Besides, he desperately needed that grandchild. It wouldn't have entered his mind that the child might not be hers. And he had a doctor's report. After our third visit to Italy we told Doctor Sartori that Mrs Callender's father was concerned about her care. At our request he wrote a reassuring medical report on the progress of the pregnancy. We went to Florence together a fortnight before the baby was due and stayed there until Mark arrived. Luckily he was a day or two before time. We'd had the foresight to put back the expected date of delivery so that it genuinely looked as if Evelyn had been caught unexpectedly by a premature birth. Dr Sartori did what was necessary with perfect competence and the three of us came home with the baby and a birth certificate in the right name.'

Cordelia said:

'And nine months later Mrs Callender was dead.'

'He didn't kill her, if that's what you're thinking. He wasn't really the monster that you imagine, at least, not then. But in a sense we did both destroy her. She should have had a specialist, certainly a better doctor than that incompetent fool Gladwin. But the three of us were desperately afraid that an efficient doctor would know that she hadn't borne a child. She was as worried as we were. She insisted that no other doctor be consulted. She had grown to love the baby, you see. So she died and was cremated and we thought we were safe for ever.'

'She left Mark a note before she died, nothing but a scribbled hieroglyphic in her prayer book. She left him her blood group.'

'We knew that the blood groups were a danger. Ronald took blood from the three of us and made the necessary tests. But after she was dead even that worry ended.'

There was a long silence. Cordelia could see a little group of tourists moving down the path towards the bridge. Miss Leaming said:

'The irony of it is that Ronald never really loved him. Mark's grandfather adored him; there was no difficulty there. He left half his fortune to Evelyn and it came automatically to her husband. Mark was to get the other half on his twenty-fifth birthday. But Ronald never cared for his son. He found that he couldn't love him, and I wasn't allowed to. I watched him grow up and go to school. But I wasn't allowed to love him. I used to knit him endless jerseys. It was almost an obsession. The patterns got more intricate and the wool thicker as he grew older. Poor Mark, he must have thought that I was mad, this strange discontented woman whom his father couldn't do without but wouldn't marry.'

'There are one or two of the jerseys at the cottage. What would you like me to do with his things?'

'Take them away and give them to anyone who needs them. Unless you think I ought to unpick the wool and knit it up into something new? Would that be a suitable gesture, do you think, symbolic of wasted effort, pathos, futility?'

'I'll find a use for them. And his books?'

'Get rid of them too. I can't go again to the cottage. Get rid of everything if you will.'

The little group of tourists was very close now but they seemed engrossed in their own chatter. Miss Leaming took an envelope out of her pocket and handed it to Cordelia.

'I've written out a brief confession. There's nothing in it about Mark, nothing about how he died or what you discovered. It's just a brief statement that I shot Ronald Callender immediately after you had left Garforth House and coerced you into supporting my story. You'd better put it somewhere safe. One day you may need it.'

Cordelia saw that the envelope was addressed to herself. She didn't open it. She said:

'It's too late now. If you regret what we did, you should have spoken earlier. The case is closed now.'

'I've no regrets. I'm glad that we acted as we did. But the case may not be over yet.'

'But it is over! The inquest has given its verdict.'

'Ronald had a number of very powerful friends. They have influence and, periodically, they like to exercise it if only to prove that they still have it.'

'But they can't get this case reopened! It practically takes an act of parliament to change a coroner's verdict.'

'I don't say that they'll try to do that. But they may ask questions. They may have what they describe as a quiet word in the right ear. And the right ears are usually available. That's how they work. That's the sort of people they are.'

Cordelia said suddenly:

'Have you a light?'

Without question or protest Miss Leaming opened her handbag and handed over an elegant silver tube. Cordelia didn't smoke and was unused to lighters. It took three clicks before the wick burst into flame. Then she leaned over the parapet of the bridge and set fire to the corner of the envelope.

The incandescent flame was invisible in the stronger light of the sun. All Cordelia could see was a narrow band of wavering purple light as the flame bit into the paper and the charred edges widened and grew. The pungent smell of burning was wafted away on the breeze. As soon as the flame tinged her fingers, Cordelia dropped the envelope, still burning, and watched it twist and turn as it floated down small and frail as a snowflake to be lost at last in the Cam. She said:

'Your lover shot himself. That is all that either of us need to remember now or ever.'

*

They didn't speak again about Ronald Callender's death, but walked silently along the elm-lined path towards the Backs. At one point Miss Leaming glanced at Cordelia and said in a tone of angry petulance:

'You look surprisingly well!'

Cordelia supposed that this brief outburst was the resentment of the middle-aged at the resilience of the young which could so quickly recover from physical disaster. It had only taken one night of long and deep sleep to return her to the state which Bernie, with irritating coyness, used to describe as bright eyed and bushy tailed. Even without the benison of a hot bath the broken skin on her shoulders and back had healed cleanly. Physically, the events of the last fortnight had left her unscathed. She wasn't so sure about Miss Leaming. The sleek platinum hair was still swathed and shaped immaculately to the bones of the head; she still carried her clothes with cool distinction as if it were important to appear the competent and unharassed helpmate of a famous man. But the pale skin was now tinged with grey; her eyes were deeply shadowed, and the incipient lines at the side of the mouth and across the forehead had deepened so that the face, for the first time, looked old and strained.

They passed through King's Gate and turned to the right. Cordelia had found a place and had parked the Mini within a few yards of the gate; Miss Leaming's Rover was further down Queen's Road. She shook hands firmly but briefly with Cordelia and said goodbye as unemotionally as if they were Cambridge acquaintances, parting with unusual formality after an unexpected meeting at Evensong. She didn't smile. Cordelia watched the tall, angular figure striding down the path under the trees towards John's Gate. She didn't look back. Cordelia wondered when, if ever, they would see each other again. It was difficult to believe that they had met only on four occasions. They had nothing in common except their sex, although Cordelia had realized during the days following Ronald Callender's murder the strength of that female allegiance. As Miss Leaming herself had said, they didn't even like each other. Yet each held the other's safety in her hands. There were moments when their secret almost horrified Cordelia by its immensity. But these were few and would get fewer. Time would inevitably diminish its importance. Life would go on. Neither of them would ever forget completely while the brain cells still lived, but she could believe that a day might come when they would glimpse each other across a theatre or restaurant or be borne unprotestingly past on an underground escalator and would wonder whether what they both recalled in the shock of recognition had really once happened. Already, only four days after the inquest, Ronald Callender's murder was beginning to take its place in the landscape of the past.

There was no longer anything to keep her at the cottage. She spent an hour obsessionally cleaning and tidying rooms which no one would enter, probably for weeks. She watered the mug of cowslips on the sitting-room table. In another three days they would be dead and no one would notice, but she couldn't bear to throw out the still living flowers. She went out to the shed and contemplated the bottle of sour milk and the beef stew. Her first impulse was to take both and empty them down the lavatory. But they were part of the evidence. She wouldn't need that evidence again, but ought it to be completely destroyed? She recalled Bernie's reiterated admonition: 'Never destroy the evidence.' The

Super had been full of cautionary tales to emphasize the importance of that maxim. In the end she decided to photograph the exhibits, setting them up on the kitchen table and paying great attention to exposure and light. It seemed a fruitless, somewhat ridiculous, exercise and she was glad when the job was done and the unsavoury contents of bottle and pan could be disposed of. Afterwards she carefully washed them both and left them in the kitchen.

Last of all she packed her bag and stowed her gear in the Mini together with Mark's jerseys and books. Folding the thick wool, she thought of Dr Gladwin sitting in his back garden, his shrunken veins indifferent to the sun. He would find the jerseys useful, but she couldn't take them to him. That kind of gesture might have been accepted from Mark, but not from her.

She locked the door and left the key under a stone. She couldn't face Miss Markland again and had no wish to hand it back to any other member of the family. She would wait until she got to London, then send a brief note to Miss Markland thanking her for her kindness and explaining where the key could be found. She walked for the last time round the garden. She wasn't sure what impulse led her to the well but she came up to it with a shock of surprise. The soil around the rim had been cleared and dug and had been planted with a circle of pansies, daisies and small clumps of alyssum and lobelia, each plant looking well established in its hollow ring of watered earth. It was a bright oasis of colour among the encroaching weeds. The effect was pretty but ridiculous and disquietingly odd. Thus strangely celebrated, the well itself looked obscene, a wooden breast topped by a monstrous nipple. How could she have seen the well cover as a harmless and slightly elegant folly?

Cordelia was torn between pity and revulsion. This must be the work of Miss Markland. The well, which for years had been to her an object of horror, remorse and reluctant fascination, was now to be tended as a shrine. It was ludicrous and pitiable and Cordelia wished that she hadn't seen it. She was suddenly terrified of meeting Miss Markland, of seeing the incipient madness in her eyes. She almost ran out of the garden, pulled the gate shut against the weight of the weeds and drove finally away from the cottage without a backward glance. The case of Mark Callender was finished.

CHAPTER SEVEN

Next morning she went to the Kingly Street office promptly at nine o'clock. The unnaturally hot weather had broken at last and, when she opened the window, a keen breeze shifted the layers of dust on desk and filing cabinet. There was only one letter. This was in a long stiff envelope and was headed with the name and address of Ronald Callender's solicitors. It was very brief.

'Dear Madam, I enclose a cheque for £30.00 being expenses due to you in respect of the investigation which you carried out at the request of the late Sir Ronald Callender into the death of his son Mark Callender. If you agree this sum, I would be grateful if you would sign and return the attached receipt.'

Well, as Miss Leaming had said, it would at least pay part of her fine. She had sufficient money to keep the Agency going for another month. If there were no further cases by that time, there was always Miss Feakins and another temporary job. Cordelia thought of the Feakins Secretarial Agency without enthusiasm. Miss Feakins operated, and that was the appropriate word, from a small office as squalid as Cordelia's own, but which had a desperate gaiety imposed upon it in the form of multi-coloured walls, paper flowers in a variety of urn-like containers, china ornaments and a poster. The poster had always fascinated Cordelia. A curvaceous blonde, clad in brief hot pants and laughing hysterically, was leap-frogging over her typewriter, a feat she managed to perform with a maximum of exposure while clutching a fistful of five pound notes in each hand. The caption read:

Be a Girl Friday and join the fun people. All the best Crusoes are on our books.

Beneath this poster Miss Feakins, emaciated, indefatigably cheerful and tinselled like a Christmas tree, interviewed a dispirited trail of the old, the ugly and the virtually unemployable. Her milch cows seldom escaped into permanent employment. Miss Feakins would warn against the unspecified dangers of accepting a permanent job much as Victorian mothers warned against sex. But Cordelia liked her. Miss Feakins would welcome her back, her defection to Bernie forgiven, and there would be another of those furtive telephone conversations with the fortunate Crusoe made with one bright eye on Cordelia, a brothel madam recommending her latest recruit to one of her fussier customers. 'Most superior girl – well educated – you'll like her – and a worker!' The emphasis of amazed wonder on the last word was justified. Few of Miss Feakins' temporaries, beguiled by advertisements, seriously expected to have to work. There were other and more efficient agencies but only one Miss Feakins. Bound by pity and an eccentric loyalty, Cordelia had little hope of escaping that glittering eye. A series of temporary jobs with Miss Feakins' Crusoes might, indeed, be all that was left to her. Didn't a conviction for illegal possession of a weapon under Section 1 of the Firearms Act 1968 count as a criminal record, barring one for life from socially responsible and safe jobs in the civil service and local government?

She settled down at the typewriter, with the yellow telephone directory to hand, to finish sending out the circular letter to the last twenty solicitors on the list. The letter itself embarrassed and depressed her. It had been concocted by Bernie after a dozen preliminary drafts and, at the time, it hadn't seemed too unreasonable. But his death and the Callender case had altered everything. The pompous phrases about a comprehensive professional service, immediate attendance in any part of the country, discreet and experienced operators and moderate fees, struck her as ridiculously, even dangerously, pretentious. Wasn't there something about false representation in the Trades Description Act? But the promise of moderate fees and absolute discretion was valid enough. It was a pity, she thought drily, that she couldn't get a reference from Miss Leaming. Alibis arranged; inquests attended; murders efficiently concealed; perjury at our own special rates.

The raucous burr of the telephone startled her. The office was so quiet and still that she had taken it for granted that no one would call. She stared at the instrument for several seconds, wide-eyed and suddenly afraid, before stretching out her hand.

The voice was calm and assured, polite but in no way deferential. It uttered no threat, yet to Cordelia, every word was explicit with menace.

'Miss Cordelia Gray? This is New Scotland Yard. We wondered whether you would be back at your office yet. Could you please make it convenient to call here sometime later today? Chief Superintendent Dalgliesh would like to see you.'

*

It was ten days later that Cordelia was called for the third time to New Scotland Yard. The bastion of concrete and glass off Victoria Street was, by now, fairly familiar to her although she still entered it with a sense of temporarily discarding part of her identity, like leaving shoes outside a mosque.

Superintendent Dalgliesh had imposed little of his own personality on his room. The books in the regulation bookcase were obviously textbooks on law, copies of regulations and Acts of Parliament, dictionaries and books of reference. The only picture was a large water colour of the old Norman Shaw building on the Embankment painted from the river, an agreeable study in greys and soft ochres lit by the bright golden wings of the R.A.F. Memorial. On this visit, as on previous occasions, there was a bowl of roses on his desk, garden roses with sturdy stems and thorns curved like strong beaks, not the etiolated scentless blooms of a West End florist.

Bernie had never described him; had only fathered on him his own obsessive, unheroic, rough-hewn philosophy. Cordelia, bored by his very name, had asked no questions. But the Superintendent she had pictured was very different from the tall, austere figure who had risen to shake her hand when she first came into this room and the dichotomy between her private imaginings and the reality had been disconcerting. Irrationally, she had felt a twinge of irritation against Bernie for so putting her at a disadvantage. He was old of course, over forty at least, but not as old as she had expected. He was dark, very tall and loose-limbed where she had expected him to be fair, thick set and stocky. He was serious and spoke to her as if she were a responsible adult, not avuncular and condescending. His face was sensitive without being weak and she liked his hands and his voice and the way she could see the structure of his bones under the skin. He sounded gentle and kind, which was cunning since she knew that he was dangerous and cruel, and she had to keep reminding herself of how he had treated Bernie. At some moments during the interrogation she had actually wondered whether he could be Adam Dalgliesh the poet.

They had never been alone together. On each of her visits a policewoman, introduced as Sergeant Mannering, had been present, seated at the side of the desk with her notebook. Cordelia felt that she knew Sergeant Mannering well having met her at school in the person of the head girl, Teresa Campion-Hook. The two girls could have been sisters. No acne had ever marked their shiningly clean skins; their fair hair curled at precisely the regulation length above their uniformed collars; their voices were calm, authoritarian, determinedly cheerful but never strident; they exuded an ineffable confidence in the justice and logic of the universe and the rightness of their own place in it. Sergeant Mannering had smiled briefly at Cordelia as she came in. The look was open, not overtly friendly since too generous a smile might prejudice the case, but not censorious either. It was a look which disposed Cordelia to imprudence; she disliked looking a fool before that competent gaze.

She had at least had time before her first visit to decide on tactics. There was little advantage and much danger in concealing facts which an intelligent man could easily discover for himself. She would disclose, if asked, that she had discussed Mark Callender with the Tillings and his tutor; that she had traced and interviewed Mrs Goddard; that she had visited Dr Gladwin. She decided to say nothing about the attempt on her life or about her visit to Somerset House. She knew which facts it would be vital to conceal: Ronald Callender's murder; the clue in the prayer book; the actual way in which Mark had died. She told herself firmly that she mustn't be drawn into discussing the case, mustn't talk about herself, her life, her present job, her ambitions. She remembered what Bernie had told her. 'In this country, if people won't talk, there's nothing you can do to make them, more's the pity. Luckily for the police most people just can't keep their mouths shut. The intelligent ones are the worst. They just have to show how clever they are, and once you've got them discussing the case, even discussing it generally, then you've got them.'

Cordelia reminded herself of the advice she had given to Elizabeth Leaming: 'Don't embroider, don't invent, don't be afraid to say you can't remember.'

Dalgliesh was speaking:

'Have you thought of consulting a solicitor, Miss Gray?'

'I haven't got a solicitor.'

'The Law Society can give you the names of some very reliable and helpful ones. I should think about it seriously if I were you.'

'But I should have to pay him, shouldn't I? Why should I need a solicitor when I'm telling the truth?'

'It's when people start telling the truth that they most often feel the need of a solicitor.'

'But I've always told the truth. Why should I lie?' The rhetorical question was a mistake. He answered it seriously as if she had really wanted to know.

'Well, it could be to protect yourself – which I don't think likely – or to protect someone else. The motive for that could be love, fear, or a sense of justice. I don't think you've known any of the people in this case long enough to care for them deeply so that rules out love, and I don't think you would be very easy to frighten. So we're left with justice. A very dangerous concept, Miss Gray.'

She had been closely questioned before. The Cambridge police had been very thorough. But this was the first time she had been questioned by someone who knew; knew that she was lying; knew that Mark Callender hadn't killed himself; knew, she felt desperately, all there was to know. She had to force herself to an acceptance of reality. He couldn't possibly be sure.

He hadn't any legal proof and he never would have. There was no one alive to tell him the truth except Elizabeth Leaming and herself. And she wasn't going to tell. Dalgliesh could beat against her will with his implacable logic, his curious kindness, his courtesy, his patience. But she wouldn't talk, and in England there was no way in which he could make her.

When she didn't reply, he said cheerfully:

'Well, let's see how far we've got. As a result of your enquiries you suspected that Mark Callender might have been murdered. You haven't admitted that to me but you made your suspicions plain when you visited Sergeant Maskell of the Cambridge police. You subsequently traced his mother's old nurse and learned from her something of his early life, of the Callender marriage, of Mrs Callender's death. Following that visit you went to see Dr Gladwin, the general practitioner who had looked after Mrs Callender before she died. By a simple ruse you ascertained the blood group of Ronald Callender. There would only be point in that if you suspected that Mark wasn't the child of his parents' marriage. You then did what I would have done in your place, visited Somerset House to examine Mr George Bottley's will. That was sensible. If you suspect murder, always consider who stands to gain by it.'

So he had found out about Somerset House and the call to Dr Venables. Well, it was to be expected. He had credited her with his own brand of intelligence. She had behaved as he would have behaved.

She still didn't speak. He said:

'You didn't tell me about your fall down the well. Miss Markland did.'

'That was an accident. I don't remember anything about it, but I must have decided to explore the well and over-balanced. I was always rather intrigued by it.'

'I don't think it was an accident, Miss Gray. You couldn't have pulled the lid free without a rope. Miss Markland tripped over a rope, but it was coiled neatly and half-hidden in the undergrowth. Would you have even troubled to detach it from the hook if you'd only been exploring?'

'I don't know. I can't remember anything that happened before I fell. My first memory is hitting the water. And I don't see what this has to do with Sir Ronald Callender's death.'

'It might have a great deal to do with it. If someone tried to kill you, and I think that they did, that person could have come from Garforth House.'

'Why?'

'Because the attempt on your life was probably connected with your investigation into Mark Callender's death. You had become a danger to someone. Killing is a serious business. The professionals don't like it unless it's absolutely essential and even the amateurs are less happy-go-lucky about murder than you might expect. You must have become a very dangerous woman to someone. Someone replaced that well lid, Miss Gray; you didn't fall through solid wood.'

Cordelia still said nothing. There was a silence, then he spoke again:

'Miss Markland told me that after your rescue from the well she was reluctant to leave you alone. But you insisted that she should go. You told her that you weren't afraid to be alone in the cottage because you had a gun.'

Cordelia was surprised how much this small betrayal hurt. Yet, how could she blame Miss Markland? The Superintendent would have known just how to handle her, probably persuaded her that frankness was in Cordelia's own interest. Well, she could at least betray in her turn. And this explanation, at least, would have the authority of truth.

'I wanted to get rid of her. She told me some dreadful story about her illegitimate child falling down the well to his death. I'd only just been rescued myself. I didn't want to hear it, I couldn't bear it just then. I told her a lie about the gun just to make her go. I didn't ask her to confide in me, it wasn't fair. It was only a way of asking for help and I hadn't any to give.'

'And didn't you want to get rid of her for another reason? Didn't you know that your assailant would have to return that night; that the well cover would have to be dragged clear again if your death were to look like an accident?'

'If I'd really thought that I was in any danger I should have begged her to take me with her to Summertrees House. I wouldn't have waited alone in the cottage without my gun.'

'No, Miss Gray, I believe that. You wouldn't have waited there alone in the cottage that night without your gun.'

For the first time Cordelia was desperately afraid. This wasn't a game. It never had been, although at Cambridge the police interrogation had held some of the unreality of a formal contest in which the result was both foreseeable and unworrying since one of the opponents didn't even know he was playing. It was real enough now. If she were tricked, persuaded, coerced into telling him the truth, she would go to prison. She was an accessory after the fact. How many years did one get for helping to conceal murder? She had read somewhere that Holloway smelt. They would take away her clothes. She would be shut up in a claustrophobic cell. There was remission for good conduct but how could one be good in prison? Perhaps they would send her to an open prison. Open. It was a contradiction in terms. And how would she live afterwards? How would she get a job? What real personal freedom could there ever be for those whom society labelled delinquent?

She was terrified for Miss Leaming. Where was she now? She had never dared ask Dalgliesh, and Miss Leaming's name had hardly been mentioned. Was she even now in some other room of New Scotland Yard being similarly questioned? How reliable would she be under pressure? Were they planning to confront the two conspirators with each other? Would the door suddenly open and Miss Leaming be brought in, apologetic, remorseful, truculent? Wasn't that the usual ploy, to interview conspirators separately until the weaker broke down? And who would prove the weaker?

She heard the Superintendent's voice. She thought he sounded rather sorry for her.

'We have some confirmation that the pistol was in your possession that night. A motorist tells us that he saw a parked car on the road about three miles from Garforth House and when he stopped to enquire if he could help he was threatened by a young woman with a gun.'

Cordelia remembered that moment, the sweetness and silence of the summer night suddenly overlaid by his hot, alcoholic breath.

'He must have been drinking. I suppose the police stopped him for a breath test later that night and now he's decided to come up with this story. I don't know what he expects to gain by it but it isn't true. I wasn't carrying a gun. Sir Ronald took the pistol from me on my first night at Garforth House.'

'The Metropolitan Police stopped him just over the force border. I think he may persist in his story. He was very definite. Of course, he hasn't identified you yet but he was able to describe the car. His story is that he thought you were having trouble with it and stopped to help. You misunderstood his motives and threatened him with a gun.'

'I understood his motives perfectly. But I didn't threaten him with a gun.'

'What did you say, Miss Gray?'

'Leave me alone or I'll kill you.'

'Without the gun, surely that was an empty threat?'

'It would always have been an empty threat. But it made him go.'

'What exactly did happen?'

'I had a spanner in the front pocket of the car and when he shoved his face in at the window I grasped that and threatened him with it. But no one in his right senses could have mistaken a spanner for a gun!'

But he hadn't been in his right senses. The only person who had seen the gun in her possession that night was a motorist who hadn't been sober. This, she knew, was a small victory. She had resisted the momentary temptation to change her story. Bernie had been right. She recalled his advice; the Superintendent's advice; this time she could almost hear it spoken in his deep, slightly husky voice: 'If you're tempted to crime, stick to your original statement. There's nothing that impresses the jury more than consistency. I've seen the most unlikely defence succeed simply because the accused stuck to his story. After all, it's only someone else's word against yours; with a competent counsel that's half-way to a reasonable doubt.'

The Superintendent was speaking again. Cordelia wished that she could concentrate more clearly on what he was saying. She hadn't been sleeping very soundly for the past ten days – perhaps that had something to do with this perpetual tiredness.

'I think that Chris Lunn paid you a visit on the night he died. There's no other reason that I could discover why he should have been on that road. One of the witnesses to the accident said that he came out in the little van from that side road as if all the devils in hell were following him. Someone was following him – you, Miss Gray.'

'We've had this conversation before. I was on my way to see Sir Ronald.'

'At that hour? And in such a hurry?'

'I wanted to see him urgently to tell him that I'd decided to drop the case. I couldn't wait.'

'But you did wait, didn't you? You went to sleep in the car on the side of the road. That's why it was nearly an hour after you'd been seen at the accident before you arrived at Garforth House.'

'I had to stop. I was tired and I knew it wasn't safe to drive on.'

'But you knew too, that it was safe to sleep. You knew that the person you had most to fear from was dead.'

Cordelia didn't reply. A silence fell on the room but it seemed to her a companionable not an accusing silence. She wished that she wasn't so tired. Most of all, she wished that she had someone to talk to about Ronald Callender's murder. Bernie wouldn't have been any help here. To him the moral dilemma at the heart of the crime would have held no interest, no validity, would have seemed a wilful confusion of straightforward facts. She could imagine his coarse and facile comment on Eliza Leaming's relations with Lunn. But the Superintendent might have understood. She could imagine herself talking to him. She recalled Ronald Callender's words that love was as destructive as hate. Would Dalgliesh assent to that bleak philosophy? She wished that she could ask him. This, she recognized, was her real danger – not the temptation to confess but the longing to confide. Did he know how she felt? Was this, too, part of his technique?

There was a knock at the door. A uniformed constable came in and handed a note to Dalgliesh. The room was very quiet while he read it. Cordelia made herself look at his face. It was grave and expressionless and he continued looking at the paper long after he must have assimilated its brief message.

She thought that he was making up his mind to something. After a minute he said:

'This concerns someone you know, Miss Gray. Elizabeth Leaming is dead. She was killed two days ago when the car she was driving went off the coast road south of Amalfi. This note is confirmation of identity.'

Cordelia was swept with relief so immense that she felt physically sick. She clenched her fist and felt the sweat start on her brow. She began to shiver with cold. It never occurred to her that he might be lying. She knew him to be ruthless and clever but she had always taken it for granted that he wouldn't lie to her. She said in a whisper:

'May I go home now?'

'Yes. I don't think there's much point in your staying, do you?'

'She didn't kill Sir Ronald. He took the gun from me. He took the gun—'

Something seemed to have happened to her throat. The words wouldn't come out.

'That's what you've been telling me. I don't think you need trouble to say it again.'

'When do I have to come back?'

'I don't think you need come back unless you decide that there's something you want to tell me. In that well-known phrase, you were asked to help the police. You have helped the police. Thank you.'

She had won. She was free. She was safe, and with Miss Leaming dead, that safety depended only on herself. She needn't come back again to this horrible place. The relief, so unexpected and so unbelievable, was too great to be borne. Cordelia burst into dramatic and uncontrollable crying. She was aware of Sergeant Mannering's low exclamation of concern and a folded white handkerchief handed to her by the Superintendent. She buried her face in the clean, laundry-smelling linen and blurted out her pent-up misery and anger. Strangely enough – and the oddness of it struck her even in the middle of her anguish – her misery was centred on Bernie. Lifting a face disfigured with tears and no longer caring what he thought of her, she blurted out a final, irrational protest:

'And after you'd sacked him, you never enquired how he got on. You didn't even come to the funeral!'

He had brought a chair over and had seated himself beside her. He handed her a glass of water. The glass was very cold but comforting and she was surprised to find how thirsty she was. She sipped the cold water and sat there hiccuping gently. The hiccups made her want to laugh hysterically but she controlled herself. After a few minutes he said gently:

'I'm sorry about your friend. I didn't realize that your partner was the Bernie Pryde who once worked with me. It's rather worse than that, actually. I'd forgotten all about him. If it's any consolation to you, this case might have ended rather differently if I hadn't.'

'You sacked him. All he ever wanted was to be a detective and you wouldn't give him a chance.'

'The Metropolitan Police hiring and firing regulations aren't quite as simple as that. But it's true that he might still have been a policeman if it hadn't been for me. But he wouldn't have been a detective.'

'He wasn't that bad.'

'Well, he was, you know. But I'm beginning to wonder if I didn't underrate him.'

Cordelia turned to hand him back the glass and met his eyes. They smiled at each other. She wished that Bernie could have heard him.

*

Half an hour later Dalgliesh was seated opposite the Assistant Commissioner in the latter's office. The two men disliked each other but only one of them knew this and he was the one to whom it didn't matter. Dalgliesh made his report, concisely, logically, without referring to his notes. This was his invariable habit. The A.C. had always thought it unorthodox and conceited and he did so now. Dalgliesh ended:

'As you can imagine, sir, I'm not proposing to commit all that to paper. There's no real evidence and as Bernie Pryde used to tell us, hunch is a good servant but a poor master. God, how that man could churn out his horrible platitudes! He wasn't unintelligent, not totally without judgement, but everything, including ideas, came apart in his hands. He had a mind like a police notebook. Do you remember the Clandon case, homicide by shooting? It was in 1954 I think.'

'Ought I to?'

'No. But it would have been helpful if I had.'

'I don't really know what you're talking about, Adam. But if I understand you aright, you suspect that Ronald Callender killed his son. Ronald Callender is dead. You suspect that Chris Lunn tried to murder Cordelia Gray. Lunn is dead. You suggest that Elizabeth Leaming killed Ronald Callender. Elizabeth Leaming is dead.'

'Yes, it's all conveniently tidy.'

'I suggest we leave it that way. The Commissioner incidentally has had a telephone call from Dr Hugh Tilling, the psychiatrist. He's outraged because his son and daughter have been questioned about Mark Callender's death. I'm prepared to explain his civil duties to

Dr Tilling, he's already well aware of his rights, if you really feel it necessary. But will anything be gained by seeing the two Tillings again?'

'I don't think so.'

'Or by bothering the Sûreté about that French girl who Miss Markland claims visited him at the cottage?'

'I think we can spare ourselves that embarrassment. There's only one person now alive who knows the truth of these crimes and she's proof against any interrogation we can use. I can comfort myself with the reason. With most suspects we have an invaluable ally lurking at the back of their minds to betray them. But whatever lies she's been telling, she's absolutely without guilt.'

'Do you think that she's deluded herself that it's all true?'

'I don't think that young woman deludes herself about anything. I took to her, but I'm glad I shan't be encountering her again. I dislike being made to feel during a perfectly ordinary interrogation that I'm corrupting the young.'

'So we can tell the Minister that his chum died by his own hand?'

'You can tell him that we are satisfied that no living finger pressed that trigger. But perhaps not. Even he might be capable of reasoning that one out. Tell him that he can safely accept the verdict of the inquest.'

'It would have saved a great deal of public time if he'd accepted it in the first place.'

The two men were silent for a moment. Then Dalgliesh said:

'Cordelia Gray was right. I ought to have enquired what happened to Bernie Pryde.'

'You couldn't be expected to. That wasn't part of your duties.'

'Of course not. But then one's more serious neglects seldom are part of one's duty. And I find it ironic and oddly satisfying that Pryde took his revenge. Whatever mischief that child was up to in Cambridge, she was working under his direction.'

'You're becoming more philosophical, Adam.'

'Only less obsessive, or perhaps merely older. It's good to be able to feel occasionally that there are some cases which are better left unsolved.'

*

The Kingly Street building looked the same, smelt the same. It always would. But there was one difference. Outside the office a man was waiting, a middle-aged man in a tight blue suit, pig eyes sharp as flint among the fleshy folds of the face.

'Miss Gray? I'd nearly given you up. My name's Fielding. I saw your plate and just came up by chance, don't you know.'

His eyes were avaricious, prurient.

'Well now, you're not quite what I expected, not the usual kind of Private Eye.'

'Is there anything I can do for you, Mr Fielding?'

He gazed furtively round the landing, seeming to find its sordidness reassuring.

'It's my lady friend. I've reason to suspect that she's getting a bit on the side. Well – a man likes to know where he stands. You get me?'

Cordelia fitted the key into the lock.

'I understand, Mr Fielding. Won't you come in?'

Also by P. D. James

THE MISTLETOE MURDER AND OTHER STORIES

As the acknowledged Queen of Crime, P. D. James was frequently commissioned by newspapers and magazines to write a short story for Christmas, and four of the best have been drawn from the archives and published here together for the first time. From the title story about a strained country-house Christmas party, to another about an illicit affair that ends in murder, plus two cases for detective Adam Dalgliesh, these are masterfully atmospheric stories, with the lure of a mystery to be solved.

'A box of crackers.' *Guardian* Books of the Year

'What a pleasure to encounter P. D. James again at the top of her form.' Shirley Hughes

www.faber.co.uk

ff

SLEEP NO MORE

P. D. James was the master of the short story, creating gripping, suspenseful tales. *Sleep No More* comprises six perfectly formed stories, published here together for the first time. As the murderous tales unfold, the dark motive of revenge is revealed at the heart of each. P. D. James shows her expert control of the short-story form, conjuring motives and scenarios with complete conviction, and delivering a satisfying twist every time.

'You're unlikely to find a book more ingeniously pleasing.' *Observer*

'It is difficult to imagine a more pleasing afternoon than one beside a fire or radiator, with a pot of tea to hand and autumn rain against the window, while settling in for a series of delightful shocks.' Sarah Perry, *Guardian*

'Sublime ... P. D. James never sets a foot wrong ... With endings sometimes shocking and never less than surprising, she leaves her readers gasping.' *Daily Mail*

www.faber.co.uk

ff

FABER

MEMBERS

Become a Faber Member and discover the best in the arts and literature.

Sign up to the Faber Members programme and enjoy specially curated events, tailored discounts, and exclusive previews of our forthcoming publications from the best novelists, poets, playwrights, thinkers, musicians and artists.

Join for free today at faber.co.uk/members

ff